THE DEAD HAND of DOMINIQUE

SIMON MARLOWE

CRANTHORPE
—MILLNER—

First published by Cranthorpe Millner Publishers (2021)

ISBN 978-1-912964-93-2 (Paperback)

www.cranthorpemillner.com

Cranthorpe Millner Publishers

Simon Marlowe is an author and artist, living and working in Essex and London. His first novel, *Zombie Park,* about a disintegrating psychiatric hospital during the social and economic turmoil of 1980's, was published in 2017. He has also had published short stories in UK magazines and a flash fiction blog: Fiction Point.

The Dead Hand of Dominique is his follow up novel.

A special thanks to: Christine, who slaps me round the chops with a dead fish; Jessica, for showing me her wonderful books; James, who lives in a world I used to live in; and Kirsty and her team.

Day 1

1

In my mind I live on a tiny island and nobody can get to me. I lie on the beach and behind me are palm trees and a mountain, with fresh water running down to the sea. I can hear the waves and the insects in the trees, and I shut my eyes, because I am looking at the blinding sun in the sky.

And all I do is breathe.

And then my phone rings and I look at the screen to see who it is.

'Yeah?'

'Is that you?'

'Yeah.'

'The End of the World. Twelve o'clock.'

'OK.'

That was Grandad.

I drop the phone back down on the bed and try not to move another muscle. I want to get back to where I was in my dream, but it is too late, the phone call has got me out of my head. I can feel my body, my long legs, my hands. I rub my face and run my fingers through my short hair. I tense all my muscles and feel my arms push against my t-shirt and my thighs push against my tracksuit bottoms. I lift my head up and look at my feet hanging over the end of the bed. God knows how I got to be so tall, how I beefed up, but I did. Perhaps it was because I had to survive. But there it was, me, fully grown, always with a grievous look on my face, always looking like I needed answers to a series of questions.

I swung my legs across the bed and put my feet on the cold tiled floor. I looked over at the dumbbells by the window but fancied a wash and a cup of tea first before I did any training. I pulled the curtains across and then farted my way to the living room and into the bathroom. I had a piss and then lent on the washbasin. It was me in the mirror. Mum always said I had an old head on young shoulders, but it looked like the old head had got into my face and made me look like ten years older. I was looking pale and pasty. I stretched my neck muscles as I moved my head from side to side. I suppose I had to be grateful for a square jaw, high cheek bones and a bit of blue in my eyes. A fine specimen, a good catch, so my mum would say. But women came and went with very little love involved. And that was the strange thing about my little island dream, because you'd think I'd be lying next to someone to make things perfect. I think I knew who that could be, but it was probably not a good idea to think like that, because it was full of pitfalls and problems. And I didn't need that; neither did she.

Once I'd brushed my teeth and washed my face, I put the kettle on and sat down on the sofa. A few years ago, I would have put some tunes on. Now I just like quiet. No TV. No noise. I like the sound of nothing. I like living in a space that has very little in it, so my flat looks like I'm getting ready to move out. And maybe I am thinking about changing things, about getting out of here and living differently. We all think about it, now and then. The thing is, not many of us do it. We just dream about it and think about it, instead of coming up with a proper plan. I just let things roll on, from one day to another, keeping things ticking over, doing things for people who need things doing. But I've got to the point where maybe that's not enough, it's not satisfying. I just don't want to end up making a big mistake if I let things carry on.

Anyway, that's the way I've been thinking for months now. Something that is a bit like an itch, that isn't going away, that tells me, if I leave it alone for too long, it's going to turn into some nasty rash. But it's not easy to get out of here and get away from things. There are people that tie me in, hold me down, but at the same time give me what I need. But there's only so much I can take of that before things catch up with me and I lose what freedom I have, which is my way of telling you, what I do is not legit. It is on the edge, or way over the edge.

I had to work out early on what I was good at, what avenues were open to me. And my avenues were narrow right from the start because my family are all class A villains, what people around here call the Mason gang. Growing up was all fists and fury, either for anyone on the estate or for me and my mum. I have my rotten old man and brother to thank for that – two nasty pieces of work. The good thing is my old man's inside and my brother is up in Manchester. It's brought calm for everyone, for my mum mainly and the estate. And there's an end to the war that was going on between my old man and Grandad's crew. It's been business as usual for some time now, which kind of makes me nervous. I keep telling myself something is bound to happen, you just don't know when, where and how. But I can feel it, just like the itch to change things. I can feel something is coming to disturb the balance.

But trust me, there's nothing to love or care about this place. You've got four blocks of flats that look at each other like gormless deadheads. Now and then the council do the place up, the latest being a new kiddies park, with swings, a climbing frame and a roundabout. But it doesn't mean the mums rush down there with their kids, because it's territory for the boy gangs, strutting around like demented ponies, wasted on skunk and booze. They want to make it big, but most of them won't get beyond crap jobs and doing time.

Everyone who lives here knows what kind of place it is. You can run down to the shops, get what you need to get wasted and head straight back up to the flats. If you go past the shops, you're going to be known for being off the estate. Not that there's anything posh around the corner, just some low-rise flats and houses, which jump in and out of dealerships, forecourts and garages. You see, this is east of London, a part of Essex that some people like to call the Thames Gateway, but it's just a rundown shithole. You won't find anyone here poncing around in some nightclub waiting to be snapped up by some off-the-scale reality TV show. You're talking about a world within a world, another planet, cut off from what anybody else would think is normal. The rules here are different. You either belong or you don't. And even if you do belong, it doesn't mean the world you live in is safe. It's like living in a fishbowl – everyone knows who everybody else is, what they're about and what they're up to. The trick is to know how to navigate, who to be friends with, who to work for and who not to get involved with. Something I've had to do, which is why I got a phone call from Grandad, who, I might add, is not my grandad, but that's what he likes to call himself.

And you must learn with Grandad that a lot of what he says is code for something else. You need to know that straight off, or else he loses patience with you, and you won't get to work for him again. So, when Grandad says, The End of the World, and you're wondering when the end of the world is, you'd be worrying about the wrong thing, because it's only a pub. Plus, Grandad will always say, The End of the World, but he doesn't want to meet you there; he wants to meet you at the old fort.

If you look out of my window, across the dual carriageway and behind the distribution warehouses, there's grassland that runs down to the river. If you follow the grassland and the tracks along the river, you can get to where the old fort is. It's only if you carry on down a concrete path that you get to The End of the World. It's probably the worst place to put a pub because its right next to a great big container park, which means a whole load of stuff is always waiting to be ripped off. That means the pub gets the workers and the villains all meeting in one place. It also means the coppers just go there and listen, take bribes and pick off a few dipsticks, as and when.

Which means you won't ever see Grandad in there, who likes to work on being unassuming. It's one of the clever things about Grandad and something he taught me early on: don't be ostentatious – always look as if you live within your means, especially if your income is not legit. But I reckon Grandad would still wear what he wears, even if he were going to be open about his money. I can't imagine him ever wearing anything else except his navy-blue anorak, which he wears whatever the weather. Probably the only difference is in the winter, when it's cold, and he'll have a jumper on underneath. He keeps his half-grey hair combed across and he wears these frameless glasses. He must have had acne or chicken pox when he was young because he has these small pits on his cheeks, like little craters.

To see him, you wouldn't spend two seconds thinking anything about him, so good is he at looking like a normal middle-aged guy, like a nothing type person. But if you were to walk up to him and ask what time it is, you wouldn't get an answer straight away. He'd just look at you, waiting to see how you'd react, before he'd tell you something that wouldn't have anything to do with the time. That's when you'd know that the guy you thought didn't look like much, had this way about him, a way of looking at you that went straight to the core. You would know then that this guy is not to be messed with, that he is capable of anything, if he felt like it. Whatever it took, he would do it.

And you need to be like that, to do whatever it takes. The knack is to do it without fear of the cost. With no fear, you do the things that a lot of other people can't. It's what gets you out of the mud and the slime; it's what gets you what you want. That's the way I see things. But we all pay a price in the end to get what we want. It is just a case of how much you want to pay. But you're going to have to give up something to get something, that's if you want something bad, so bad you'll do anything to get it.

Which kind of brings things full circle and back to Grandad phoning me. I'm pretty sure I know why, and I bet it's about Dominique, who's gone AWOL again. She's a live one, a real force of nature, if you know what I mean. She's a beautiful woman – a natural, nothing false. She's got this long, flowing blonde hair, piercing blue eyes, and she's French, so she's got this sexy accent that makes her even more attractive. I'm sure she could easily have been a top model or an actress, if she weren't a bit wobbly. She has this habit of going missing, and that's when Grandad usually freaks out and wants her brought back in. It's not that he's her keeper. He loves her and cares for her, which is why he does what he does. But if he admitted it, not that he ever would, but if he were honest, he would have to say she can be a bit crazy. That's when she wanders off like she's on a mission or something. And that's when she's at risk, when she can fall prey to other people.

Now, it's probably worth saying that Grandad is not really the possessive type. His concerns for Dominique are honest, because when he found out she was bipolar, he could have dumped her. But when she's manic, that's when she goes walkabout and doesn't always know what's she's doing. I've found her with people keen on using and abusing her. Grandad's way of thinking is there's no point in being hands-off about this; the services are all shit and you're better off doing things yourself. After all, most of the people on the estate have depression and anxiety. All they get off the doctor is pills to keep them straight. And, at the end of the day, she has stood by Grandad with him fighting cancer.

One thing, though: I'm not sure how much his wife knows about Dominique. She's always off the radar, keeps quiet and likes the benefits of everything. But there isn't much left, as far as I can tell, when it comes to romance. But Grandad likes to keep things all hush hush, having an on/off thing with Dominique.

Anyway, I don't see how you can tie down a free spirit, because that's what she is. And as I said, she can go a bit crazy. So, my bet is, the reason why he phoned me is he will want me to go and look for her again.

2

As I double locked my flat, I checked both sides of the walkway to see if anyone was about. The kid's play area was cold and empty, and a mist was hanging just below the top-floor flats. I did the four flights of stairs one step at a time because I like to be ready for anything around the corner. I then walked along the side of the flats and through a line of conifers, which covered up the dual carriageway. The trick of getting across the road is to walk out calmly and not run. If you run, they tend to go for you; if you walk, they slow down and you get across in one piece. I like to look at one car coming close and give the driver a real mean look, so they know I will beat the crap out of them if they hit me and I live.

I headed along a path surrounded by warehousing, jumped over another fence, onto the path that took me down to the river. This is where we'd played as kids, where the noise of the traffic stopped, and the tall thick grasses locked us away from all the concrete. That's where I would go to play or hide there from my old man and my brother. Weird, but that's when I liked it most, even in the cold and rain, sitting down, out of sight, listening to the grass.

I carried on walking down to the river and then along a path that cut inside and took me through more grass and bushes. It was all signposted footpaths and nature signs because they look after the wild birds who fly in and out of the wetlands. I suppose, when I was a kid, I could have done with some of that protection. But it wasn't all doom and gloom. We had a crazy time playing war and pirates, probably because we had the old fort next to the river. It also meant we always wanted to get out on the water, with all sorts of dodgy boats that sank after five minutes. None of us had a clue about anything nautical. It was only me and Anthony, who went a step further and nicked an inflatable and took it down to the coast. It was always a trek, two or three buses, but you could fart around and get it out onto an island, and a million miles away from all the misery we had to put up with.

Anthony was different from the rest of us – tall and thin, black curly hair, his face covered in spots, a stonking big nose and thick glasses with lenses like binoculars. He was pretty much blind as bat, but he was good at drawing, even if he couldn't see a thing. I watched him once in an art class, with his face pressed up against the paper, drawing this girl he fancied. I remember the art teacher always used to give him a hard time and tell him he wasn't good enough. God knows why because he was the only one in the school who could draw anything. He was either trying to push him to do better or else he couldn't cope with the fact someone off the estate had talent.

Anyway, it wasn't until later, when we'd all left school, that Anthony got involved with Grandad, when he found out, through Anthony's old man, that there were all these paintings clogging up the place and he had nowhere to put them. Now you wouldn't think that Grandad was the type of person to have any interest in art, but he went straight around there and struck a deal with him. All Anthony had to do was carry on painting and let Grandad do the retailing. It was perfect for Grandad because he was always looking for ways to make his money legit, by making up invoices for sales that never happened. And it kept Anthony fed with gear. It meant he could paint all day without his mum and old man bugging him about getting a job. But for Grandad to make sure he had transactions that looked legit, he had to use his connections in the city to put on a show to promote Anthony's artwork. That's how Grandad came across Dominique. She was there with a load of other oddballs and Grandad was doing his sales pitch about how afflicted Anthony was, and how it was doing a load of good for the community. I don't think Dominique was fooled by any of it, but she took to Grandad, and that's how their affair got started, and she took to Anthony, and that's how they became friends.

She did a lot for Anthony. She'd take him to the galleries or tell him there's some new exhibition in town that he must check out. I still can't figure how he managed to see anything without sticking his face right up against the pictures. Anyway, Grandad was all for it because it gave him cover for seeing Dominique. All Anthony had to do was stay out of the way when Grandad turned up, or sometimes he would take Anthony with him, so he could keep her company until he had finished some business.

I checked my phone. It was twelve. I was just on time as I walked into the barrack square of the old fort. There was a small shop in one of the buildings to buy tickets if you wanted to do a bit of a tour. That is if you were into dummies dressed up for war, massive gun shells stacked up in the defensive walls or a load of old naval guns on the top of the fortifications. But being the middle of winter, there was hardly anyone around. You just got the odd military nut having a look. Grandad was big on it, he loved it. So I knew where to find him, always sitting with his legs hanging over the brick wall, looking out across the Thames.

'All right, Steven,' he said, his thin lips and eyebrows looking like he was thinking about things.

'Yeah,' I said, shivering, as I stood next to him. 'You're looking better.'

'Remission,' he said. 'About time too.'

I nodded as I looked across the river at the old docks and black timbers sticking out with no purpose.

'Yous cold?' he said, looking up at me.

'Yeah, its winter.'

'Don't your mum feed you no more?'

'Yeah... she does. When I see her.'

'Yous don't see 'er enough then, do yer, or else yous wouldn't be standing there freezing your bollocks off.'

I shrugged.

'I didn't wear a coat.'

'I can see that, Steven,' he said. 'Right, well, yous 'ere on time for once. So, sit down.'

I wanted to avoid the cold brick getting up my arse, but I knew he wanted me close, even though there was no one around to hear us.

'It's great this place,' he said. 'I love it 'ere. All the 'istory. It's good they keep places like this running.'

'We used to play war here.'

Grandad smiled.

'Good practice then, weren't it?'

'Kind of.'

'Yous see that?' said Grandad, pointing up at a red brick tower behind us.

I turned my head.

'Yous looking, Steven?'

'Yeah.'

'That's the first bit they built, in 'enry the eights time, to stop the invasion coming up the river. Then all this, what we're sitting on, all this is Napoleonic, keeping the Frenchies out up until the First World War. Then it was the Germans. I tell yous, Steven, they's always been invading. Now, it's a different kind of invasion. They's all coming over 'ere, even on inflatable donkeys!'

I shivered and nodded. It wasn't my place to disagree with anything.

'We's a mongrel race, though, ain't that right, all mixed up over the ages. 'owever, who knows why anyone wants to come 'ere, eh?'

'Not in the winter.'

'That's right, too bloody cold over 'ere. We should all be trying to get out, find some nice beach on the Mediterranean. Then they can all come 'ere and we can go back the other way!'

'That would be nice.'

'Yeah, Steven, that would be lovely.'

Grandad paused. We both looked back across the Thames.

'So,' he said, 'I've got a job for yer.'

'Yeah?'

'That's right. I need you to find Dominique. She's gone off again.'

'How long?'

'Two weeks, which normally I wouldn't worry about either, but this time I am worried, not that she ever answers 'er phone. I want yous to go and see Anthony first, take 'im with you. She likes 'im so it might 'elp.'

'OK.'

'Where's your phone?'

I pulled it out of my tracksuit pocket.

'Right, let's sling that.'

The phone landed a good twenty yards or so in the river, just like a stone.

'Now, use this one,' he said. 'Log back into the app and let me know what yous find out.'

'Do you want me to bring her back?'

'We'll see,' said Grandad.

'So, you just want me to find her?'

'Yeah, that's right, Steven. Find 'er and let me know.'

'OK.'

'All right, Steven, good 'unting.'

I nodded and pushed myself back up onto my feet.

'I'll let you know later,' I said.

'Good boy, yous do that.'

I knew he'd stay there for a bit longer because he probably had a few more people to see. I walked back down into the barrack square and had to get back to the estate to grab hold of Anthony. Just as I was about to hit the riverbank, there was this guy in front of me, dressed a bit like Grandad, and as I walked past him, he had this wooden cage strapped to his back with a parrot in it. As he went past, I had to turn around and look. The parrot was well over two feet tall and made up of all the colours. Now that's weird, I thought, because why would anyone be wandering around with a caged parrot on their back? Were they taking it to the vets, or were they on the way back from the vets and wanted to take a sightseeing tour of the fort? Or were they so paranoid someone would nick it whenever they went out, they always took it with them? Were parrots worth a lot? Or was it just a strange love and devotion?

3

I call Anthony's mum Mrs C because their name is Crabbe. They live in a block of flats opposite, on the ground floor, because Anthony's old man needs to avoid the stairs, after he was told he had asbestosis. The hospital said he probably got it from working down on the docks and he's been trying to get money for it for years. But like most of us here, there's just the Social and that's it. Mrs C has always been good to me. She's been like my second mum. In fact, if I was honest, she was better than my real mum. Whenever things got crazy with my old man and my brother, fighting each other or having a go at Mum, I would escape round theirs. She'd feed me up and let me sleep in Anthony's bedroom on the floor. Funny what things you remember, but I never forget when we had fish fingers and she put six of them on my plate. I was like, Six... six fish fingers! We only ever had six fish fingers between the four of us, and even then, my brother would nick them off my plate.

I sat in the kitchen with Mrs C, waiting for Anthony, who she said had gone round to the shops. What that means is, he had gone to score from the greengrocers. It's one of Grandad's businesses. You can get fruit and veg of course, but if you're into gear, it's the best place to go – come away with a pound of apples and your dope for the day.

Mrs C was ironing some clothes, and I think that was all she ever did, iron her husband's clothes and Anthony's clothes. It was like her slave thing, she had no choice – ironing, cooking and looking after Anthony's old man, who was on the oxygen when he was at home and down the pub when he wasn't. I could see him sitting in the living room, watching a load of crap on the TV, breathing through his mask and looking like it was only a matter of time before he ended up in hospital again. But whatever Mrs C had to put up with, she was full of heart, full of giving – what I thought a proper mum should be.

Anyway, I knew there was something on her mind because she was taking her time on the shirt she was ironing.

'You should go and see him, Steven,' she said, steaming the collar.

'Who? Anthony?'

'No, Steven, I mean your dad.'

I laughed.

'That's a blood thing,' I said. 'That's the only thing that connects me and him.'

'Thicker than water, dear. You should know that. Whatever my Anthony's like, I still love him.'

'There's plenty to like about Anthony,' I said, 'but my old man is in prison because he's a nasty piece of work.'

'Well, dear, I don't know if you know, but I saw your brother the other day.'

'You saw Greg?' I said, wondering what the hell he was doing sneaking back here.

'Haven't you seen him?'

'No.'

'He must have gone to see your mum.'

'He'd only go to see her if he wanted something.'

'Well, he was with Mickey Finn,' she said, finishing the collars of the shirt.

'Mickey Finn... He must be out then.'

'Well, I don't have any time for his kind,' she said, putting the shirt over the back of a chair, which was loaded with other shirts.

Hearing that Mickey Finn was a free man made everything a bit more interesting. His real name was Mickey, but he'd got the full nickname because they had put him away for drugging women. He claimed he never did anything to them, but the one that got him convicted had woken up in his flat and run screaming through the estate half naked. He claimed at his trial that he just liked looking and never did anything to them. But Mickey Finn hanging around with my brother was not good.

'I tell you what, Mrs C, I've just got to pop out. Tell Anthony I'll ring him.'

'He hardly goes anywhere, dear. You know that.'

I smiled.

'Catch you later,' I said, as I rushed out of the door.

I took a shortcut through the garages, across some grass and over the railings. Mickey's flat was on the top floor of some low rises. He was lucky Housing hadn't taken it off him while he was inside. I know he'd been renting it out until they'd got suspicious, so I reckoned it had to be empty. I went up the fire escape to have a quick look through the window. I couldn't see anything through the blinds. I tried the back door. My lucky day – it wasn't locked. I walked through the kitchen and into the living room. The place stank of cat piss. Whatever Mickey was up to with my brother, he hadn't bothered to move back into his flat. There was no furniture, just a mattress standing up on its side in the bedroom.

I stood there looking around. No curtains on the windows, no nothing. But there was something not right about the place. I stood there, just stuck in a moment, waiting for something to happen, and then nothing did. I was going to leave it when the fridge in the kitchen started humming. Why, I thought, keep the fridge going? I went back into the kitchen and yanked open the fridge door. There was a tin of sweetcorn on the top shelf and some milk. I would have just closed the door again when I thought I better just check the small freezer. The inside was covered in ice with a blue freezer bag and something in it. Mickey and my brother must have stashed some drugs in there, but when I took a closer look, it looked like frozen meat wrapped up in a freezer bag. Being nosey, I pulled it out.

'Fuck!'

I dropped the whole thing on the floor.

And then I said out loud to myself again, 'What the fuck!'

I stared at it, but no doubt about it, it was a severed hand, and I reckoned a woman's hand. I bent down and looked at the thing through the blue plastic. It had landed palm down and there was a clean cut from the wrist. The plastic had almost sealed itself around the hand so I could see a bit of detail. That's when the bad news hit me, but I was pretty sure, unless I was dreaming, it was Grandad's ring on the finger, because he had given her a gold-band wedding ring, and Dominique being Dominique, she had put it on the wrong hand on the right finger.

Now in these kinds of situations, there are rational things you should do and irrational. I don't live in a rational world; I live in a dirty world, full of grime and shit, and finding Dominique's severed hand meant a whole load of things all at once. But there was no way I was going to leave it lying on the floor and tell Grandad I've found a piece of his girlfriend in Mickey Finn's fridge. All hell would break loose. What I had to do was get hold of Anthony.

So, I rang him.

'Anthony.'

'Yeah?'

'It's me,' I said.

'All right, what are you up to? Why didn't you stay? My mum said you left?'

'Yeah, don't worry about that. I need you to get your mum's icebox, fill it up with ice and come round to Mickey

Finn's old flat.'

'What?'

'Anthony, I ain't repeating myself.'

'Right, OK, but is Mickey there?'

'No, just come up the fire exit and knock.'

'OK, give me five minutes.'

'All right, don't be long because I need you here now!'

I then picked the freezer bag up, so I wasn't touching the hand, and placed it back in the freezer. As I waited, I did a few calculations, all of which added up to what I was going to do next and what I wasn't.

First things first, I wasn't going to let Anthony know anything, not yet, so he was just going to have to be in the dark. I was also sure it was Dominique's hand, but it didn't mean she was dead. And finding her hand in Mickey Finn's fridge didn't mean he was the one that had cut her hand off, or did anything else to her. But, given his previous, he would be a prime suspect, seeing as Mrs C had said she had seen him hanging about with my brother.

Now, Greg is capable of anything, such as chopping people's hands off, which is very much his thing. However, running to Grandad and telling him all of this would be a bad idea because there was still a lot to find out before I let him know anything. But why was her hand in Mickey Finn's flat? There were no calls to Grandad to pick it up, go see what we've done to your girlfriend. It was just here, like it was a piece of meat for dinner later. Also no one would have known I was going to stick my nose in through the door. So, there had to be some other reason why the hand was here. It had to be for someone else to find and collect. But whoever had been keeping the hand, or wanted it, was going to be pissed off, because it was coming with me in an icebox. And with eyes everywhere on the estate, they would work out I had the hand and then they would come looking for me.

4

I could tell Anthony had scored and injected. He had the pinprick eyes and jogging leg, which made me wonder if he'd keep it together until we got up to London. He kept looking at his mum's icebox in between my legs. But for now, I was going to keep it simple with him, which was instructions from Grandad to find Dominique.

'How long did Grandad say she's been missing?' he asked, slipping on his seat as the train crossed over some points.

'Two weeks,' I said, looking up and down the carriage to check people out.

'Two weeks?'

'Yeah.'

'You know, she's gone and done her own thing before. I mean, I've known her go away for a month and not say anything.'

'Yeah, I know.'

'She's been all the way to France and back again. Perhaps that's what she's done?'

'Well, Grandad's worried, and we don't know if she's doing it because she's gone crazy.'

'Why do you say she's crazy?'

'Because she is, Anthony. She's not well is she sometimes.'

Anthony was fidgety, swaying around, as he looked out

of the window. Something was not right with him, which was either to do with the gear or he was uneasy about being told earlier to wait outside Mickey's while I sorted out the hand and put it in the icebox.

'Are we going to help her then, if we find her?' he asked, still looking out the window.

'Yeah,' I said, but it would also be a case of what Grandad wanted.

'Has Mickey Finn done anything, do you think?'

'I don't know, but he'd be an idiot if he has.'

He then looked down at my feet. I could tell he was dying to know what was in his mum's icebox.

'It's a clue,' I said.

'What's in it?'

'Just something that needs to be kept fresh.'

'What, like fish?'

'Yeah, a bit like that.'

'OK,' said Anthony, sitting back, knowing he was not going to get a straight answer from me. 'Do you think she'll be there?'

'In her flat?'

'Yeah.'

'I don't know, but it's a good place to start.'

'I don't think she'll be there.'

'Why's that?'

'Because Grandad would know, wouldn't he? He would know if she was there, or why ask us to look for her?'

'I don't know, Anthony. Let's just see.'

He went back to looking out of the window, wrapped up in his coat. He was all sweaty and pale and was going to be useless by the time we got into London.

It was Grandad who had sorted Dominique out with a

bedsit north of the river.. He employed an Irish guy called Tommy to look after his properties, and Grandad had messaged me to get Tommy to let us into the house. That wouldn't be a problem for Tommy because he lived in the basement, where he kept his young boys.

Anthony had shut his eyes and was drifting off. It gave me time to think. I knew I had to be real careful about things because I was not just sitting on Dominique's severed hand. I was sitting on a powder keg, which could start another turf war between my old man and Grandad's crew. Both had been at it before my old man went inside. That's when I had to choose whose side I was on, and I decided to come down on the side that was going to win. But I didn't want the whole thing kicking off again, upsetting the apple cart. It would only start to mess things up for me - get all the split loyalty stuff going. I needed to keep things as they were, but what I'd found was trying to unsettle everything.

I kicked Anthony's leg and didn't get anything back from him. That left me looking out of the window, trying to think what benefit Greg would get from kidnapping Dominique and cutting off her hand. It would spite Grandad and would get the whole war thing up and running. But there was nothing left of the Mason gang, apart from me, and I was always going to be part of Grandad's crew.

We were getting up speed and flying past blocks of flats, old warehouses and offices. It made me close my eyes and I drifted off.

5

Dominique's bedsit was in one of those converted old town houses that had every room, cupboard and corner, turned into

21

rentable space. It was about four or five doors down from a long street of terraces. As we strolled up, Tommy was waiting outside for us. He was a squat little git, with a fat round head, a squinting smile and a devious glint in his eyes. He had a thick, dark-green overcoat on, which half covered his stained pinstriped collared shirt, with a thick gold chain around his neck, which I always felt like ripping off him. I wasn't going to waste my time on being nice because I didn't like him.

Tommy just nodded at me as he let us in. The hallway stank of cooking.. The walls were peeling a bit, but the place wasn't in too bad a nick. I knew there were three floors, with two bedsits on each floor, and Tommy's little den tucked down in the basement.

I followed Tommy as we walked up the stairs to the top floor, with Anthony behind me, half asleep and looking a total wreck.

'Who's in there?' I asked, looking at the door next to Dominique's.

'Who's in there you say?' said Tommy, fiddling with a bunch of keys. 'Well, he's a chef. Likes a drink, you know.'

'Right. And when did you last see Dominique?'

'The French lady you say? Oh, you know, about two weeks ago. Maybe three weeks ago.'

'So, you not seen her since?'

'No, no, no, I've not seen her. Have you lost her, then?'

I didn't answer. He'd been looking at the icebox desperate to say something, but I wasn't going to give him a chance.

'OK, Tommy. That's it now. Bye bye.'

'Well, you know,' he said, knowing only too well he wasn't wanted. 'I'm only downstairs in the basement for yers, if you want me for anything.'

Anthony was leaning against the wall in the corridor, looking as if he might fall down any minute.

'Is he another one, you know,' said Tommy, 'who likes a drink like?'

'No, he doesn't drink.'

'Oh, I see. Well, you know, here's the key, and as I said, I'll be in me flat if you want something.'

I nodded, waiting for the creepy pervert to make his way downstairs. I looked over at Anthony, who was looking like shit.

'Heh,' I said, 'your mum wouldn't be happy if she saw you like that.'

He smiled, doing his best to make out he was still with it.

'Are you going to knock?' he asked.

'No,' I said, inserting the key into her door. 'Just stay out here.'

There's never that much to a bedsit and Dominique's was no different. Also, there was no Dominique or body parts lying around. Anthony had pretty much followed me in after my little survey and headed straight for the bean bag on the floor.

'Man, I don't feel right,' he said, falling into the foam.

'You don't say,' I said, putting the door on the latch and placing the icebox next to the fridge.

'She's not here then. Won't she get mad if she finds us in her room?'

'Well, that's why you're here isn't it.'

'Trust me,' said Anthony, dragging his hand through his hair, 'she'll be mad as hell.'

'Well, she might already be a bit like that, but I reckon we can have a cup of tea though.'

'Oh yeah, tea. I could do with a cuppa.'

I opened the door to the fridge and then opened the door to the small freezer. No frozen fingers, hands, limbs, tongues, eyes or any other body part. There was half a bottle of wine, a few cans of beer, some cold meat and some butter. The milk had gone off, but I couldn't be arsed to go back down and get a pint.

I went over to the tall window and looked down into the back gardens. It was almost dark outside, as I watched a bunch of feral cats running across the top of the fences. I pulled the curtains across, which made the room a bit dim. Dominique had done her best to make the room cosy, but I knew she was always out and about, or shagging Grandad in hotel rooms. She had covered the walls in pictures and there was a painting over the bed, one of Anthony's – the sunny Caribbean-type island he always painted.

'She's a fan of yours, isn't she?' I said, as I bent down and opened the cabinet next to the fridge and found some of Grandad's favourite tea bags.

'She likes my stuff,' he said, looking up at his painting.

'I like it,' I said, as I searched for a couple of mugs. 'I would have liked it for myself.'

'Oh yeah, that one. I've painted a lot of those. It's a cliché but people like it.'

'Don't knock it, Anthony,' I said, as I started rinsing out the cups in a small wash basin. 'You've got talent.'

He never liked me saying that. I don't think he knew how good an artist he was.

I turned the kettle on.

'There's no milk and no sugar,' I said, turning around to see Anthony was doing his best to keep his eyes open, but the gear was sending him off to la la land.

I was happy with that because I didn't want him to see me

poking my nose around. I had a look in her chest of drawers, which had knickers and bras in one, a few tops and a few pairs of jeans. The wardrobe had some dresses hanging up and there were shoes in the bottom, but not much else. I looked underneath the bed and some sweet wrappers and a magazine were hiding under there, which all told me what I already knew: that she didn't live here that much. Why would you when you had a boyfriend who paid for everything.

I finished making my tea and turned her small TV on with the sound down. I lifted myself onto to her bed and put my feet up. All in all, there were no clues to where she might have wandered off to, and there was no sign of any disturbances. I lay there thinking, sipping my tea, wondering what I should do next. If she was dead, I wanted to know for sure, and I needed to know who had done it. The best thing for now was to rest here and wait and see what turns up. I would keep Grandad posted on where we were at, but I wasn't going to say anything about the hand.

I checked on Anthony and he was fast asleep. It was still early but there was some stupid film coming on. If we were event-free tonight, the next best thing, was to chat to one of the residents in the morning.

Day 2

1

I'd kept things simple for Grandad last night and he was happy with me and Anthony staying put in Dominique's bedsit. I warned him about Greg being back and hanging around with Mickey Finn. We messaged about what I should do next and came up with a bit of a plan for the morning, but it wasn't going to include Anthony, who was sweating like a pig and sounding well ill. There's not much you can do for somebody when they're like that. They just need to get through it and come out the other end. So, I had been out and about in the morning, doing a little bit of shopping and had got Anthony some pills, ice for the icebox and milk for my morning cup of tea.

I got back and was just about to run back upstairs, when I could sense someone behind me. I turned my head to see a door open by a few inches.

'Hello,' she said, as I looked at dark skin and dirty teeth.

'All right,' I said, keeping my foot on the first step and

noticing a massive mole close to her lip.

'Have you moved in upstairs?'

'Yes and no…'

She smiled at me and I got a good look at all her teeth, stained brown and matching the colour of her long brown dress. She had these thick black curls of hair, which looked like a wig, with the brownest eyes I had ever seen behind her glasses.

'Would you like a cup of tea?'

'OK, thanks,' I said, taking a step down.

It was a way in, I thought, to see what she knew about Dominique.

She left her door open and I walked into her room, which was no more than a cupboard, enough space for a bed, an old wardrobe and a few suitcases stuffed up against the wall under a washbasin. There was an armchair squashed up against the door of the wardrobe, which she said I could sit on. That's when I noticed, leaning against her bed, a stone carving about half the size of a car wheel.

'Have you just moved to London?' she asked, filling the kettle behind me.

'No, I live just outside, down in Essex,' I said.

'I moved here many years ago,' she said, turning on the kettle. 'I am Greek. Have you been to Greece?'

'No,' I said, trying to work out why she'd have a lump of stone in her room. 'But I'd like to live on a Greek island.'

'They are very old,' she said.

'Yeah, so I hear.'

'Would you like some cake?' she asked, bending down to pull out a box of Kipling's from under her bed.

She took out all the Battenberg and put them on a glass cake stand sitting on her bedside cabinet. The kettle started to boil and she asked if I didn't mind moving. I stood up and looked through the window into the overgrown back garden.

'I just need to find the teapot,' she said, bending down again to get under the bed and pull out a cardboard box.

A teapot came out. She shuffled around me and I sat back down in the armchair.

'Do you have a job?' she asked, as she made the pot of tea.

'On and off,' I said. 'I wait for things to come up.'

'But you need a job to the pay rent,' she said, as if she thought I had still moved in upstairs.

'It's casual work,' I said, 'but I wouldn't say I know what I want to do, you know, for a job.'

'Oh, you are still young. You can always get different jobs before you know what you want to do.'

I could tell she was kind a woman, but I thought she was cut off from the world, not really with it. She was certainly too old to be living in some pokey bedsit; this was no way to live, not for someone of her age.

'Do you like cake with your tea?' she asked.

'Thanks,' I said, and balanced it on the armchair.

'I think they are still fresh,' she said. 'But you can't keep much in a small room.'

'No, there's not much space for you is there. This must be the smallest place in the house.'

'He keeps saying I can have a bigger room, but then he says I have to pay more rent.'

'You mean Tommy?'

'Yes, Tommy,' she said, as the kettle clicked. 'I think the water's ready.'

'He lives downstairs, doesn't he?' I said, keen to know what he got up to.

'Tommy rules the roost. He won't do anything for you, even when you keep asking him to fix it, but he's always on about the rent.'

'That sounds like Tommy.'

'I will let it brew,' she said, as she sat down on the bed with her knees close to mine. 'My name's Mary.'

'Steven,' I said. 'Steven Mason.'

Then she offered me her toothy grin.

'Don't you like your cake?' she asked.

'Oh, no, Battenburg's all right. I'll have it with my tea.'

'Perhaps they are a bit too old… It's difficult to keep things fresh.'

'No, I think it's all right,' I said, thinking I had better start eating it or she would never stop.

I took a large bite. I made the right sounds to let her know I was enjoying it. As I chewed and swallowed, she said the tea was ready and poured me a cuppa.

'Do you have sugar?'

'Two, thanks.'

'Well, I'll have to go out and get some,' she said.

'You're all right,' I said, not wanting this to go on for too long. 'I can drink it without sugar.'

'If you're sure?'

'Yes,' I said. 'Tea and cake are good, don't you worry.'

I got my tea, but she didn't pour one for herself. She just looked at me, like it was my turn to say something.

'Do you work?' I asked.

'I do,' she said. 'In the city. I clean the offices in the mornings.'

I nodded but there was something about her that was making me feel vacant.

'My boyfriend,' she said, 'he's a stonemason.'

'Right,' I said, thinking I must get a grip.

'He works on churches. That's one of his stones,' she said, pointing at the lump next to her feet. 'He likes to work on it. Do you like it? He's very good, you know, and does a lot of work for free.'

'OK,' I said. 'Why doesn't he want to get paid then?'

'We all do it for the church,' she said, smiling.

This was beginning to get a bit weird, sitting in a tiny room with the Jesus brigade, telling me how her boyfriend likes to carve stone from churches when he visits.

'Do you believe in angels?' she asked, looking at me like I should know one way or the other.

'Eh... I'm not really a believer,' I said, wondering where all this was going.

'We are all angels,' she said, looking like she was ready for a good old sermon. 'Even the fallen angel can find redemption when we seek forgiveness from the Lord for our sins.'

'That's if we have sinned,' I said, thinking I had plenty of sin piled up somewhere.

'If we harbour sin, we can turn in on ourselves,' she said, touching one of the Battenburg on the plate next to her. 'I see angels at night, who need the comfort of the Lord and our forgiveness. We must always try to find in our heart the words of forgiveness and forgive those who have done us most harm.'

This was interesting, I thought, if it had anything to do with Dominique.

'Yeah, who do we need to forgive then?'

'Your parents, perhaps?'

I burst out laughing, which was the wrong thing to do because I needed her to trust me if I was going to find anything out.

'I'm sorry,' I said. 'You're right, my parents do need a lot of forgiveness.'

'We don't often think it,' she said, 'but we are lucky to have parents to help guide us.'

'I suppose they only wanted the best for me,' I said, deciding it was in my interest to let her think I cared.

'And whatever our sins, we will one day have to face the Lord and seek redemption.'

'It's a sinful world, that's for sure.'

'We must remember, there are so many who have nothing, not even love. They use their flesh like water.'

I think I knew what she meant but I didn't want to listen to a load of guff.

'So,' I said, 'have you lived here long? You seem to know Tommy?'

Her face changed and she looked angry.

'Look, see,' she said, getting up and grabbing the door handle. 'My wrist is damaged from doing this, you see?'

She twisted the door handle, thrashing the door until it burst open, pushing her back.

'Now I can't close it and the people here think I leave the door open because I am looking into their lives, but I need help to shut the door.'

She pulled up her sleeve and showed me a useless looking bandage around her wrist.

'My doctor told me to wear this but I don't think it works. I have asked Tommy so many times to fix the door and he says there is nothing wrong with it.'

'That's not good,' I said.

'Now you can tell him that the door does not work properly.'

'What does he get up to then, Tommy?'

'He's not a nice man.'

'No, why's that?'

'He always wants his rent and I can't always give him the rent. I can't clean, you see, if my hand cannot work. If I cannot work, I cannot pay the rent.'

'Well, he should fix your door, shouldn't he.'

'And he is noisy.'

'Is he?'

'Yes, he has all those boys running around down there.'

'Really? What do they get up to?'

She raised an eyebrow.

'Do you see much of them, the boy's downstairs?' I asked. She shook her head.

'But they get on your nerves?'

'I go out,' she said, sitting back down on the bed and putting her hands flat on her thighs.

'OK, is that to get away from them?'

'It is a mission,' she said, 'to help the fallen. They are only children really, left on the godless streets.'

'You help children?'

'They are children inside, all angels, who have the hearts and minds of the child.'

I didn't know if she was tripping out on angels or talking about prostitutes.

She got up and pulled out from the wardrobe a thick fur coat.

'That's a nice coat,' I said. 'For when you go out at night?'

'This keeps me warm,' she said, laying it on the bed and stroking the fur, which I guessed was fake. 'We are all lost until we find God. He is the heart that is missing.'

I felt sorry for her. She didn't have much in life, apart

from a cleaning job, some freaky boyfriend, angels for friends and a God who doesn't exist.

'Will you speak to him?' she asked.

'Who, God?'

'About the door?'

'Oh, you mean Tommy? No, you see, I'm not staying here for long. I'm just looking for my friend, Dominique, the French lady who lives upstairs.'

'Has she left you?'

'No, I'm not her boyfriend. I'm a friend. You see, we were expecting her the other day, to come down and see us, but she never turned up. Which is odd, not really like her. She's not answering her phone. You know, we're a bit worried.'

She looked at me like she thought I was lying.

'Do you know her?' I asked. 'Do you know who I mean, the blonde French lady who lives upstairs?'

She smiled, again not saying anything, which was even more strange. All she had to do was say she saw her or she hadn't seen her.

'How long have you lived here, Mary?' I asked, taking a large gulp of tea so I could leave as soon as I had finished.

'A long time.'

'And you've never seen Dominique?'

'She has been with me,' she said, stroking her fur again.

'Really?'

'She went with me and we found an angel.'

'An angel? Do you mean a real angel or someone who is like an angel?'

'You don't know much about God, do you, Steven. These are the fallen angels, the ones who have been cast out and seek redemption. They can do good and find salvation in the reflection of the Lord.'

33

It sounded like more crazy stuff, but if she was trying to tell me something I didn't know, I needed her to be straight with me and stop talking in riddles.

'Did Dominique meet somebody when you went out together at night?'

But before she could answer there was a knock on the door.

'I'll get it,' I said, jumping up. 'You can't use that hand, can you.'

It was Tommy and he was all sweaty and twitchy.

'Oh, I heard voices in there and so thought I'd knock and just let you know, your man there, your friend in the room, he's not looking too good.'

I pulled a face.

'You know, I was just knocking on the door upstairs and he couldn't really get to the door probably and so I just used the key to check on things. You know, he must be ill with something.'

'Yeah, he's got a cold.'

'OK, so you know, and if you need anything you can let me know.'

'Yeah.'

'OK, so he could go see a doctor if he needs to see a doctor.'

'Yeah.'

'OK, so…'

'Yeah, it's not a problem.'

'Right, OK.'

By now he was trying to look past me to get a look at Mary.

'She's a saint that one.'

I was going to punch him.

'But I'll be off…'

'Yeah.'

I shut the door.

'Listen,' I said, 'I've got to go, and thanks for the tea and cake. You know, if there's anything you can tell me about Dominique, where's she gone, anything, that would really help.'

'Don't you like my tea?' she asked, noticing my cup was half full.

'No, Mary, that's a lovely cuppa, but I've got to go, really, but thanks for the tea.'

She was looking up at me like I was the only one who could help her with her hand and her door and the noisy kids.

'Please come again,' she said. 'Just knock on the door. I like to leave it open, but no one else in the house wants to talk.'

'Of course,' I said. 'I would like to talk to you again, but I've got to check on my friend, he's not well, then I've got to pop out and see someone who knows Dominique.'

'She's an angel,' she said.

'In what way, Mary, is she an angel?'

'Descended from heaven, to bring peace and love.'

'She's a very nice lady, I know that,' I said. 'And has she helped you, with the other ladies?'

She just did a toothy smile. Why it was such a secret?

I twisted the doorknob both ways as I tried to open it again. She was right, it did get stuck.

'Well, thanks,' I said, as I put my foot on the step to go back upstairs. 'I'll come and see you again, maybe tomorrow.'

Saint Mary, with angels in her head, stood in her doorway. I thought she'd just stand there and watch me walk back up the stairs, but I heard her slam the door like she was angry. I could've knocked on Tommy's basement behind the stairs and told him to fix her door, but she should have told me a lot more and for whatever reason, she was keeping things to herself.

2

Anthony was crashed out, so I loaded up the icebox with fresh ice. As far as I could tell, the hand was looking as good as when I had found it. The only thing that bugged me was walking around with the icebox all day, looking as if I was going for a picnic in the middle of winter. But I had to take it with me because I was going to find out when Dominique's husband had last seen her.

Grandad had told me the story about how Dominique and Texas had got married, before Grandad and Dominique became a thing. She did it, so Grandad said, out of the kindness of her heart because the guy's papers were only going to last a few more weeks. It was just meant to be a marriage for staying here, but it turned into a romance thing, until Dominique took a turn for the worse and ended up in a looney bin. After that, they stayed together so Texas could get his right to stay, living together in some arty squat for years. They were supposed to be divorced by now, but Grandad said Dominique was being a bit funny about the paperwork.

It was a right old trek, getting the tube all the way out West to where all the museums were, but just a short walk from the tube to the house Texas had bedded down in. It was a high-end terrace that looked out on a neat square of railings and trees. The street and the house were a million miles away from the estate, but in my line of work, you run into all types, rich and poor. And the rich thing was like a worm that got inside me sometimes, wondering if I should be after more money so I could get away from all the shit I had to put up with.

Texas answered the door and did a great big grin, like the cat who had got the cream. He was a tall guy, like a beanpole, with a small head on wide shoulders. And he was as black as anything, as black as any African I had seen, so his eyes shone out like white laser beams.

He shook my hand and laughed like a crazy guy.

'Come, come,' he said, in his thick French accent.

I walked behind him, up a steep flight of stairs and into his little palace.

'See!' he said, laughing, as I walked in.

He was congratulating himself on having made it.

'Nice!' I said, looking around.

'It is!' he said, excited as hell.

It was all open plan, with a view of the treetops in the square below. Smack bang in the middle of the room was a black, shiny grand piano. She was also into her art, his German money ticket, because the walls were painted white with two massive colour splodges spaced on either side. I looked behind me and she'd put some wood carvings on glass shelves, that looked like the type of thing tourists would go for after ten days on safari.

I sat down on a large, black leather sofa with the icebox between my legs. Texas would want to know what it was, but I wasn't going to say anything. He didn't need to know I might have his wife's severed hand.

37

'So, it's good, no?' said Texas, as he plonked himself opposite me.

'Very nice,' I said. 'Do you tickle the ivories?'

He didn't know what I meant, so I pretended to play the piano, using both hands on the glass coffee table.

'No, no,' he said, all serious. 'She invites musician and 'e play, at parties.'

'No kids then?' I said.

'No, no, no,' said Texas, laughing. 'But she very rich...'

'I can see,' I said. 'How did you meet her?'

He didn't like the question, but it seemed simple enough.

'She loves art,' he said, giving me a shifty look. 'We meet in the gallery. She come to me and talk to me and she like me.'

'Yeah, all in a day then?' I said, grinning at him.

He burst out laughing, then sucked his teeth.

'She talks to me about Africa. She loves Africa. We talk a lot and a lot.'

'Right, so you have things in common, it's not just about the money?'

'You a naughty man, Steven!'

'Heh?' I said, thinking I didn't really care what he did to put a roof over his head. 'I hope it works out for you.'

'Yes, it is good. She so rich,' he said, getting up. 'Look, you see, she paints the door in art!'

I twisted my neck around again. There was another door next to the one where we had come in, covered in a thick stew of oil paint.

'Very expensive,' he said.

'What if she moves, will she take the door with her?'

He laughed, wagging his finger at me for being a naughty

boy.

'You will see everything,' he said, ready to show off his honey pot.

I decided to go along with it, just for now. I picked up the icebox, as he told me to follow him through the arty door. He turned on the lights, which lit up the stairs. For whatever reason, everything had been painted black. We walked like a corkscrew down a couple of flights. At the bottom were two more doors, left and right, and Texas went right into a basement kitchen. There were bars across the window, which I didn't like. Copper pots, pans, spoons and other stuff hanging down over a large island in the middle. A chef would be happy with this, I thought. Texas couldn't help himself as he opened a few drawers to show me knives and forks, all made of silver, so he said.

'How do you make a cup of tea?' I asked.

Texas laughed and wagged his finger at me, again.

'You want tea?' he said, grabbing hold of an electric kettle.

'No, you're all right,' I said.

That was enough for him to lead me through the kitchen and through another bloody door.

'Come, you see the bedroom. It is beautiful.'

I really didn't need to see it, but there was no stopping him proving to me that all his sacrifice had been worth it. As soon as he turned on the light, Texas was full of himself. There was great pride in the way he looked at the walls, covered in a shiny red silk, and on the floor was a queen size mattress, covered in a sheet of the same shiny red. Texas sat down on the bed and rubbed the sheet between his fingers, like it was cash. I didn't want to know what he got up to in his gigolo temple, and was ready to leave the love nest behind when I noticed another door at the back of the bedroom.

'What's through there then?' I asked, pretty sure it wasn't a cupboard.

'No, no, no, not through there! 'e lives there.'

'Who?'

''er boyfriend.'

'She's got more than one boyfriend?'

'No, she finished now, but she gives 'im the flat.'

'Oh right, so that's a flat?'

'Yes,' said Texas, still touching the sheet on the bed. 'She gives all 'er boyfriends something, even when she finishes with them. And you know, they all African, like me.'

'Really?' I said, thinking it would freak me out if I let my ex have a connecting door.

'Yes, if she leaves me, I will win, you see.'

'OK,' I said, working out the returns. 'So, she will give you a flat if she wants to end it. But what if you don't want to end it?'

Texas burst out laughing, as if that was a stupid question. Then he was all serious.

'She is very sensitive. Very, very sensitive. You must be nice, very nice, very gentle with 'er.'

'You mean in bed?'

'Yes, she takes a long time…'

I had an image.

'But it's worth it,' I said. 'You have a win-win.'

'Yes, she does it for Africans. She gives.'

I was tempted to say that she does it for herself, but I didn't want to burst his bubble. It was clear to me Texas had gone back to what he knew, what had kept him going in Africa – a dancing gigolo for the white women past their sell-by date.

'Well,' I said, still trying to figure out why anyone would have a door to their ex's in their bedroom, 'what's your girlfriends name?'

'Ann,' he said, proudly.

'OK. And what about Dominique?' I said, keen to get to the point of my little visit. 'Have you seen her?'

'She can go!' said Texas, who was back to looking serious.

'What does that mean?' I said, as I watched him keep his hands on the bedsheets.

'She can go when she please.'

'We know that,' I said, keeping a close eye on how he would react. 'But we don't know where she is.'

'Why you need to find 'er?'

'I just wondered, in case you killed her.'

'No, I do not kill 'er,' said Texas, who didn't shrink from the question. 'She kills me.'

'Oh, so you're dead.'

'No, I'm not dead, but she kills me, inside…'

And he pointed at his chest, wanting me to think, in there, somewhere, was his heart.

'I think she run away this time,' he said, shaking his head. 'She does nothing for me.'

'What do you mean?'

'I show 'er the papers, then she run.'

'Oh, I see,' I said. 'She doesn't want to get divorced then?'

Texas shook his head. He was feeling sorry for himself. He was so close and yet so far from getting what he wanted, what he needed from the marriage.

'You never know,' I said, 'she might turn up again.'

Although in how many pieces, I wasn't sure.

Texas pushed himself up and went into the kitchen. I stayed for a second or two, giving the place the once over, but there was nothing that caught my eye, apart from the door to one of Ann's ex-boyfriend's.

I could hear the kettle boiling so I went back into the kitchen.

'I make you tea, Steven,' he said, finding mugs in a cupboard.

'Yeah, not a bad idea,' I said, pulling out a stool from underneath the breakfast bar and putting the icebox next to me.

The kettle boiled and he made us both a cuppa. He then stood by the window with the sun cut by the bars across the window.

'You know I make filum?' he said.

I nodded. I knew he pestered people to be in his films, which as far as I knew were a tragic mistake.

'What are they are about?' I asked, doing my best to sound interested.

'Yes, come, I 'ave filum,' he said, walking back into the bedroom and returning with a DVD. 'You can see...'

On the front of the case was some writing in French. It meant nothing to me.

'I 'ave a party for my filum. They show it 'ere. We 'ave lots of people come and they clap for me.'

'Why did you show it here?'

'They 'elp me,' he said. 'When I come 'ere, Ann and 'er friends say I can make filum. They said they wanted filum about what it is like to come 'ere. I see all my friends and we make the filum.'

'OK, I see. So, this film,' I said, raising the DVD up in my hand, 'is a documentary?'

'No, it's filum. It tells a story.'

'But you said your friends were in it?'

'Yes, they act for me.'

'Oh right, so your friends were the actors?'

'Oh yes, they love it, they all love it.'

Putting the pieces together, his girlfriend must have encouraged him to tell his story.

'So, do you want me to see it?'

'Yes, you can see, you see the filum. You like the filum and we make another filum.'

I laughed.

'Listen, mate,' I said, sipping the cup of tea that wasn't up to it, 'this is not really what I was expecting. You know, I'm looking for Dominique.'

And as I said this, I knew he was upset because I wasn't showing a great deal of interest.

'It is good. She 'as the child, and they take the child and they sell the woman.'

'I tell you what,' I said. 'I will watch it, but you must promise to be honest with me about Dominique.'

Texas had a broad smile.

'You will watch the filum. You see I am 'onest, you will see Dominique.'

3

I'd spent way too long listening to Texas prattle on about his effing 'filums', like I was some kind of film critic interested in what he had to say. It meant I was on my way back to Dominique's bedsit a lot later than I'd planned, stuck on a tube stuffed full of commuters. But I had learnt one thing, which was Texas and his honeypot were not the kind of people who would chop off hands and leave them in fridges of convicted sex offenders. And they were both as keen as I was to track down Dominique, because she was not signing off on the divorce, something Texas needed to get his status sorted. Now I can understand his frustrations because Texas will be thinking he had kept his side of the bargain. The way he sees it, he's given Dominique five years of his life, when most people, apart from Grandad, would have walked away. He gave her love, as far he is concerned, and all she had to do was sign on the dotted line for the love he had provided.

I don't know if Texas was a good husband. All I do know is he had moved on to sell more of himself, with a far better return than he had with Dominique. Even if it looked like Dominique was hanging on, I didn't think she'd be doing it for any serious reason except to wind up Texas. But I had found out one good thing from that little trip: the last time Texas had seen Dominique was a few weeks ago at a wedding he had filmed. He'd said there was nothing wrong with her, she wasn't going nuts, she was as normal as you and me.

Anyway, I was fed up with all the looks I was getting on the tube, from people who must have thought, why is this guy who looks like a villain carrying around an icebox? It was tempting just to open it up and charge a fiver to let them see it, which got me thinking. I was being slack about the threat from Greg and Mickey. I was wandering around with a severed hand that must have been meant for them. There was a load of questions I should have been asking myself. I was being dumb, no doubt about it, and I needed to wise up. This made me think: the one thing I didn't want was those two Herberts getting hold of it. And this meant me taking a little diversion, as I got off the tube and headed down the street to Dominique's.

I checked out a footpath, which ran down the back of the terrace gardens. I pushed through all the foliage and rubbish down a narrow passage and found my way to the back of the house, where I could see the light on in Dominique's bedsit. There was a pile of furniture covered in grass and weeds, so I shoved the icebox under a rotting table. It was a risk, leaving it there, but a risk worth taking. There was also another bonus to hiding it because Anthony would start asking questions if he had got his shit together, and as I've said, I didn't trust anybody. I checked the back door but it was locked, so I trudged all the way around to the front of the terraces.

That's when I made the mistake, which my instincts had been telling me about. I opened the door to the bedsit and thought it was Anthony on the bed, which gave Mickey Finn enough time to come from behind, put me in a headlock and put me on the floor.

'Don't fucking move! Hold him there, Mickey.'

That was the voice of Greg, lying on the bed, but I couldn't see him with my face pressed down into the floor. How I could mistake the bulky dwarf for anything like a skinny junkie like Anthony, God knows!

I tried testing the strength of Mickey, wriggling and pushing up, but he only pressed his knee harder into my back and twisted my arm like crazy. He felt strong, but that's the problem with putting people in jail – they get bigger and stronger. But worse than that, I could feel his greasy long hair touch the back of my neck. He must still be into his heavy metal look; all grunge and no rap with Mickey.

'Don't do it, Steven,' said Greg. 'Mickey's got you good and proper, so you just stay there nice and quiet.'

'Christ, he's wriggly,' said Mickey.

'Not any more,' said Greg, as I heard him jump down off the bed.

I caught sight of him as he bent his head down and smiled at me, his hair like a razor-sharp bristle and the same nasty grin as he always had, which meant you weren't ever going to mess with him unless you needed to. Then Greg's boot went straight into my face. My nose sprayed blood everywhere and a thumping pain went right through my head.

'Nice one,' said Mickey, as he started laughing, pushing my arm up so it felt like he was going to break it.

They wanted me to know that things were serious.

'He's used to it,' said Greg. 'Aren't you, little bro?' I heard him jump back onto the bed. 'Anyway, how's Mum?'

I was breathing hard, trying to clear the blood out of my nose, which was throbbing like hell.

'He ain't answering,' said Mickey, who wasn't the brightest tool in the box.

'No, maybe he can't right now,' said Greg, who must have been dying to do that to me ever since he ran off up to Manchester.

Anyway, I needed to get my head together, before these two monkeys made mincemeat out of me.

'She's OK,' I said, spitting out blood.

'Yeah?' said Greg, who didn't care about Mum and would do the same to her if he thought she deserved it. 'Well, you know, little bro, you should think about going to see the old man. He'd like to see you.'

'What, right now?'

That's when Mickey's fist came down on the side of my head, hitting most of my cheekbone.

'I think that's for trying to be clever,' said Greg, who was enjoying me getting this. 'But we don't need that, do we, Mickey? Some clever arse trying to think he's better than us. No, we need order, my little bro. You see, Mickey has learnt a few things being in jail and one of them is order. He knows the rules like everyone else now, so he knows how to comply with things, don't you, Mickey?'

Mickey didn't answer, probably because he didn't understand, but he knew enough to hit me in the face again.

'It's a weird and wonderful world, Steven,' said Greg, 'and there's all sorts of strange shit going on. Now, it's not like being back on the estate up here, is it? No, it's all different up here in London Town. You don't know who's who or nothing. Crazy, isn't it, but I tell yer, it takes ages to find someone who looks English and speaks English. Isn't that a crazy thing? In yer own country, come up here and it's all fucking foreign.'

This was classic Greg, taking time and pleasure out of what he wanted.

'So, you see,' said Greg, 'I don't like this place, and I am only here because I need you to comply, just like the olden days, when you were also my little bro but you was not as tall as you are now. So, as I've got you on the floor, you're going to tell me what I need to know.'

'What's that?' I asked.

The answer was a few more blows to the head, but this time I tried to avoid the fists on my face.

'You are a cheeky fucker, aren't you, Steven?' said Greg. 'I told yer, Mickey, my little bro thinks he's the dog's bollocks now. He thinks he's king of the fucking castle. But the thing is, Steven, what are you doing here, eh? What are you doing in Grandad's shag pad? Are you here to fuck that crazy French chick? Is that what you do now, Steven? Are you fucking other people's birds behind their backs? Now that's not nice, is it, Mickey? Not playing by the rules. I'd say that's almost deceitful, don't you think, Mickey?'

Greg's hard man then pushed his knee again into my back, which was more painful than the beatings on my head.

'You need to know, Steven, that you are out of your league,' said Greg. 'You don't just start sticking your nose in and think everything's going to be hunky dory because you're on Grandad's side. Because let me tell yer, you ain't just going to get your nose broken, you're going to end up dead, ashes to ashes, with a fucking rose bush growing out your fucking arse. It's simple for you, little bro. All you need to do is tell me what have you done with my little package?'

I looked at a magazine under the bed. It was a kind of comfort as I weighed up what to tell him. But I wanted to test the water first, before I said anything about the hand.

'I'm looking for Dominique,' I said, which was pretty much the truth.

'Yeah...' said Greg. 'And have you found her?'

'No,' I said, which again was the truth.

'So, Grandad asked you to look for her then?'

'Yeah.'

There was a pause. As I suspected, both Greg and Mickey were working out how much they could ask without giving anything away.

'So, why the fuck was you in my flat?' asked Mickey.

My next answer probably meant I would live or die.

'I didn't know about the package,' I said. 'I just picked it up.'

I was expecting the knife. Even I thought it sounded like I was lying. But nothing happened. They were both still thinking.

'Where is it?' said Greg.

'I had it, but it's gone.'

'Yeah, where's it gone?'

'I don't know. I left it here. So, unless you've found it, which I suppose you haven't, it means someone else has got it.'

'I don't believe him,' said Mickey, which for a man who had a half a brain, was almost intelligent.

I could hear the cogs going around in Greg's violent mind. He wasn't going to let me get away with just saying his wandering severed hand had just floated away. He would need a name.

'So, where's you junkie friend then?' asked Greg. 'We haven't seen him, have we, Mickey?'

'Nah.'

'And I would have thought,' said Greg, 'seeing as how close him and Grandad's bit of fluff were, that Grandad would get you two to look together.'

'I don't know,' I said. 'I haven't seen him.'

Mickey applied pressure.

'He's going to snap it off, little bro, if you don't stop telling us porky pies. Mrs C told us you two had been holding hands yesterday.'

'I don't know where he is. He's gone.'

'With our package?'

'No,' I said.

'So, that means you have it, doesn't it, little bro?'

'I did,' I said, hoping what I said next would save my arse. 'But someone's taken it.'

The arm went up again.

'Who has it, Steven?' said Greg, almost spelling out every word.

49

'Whoever let you in.'

They both paused – Greg, so he could think and Mickey, so he didn't have to think.

'It's the Paddy,' said Greg, the words seething as he said them.

'He's gone out,' said Mickey, 'with those kids.'

I heard Greg get off the bed. He then stuck his pockmarked face right next to mine. He always had dead eyes and his eyes were colder than I had ever seen them before.

'You know, Steven,' said Greg, who sounded like he had accepted my story, 'you working for Grandad ain't going to work out. You think he treats you like his son, but that's all bullshit. You need to think about whose side you're on, Steven. That means you're on the wrong side, the wrong side of everything.'

I spat some blood out as Greg carried on with his little sermon.

'Just so you know, little bro, I don't care about you, and if you get in my way, I will kill you. You see, it's like football: Grandad is going to get relegated and you need to think about who you want to be playing for. No one wants to be a loser. It's dog eat dog, and if you're not careful, you're going to get eaten.'

Greg picked himself up and I got a few kicks to my chest before one god almighty kick to my head, which pretty much knocked me unconscious.

The next thing I remember was a woman's voice. She was saying, 'Help me, help me. Help me get him on the bed.' I could hear them talking about an ambulance. All I remember is saying, they can't do anything like that, I was OK, I just needed rest. I needed sleep or something like that. But I was passing in and out, and for all I knew, I probably did need an ambulance and a doctor. The only thing that stopped me worrying was when I recognised the woman's voice. It was Britney, Anthony's girlfriend, and then I knew I would be all right.

Day 3

1

It wasn't until the morning that I started to come around. As I lay on the bed, I was happy to see Britney had stayed all night with me. She gave me this beautiful smile and it was great just to stare at her, admire her perfect skin, no blemishes, and her stunning eyes. They seemed to glisten and shine at me. Of course, she kept asking if I knew where Anthony was, and how his mum was worried because she hadn't heard from him, but I think Britney knew there wasn't much point in asking me too much. It must have been hard for her because I knew she would have been told by Mrs C to find out what we were up to. But there wasn't a lot I could say and I didn't want to start dragging Britney into things. As for Anthony, he must have just got lucky, or worked things out and was keeping a low profile somewhere.

She was good enough to clean up my face, getting all the blood off. She also kept banging on about seeing a doctor, but that was when I would always say, 'No, no, no, nothing like that.' Anyway, Britney said she would stay and wait for Anthony. It was a risk because I had no idea what Greg and Mickey had found out last night, and I was sure they would be back wanting to know why I was lying.

A bit later I started to come around and think about next steps. I gave Britney my card and asked her if she could do some shopping. I had a list that had been coming together in my head.

'A phone charger,' I said. 'And some clothes, paracetamol and lots of water.'

'Do you want some soup?'

'No, but thanks,' I said. 'But get a load of sausages, and bread and butter. We can cook them on that thing.'

I pointed at the two electric rings sitting on the chest of drawers.

'And can you get a DVD player?' I said.

Britney was looking at me a bit funny.

'Listen,' I said, 'if it's too much, don't worry about it.'

'That's all right,' she said. 'Did you want to watch some films then?'

'Yeah.'

I think that made sense to Britney.

She was ready to make her way out, when I said, 'Thanks for staying. Honest, I don't know where Anthony is, but I am sure he's OK.'

'I hope so,' she said.

'Yeah, he'll be fine.'

'But he's not answering me. I've tried texting and everything.'

'Yeah, well, don't you worry. He'll be all right; he can look after himself. He's better at avoiding things than me.'

'But it's dead, his phone. There's no connection.'

'I think that's Anthony playing safe.'

Britney paused.

'Is it your brother?' she asked. 'Is he the one who hurt you?'

'Yeah, it was Greg.'

Britney nodded, as if she already knew.

Just as she was going out the door, I had to ask, 'Who helped you?'

'What do you mean?'

'How did you get in?'

'Oh, it was a funny looking lady. She had really horrible teeth.'

'That's Mary,' I said. 'So, who helped you get me off the floor last night, onto the bed?'

'Oh, no one.'

'Yeah?'

'You're heavy.'

'I know.'

'But I'm strong,' she said, raising her arms like a body builder.

'Yeah, you're stronger than I thought.'

Then she smiled. Just as she was almost out of the door, she poked her head back in.

'I forgot,' she said, casually. 'It was that Irish man, Tommy, he helped. I think he's a bit scared of you, so he said not to say anything about helping.'

'Well, I look scary now.'

'Don't worry, I'll get you something for your nose, so it doesn't look all mashed up.'

'Thanks.'

'And don't get up or look in the mirror till I've come back,' she said swinging on the door handle. 'But you still look nice.'

'Do I?'

'Yeah, you've always looked nice, Steven.'

'Thanks.'

Then she smiled again and shut the door.

There was no denying it, she was attractive. When I thought about her like that, I knew I also fancied her. And I also struggled to figure why she and Anthony were an item? I always thought she went for him because he was nice and gentle, something different on the estate, because he had a talent for painting. Perhaps she thought he'd be famous one day and make loads of money. But when it came to the physical side of things, looks and everything, I would have to say, the two of them didn't match up.

Out of respect for Anthony, I all ways kept my distance. I didn't want to muck things up for him. I never made any moves. And perhaps she knew I would never do anything because of Anthony, probably because I missed my chance.

She'd come round my flat one day, which was a bit of a surprise because she normally would've texted to say she wanted something, but she came round my flat and I thought she looked a bit high. She was full of herself, excited, like something good had happened in her life. I made a cuppa and then she was looking through my CD collection and asking if I had some sounds that I'd never heard of. Then she asked if I could look, so I got down on my knees and was flipping through the discs, when I felt her hand go right up the back of my t-shirt.

That was when I had to decide: do I go for it?

I could have turned around and kissed her there and then, and the whole affair thing would have started up. It was tempting. I was tempted. But then there was this whole honesty thing. I knew I wouldn't feel good if I stepped on Anthony's toes. I mean, the poor guy was lucky to have Britney, and I didn't think he'd recover from me crapping on him like that. He was so into his gear he'd probably overdose and kill himself. Not that I had all those thoughts at the same time, as Britney was rubbing her hand up and down and over my shoulder blades. It was just instinct, gut. I wanted to, I could have done it, but it just didn't seem right. And when I did turn around, after Britney had taken her hand away, she smiled. It wasn't a smile of embarrassment, or pissed at being rejected. I think she just wanted to let me know she was interested, and if anything was going to happen, it was up to me to do it.

I left it like that, but it was on my mind, a lot. And it was on my mind, lying on the bed with Britney being all nursey. OK, she was worried about Anthony, but she wasn't begging me to track him down. True, I hadn't a clue what had happened to him, but he must have managed to miss Greg and Mickey and gone to ground. He'd be daft to turn up anywhere with those two on the prowl.

Then the next thought entered my head, something I needed to get my half-concussed brain around: how long did I have before Greg and Mickey came back? I had no doubt they would be coming to finish the job they'd done on me and I was in no fit state to take those two on. All I could feel was pain, throbbing pain all around my nose, the back of my head and all over my chest. All I could do was hate Greg more than I'd ever done before. He was making me feel violent. I was thinking good and hard about how I was going to kill him, make him suffer first, and then do what he thinks I would never do, and stick a knife right in him, right in his gut, so I could look at his face and think how good it was to see his ugly dying mug.

Of course, things are never that simple, but that's what kept going around and around in my head. And at the end of the day, it would be no loss to the human race, to have either Greg or Mickey despatched for all their sins and misdemeanours. After all, Greg was a full-blown psycho nutjob, who had spent years taking pleasure in beating the crap out of me and my mum. That's the kind of sick-job Greg was, right from the beginning. He loved violence. He got a buzz out of it, just like my old man did. They were cut from the same cloth and all that – drinking and fighting. It was simple. But there was one thing Greg wasn't good at, and that was thinking. I mean, it must have taken all his brain power to work out Mickey should sneak up behind me. But I think that's why Greg hated me, because I was always thinking, and that was a threat.

So, I decided, seeing as Greg couldn't really think for himself, it must have been my old man who told him to fuck things up for Grandad..

Which left me with one more thought.

What had happened to Tommy and why would that two-faced pervert do anything for me, if he was still alive?

2

I swung my legs over onto the floor and the pain in my chest shot right through me. Maybe they had busted a few ribs? It was even more painful when I stood up. However, the best cure for taking a beating is always to get going again. So, I moved like Frankenstein over to the door, holding the right side of my ribs because that was where all the pain was coming from. Out on the landing, I then I eased myself down the stairs, checking the bathroom on the first floor – which I decided I would have to use because I could seriously smell myself – and down on the ground floor. I listened. Mary's was all quiet, but there was plenty of noise coming from behind Tommy's door, which sounded like a bunch of toddlers running around. I gave it a police knock and the noise stopped. I left it a few more seconds before giving it another. There was more silence. If they thought I was going away they were wrong, and so to make sure they got the message, I gave it one hard kick, which wasn't too good for my ribs. It was making their mind up time.

They made the right decision.

I heard a bolt on the door being unlocked. A kid stuck his face out, no more than twelve I reckoned, with black smudges on his face, his hair all gelled and spiked.

'There's no one here,' he said, looking at me as if I was from social services.

I laughed, which only made my chest hurt.

'Really?' I said, moving closer so I could shove my foot in the door.

'You're not allowed in,' he said, keeping his naughty-looking face poking out.

'I'm a friend of Tommy's,' I said.

'Tommy's not here.'

'No, but you are. Who's with you?'

The kid delayed.

'A friend.'

'Yeah, well, I'm thirsty. Why don't you or your friend make me a nice cup of tea?'

The kid got the message and left the door open as he ran

back down the stairs. There were about ten steps to walk down before I got to see how Tommy lived with the kids.

He had turned his little bunker into an American diner. It was all red, white and blue, with photo frames of Harleys, fifties rock and rollers, candy and ice-cream. It was a sparkly little haven, a young boy's dream. In the middle of the room was a large red table with moulded plastic chairs. So, I sat on one side of the table, opposite the kid who had opened the door, and another kid, who looked just like his twin brother. Seeing them both together, blonde hair, dirty faces, sitting in their underpants, there was only one thing these kids did for a living.

'Have you put the kettle on?' I asked.

The kid who had opened the door shook his head.

'Is the kitchen through there?' I said, pointing at a closed curtain behind them.

The kid nodded.

I noticed another curtain to the side of me. I was going to keep my eye on that, and the kitchen, seeing as people liked jumping out and surprising me.

'Well, I tell you what, all you need do is answer my questions, and you won't need to make me a cup of tea, because this should be quick and easy for you.'

The other kid didn't look like he was going to talk. He was starting to shake, which must have been nerves, because it felt like a hundred degrees in Tommy's den.

'What happened to you?' asked the kid, who didn't like me looking too closely at his little friend.

'My brother,' I said.

'Does it hurt?' he asked.

'Yeah.'

Then both kids went quiet, looking at me, fidgeting.

'Do you know when Tommy's back then?' I asked.

The kid shook his head. I sat back, which set off the pain in my chest.

'How long you two been here?' I asked, puffing out my cheeks.

They both shrugged. It either didn't matter to them or they didn't know.

'Do you just live down here then, running around playing games?'

Again, they didn't say anything. They were used to playing dumb.

'I tell you what,' I said, easing myself forward, 'you just answer my questions and I won't report you to social services.'

'You can tell 'em what you want,' said the kid who could talk. 'They won't do anything.'

I gave him a mean look. I might be beaten up, but I wanted him to know I was more than capable of being a bastard.

'Listen you two,' I said, hoping this would help them focus. 'We can play games for a bit, but you don't want me coming back down here again, because I will do to you what my brother likes doing to me, and that's not very nice.'

The kids had balls because they didn't blink once.

'OK,' I said, hoping I'd get a straight answer. 'I am looking for my friend. The French lady who lives upstairs.'

'We don't know her,' said the kid.

'You don't have to know her, you just need to tell me when you last saw her.'

'We haven't seen her.'

This wasn't going to be easy.

'What about Mary?' I said. 'Do you know Mary, who

lives at the top of your stairs? I bet Tommy goes on about her?'

'Tommy doesn't like her,' said the kid.

'Why's that? Is she always complaining?'

'Yeah.'

'Does she complain about you?'

'Don't know.'

'That means yes then,' I said, looking at the kid's friend, who had his eyes down on the table. 'She was telling me Tommy wouldn't mend her door handle for her.'

'She's nutty.'

'She's lonely,' I said.

'She's into God and all that shit.'

'You're not a believer then?'

'Don't care.'

'No,' I said, smiling at the kid's sharpness. 'Not many people do.'

The kid relaxed, feeling good about himself because he thought he'd handled things.

'But I reckon,' I said, 'Mary doesn't like the way you and Tommy live together. Perhaps that's why she's always complaining?'

'She can't complain,' said the kid. 'She never pays her rent.'

'I thought she worked?'

The kid shook his head.

'She doesn't work. She doesn't do anything.'

'She's a hypocrite,' said the kid who had said nothing.

'Wow, that's a big word to use,' I said. 'Sounds like you've been to school.'

'He means the shaggers,' said the kid.

'What about them?'

'She likes them.'

'What does she like about them?'

'She keeps them in her room.'

'But she lives in a cupboard. You can't fit a midget in there.'

They both looked at me as if they had told me the truth and they shouldn't have to prove it. But it made sense – only religious nutjobs like her would call prostitutes fallen angels.

'What about my friend, the French lady upstairs, did she ever get involved?'

I got the twin-brother shrug.

It looked like Tommy had told them to say nothing about Dominique, but if they knew a few things about Mary, they might also know what Dominique got up to.

'OK,' I said. 'You need to tell me about my friend because if I go and look behind those curtains and I find Tommy there, I am going to beat the fucking crap out of you, and then I am going to cut Tommy so bad he'll look like a fucking car crash.'

It was Weak Spot who spoke.

'Your friend's gone,' he said. 'So you don't need to hang around here.'

'Yeah, where's she gone then?'

'We don't know,' they said together.

'And what did she do with Mary then?'

'They would go out together, at night, and bring them back.'

'Really?'

'Yeah.'

I looked at the kitchen curtain and the other curtain, just to see if there was any twitching.

'What about last night? Did you see anything going on?'

'We went out,' said the kid, 'to a party.'

'What time was that?'

'Before your brother came round.'

'How do you know that?'

'Because Tommy said we had to leave.'

I leaned across the table. I needed to know the kid wasn't lying to me.

'Tell me again,' I said, 'just to make sure. You and Tommy were not in the house when my brother and his ugly friend turned up?'

'No,' said the kid. 'We got back this morning.'

I sat back and had to think. In fact, I had a lot of thinking to do.

3

I stood in the pokey shower room, waiting for the hot water to come on, and looked at my face in the mirror. Britney was right about not looking because my nose was a mess and the side of my face was turning from red to yellow. I wondered if I could pass it off as a serious case of jaundice, but it was the nose that gave the beating away.

I stripped off and stepped into the shower, and just let the water run over me, as I tried to think through everything. Yeah, there was no doubt I had stuck my head in a wasp nest and the nasty buggers were out to sting me as much as they could. But what I didn't know was who was going to sting me next.

You see, when I said at the beginning of all this I didn't trust anybody, well, perhaps you can see why. Because if I believed the kids when they said it wasn't Tommy who had helped Britney last night, then who was it and why would she lie? But then I couldn't be sure those kids were telling me the truth because making out Tommy hadn't been round let him off the hook; it meant he couldn't have let Greg and Mickey in. But then, there was nothing stopping Tommy handing over a key and keeping out of the way. Whatever the truth, it meant I needed to keep Britney close because if she had got herself into something, she would need my kind of help. I think that was because I was beginning to have feelings for her, even if it meant stepping on Anthony's flat feet.

Which then got me thinking about Anthony. It was not like him to just disappear like that, unless he'd had some sort of warning about the Chuckle Brothers. The thing is, how did he know they were coming? Someone must have told him. And then I wondered if it was Anthony who had helped Britney last night. But if that's what they did, why were they pretending and what were they trying to hide?

My thinking is, when the water is all muddy, it's best just to wait and see and let the mud settle, so to speak. After all, something that should be simple – just tracking down Dominique – was turning into a bit of a jigsaw puzzle. And I was pretty sure Grandad knew a lot more before he got me roped in. He'd also know by now Greg and Mickey were around. He could easily put two and two together and there could be some great almighty turf war breaking out again.

The thing is, with Grandad and my old man, it was my old man who had lost a lot of ground. It's always a matter of time, in my line of business, before you end up inside, and once my old man had to do his time, it was a lot easier for me to move over to the other side. And that's why Greg thinks I'm a traitor, which is a load of BS, but it suits Greg to see it that way, to make me enemy number one, so he can have more for himself, or so he thinks. But Greg can't see beyond the end of his nose. He's just good at being a right nasty piece of work. The thing is, it can only get you so far in this game, which only proves Grandad was the right person to go with because he thinks about everything. That means you choose when to be violent and who is on the receiving end of the violence. That way, you tend to get a far better return. But Greg and Mickey were always random and out of control, even if they thought they knew what they were supposed to be doing. The only thing I really knew for sure was there must be high value on that piece of anatomy, and if Greg and Mickey weren't into Hannibal-type things, the only value on that hand was Grandad's ring. But that's a lot of hassle to go through, just to get hold of a gold wedding ring, something they could nick from a jeweller without giving it a second thought. And even if they wanted the ring, why get someone to chop off her hand? Why not just take it? Yeah, if you want the hand, you probably want it as proof – proof they were dead, or at least missing some vital parts. Whoever did it, and if it wasn't Greg or Mickey, they wanted to show they'd been seriously nasty.

As I turned off the shower, there was one more little thing that was bugging me: Mary downstairs. Even more than Tommy, who was just some pervert elf shagging little boys, Mary was a bit out there. Somehow, Dominique had got herself involved with the religious nutjob, although I had no idea why either of them would want to be spending time with prostitutes.

Out of the shower, I felt clean again. But all this moving around, upstairs and downstairs, was taking its toll on me.

Back in Dominique's room, I lay the wrong way up on the

bed so I could stare at Anthony's island painting. Grandad said they were good sellers. That's why Anthony probably painted them, unless he was like me and it was a way of dreaming about a better place, getting away from everybody and everything. But I'd never thought Anthony ever wanted to get away from the estate. He liked living with his parents, he had his gear on tap and Britney lived around the corner.

And that's when I stopped thinking. I was feeling tired and the island was helping me drift off to a good place.

4

I woke up and it was turning dark outside. Britney was lying on the beanbag smiling at me, with things she'd bought lying in front her feet. She hadn't bothered with the sausages , but she threw me a BLT and some crisps, which I ripped into.

'Why don't we have a drink?' she said, pulling herself up. 'I've got a bottle of vodka and some orange juice.'

'What's the time?' I said, because my first thought was about Greg and Mickey crashing through the door.

'Four o'clock,' she said, without looking at her watch.

Too early for the Chuckle Brothers to do anything, I decided. Britney looked like she needed alcohol and so did I, to ease the pain, which I could feel right across my face and my chest.

'So, how did you get back in?'

'Oh, I had to ask Tommy again.'

'He's alive then!'

'What's that?'

'Nothing. Well, I need to see him.'

'Oh, he said he was going out,' she said, pulling stuff from a shopping bag. 'I've got a plaster for your nose. Stay there.'

She stood by the bed and looked down at me, and pulled out a white plaster from a box.

'I asked at the pharmacy and they said this should help, but they said you should go and see a doctor if you think its broken.'

'All I know is it hurts like hell.'

Britney sighed and pulled the thick white plaster apart.

'I suppose this might hurt,' she said.

'Give it a go. I'm sure it's better than the way I look now.'

'OK… stay still.'

Britney bent over and her hair tickled the side of my face.

'It's OK,' I said, as she paused.

She smoothed it out and leaned back, pleased with her handy work.

'Thanks,' I said, feeling around the sides of my nose.

'I don't think you should get into any more fights,' she said, turning around and looking on the floor for the carton of orange juice and bottle of vodka. 'Does she have any glasses?'

'Try in there,' I said, pointing to the cabinet by the fridge.

She pulled out a couple of mugs.

'I got some clothes for you. I had to guess your size. Shirt and trousers, and a nice coat.'

I looked down at the bags and took out the clothes she'd bought. I was never that interested in the way I looked, which is why I wore tracksuits, but it looked like she'd given it some thought. I kept it decent as I put the clothes on.

'You look nice,' she said, pouring out an equal measure of vodka and orange juice.

'Yeah, feels better,' I said.

Britney gave me the drink and she sat back down on the beanbag.

'So, do you know where she is?' she asked.

'Who, Dominique? No,' I said, easing myself back onto the bed. 'I've done it a few times before, look for her, but it's never been like this.'

'Is she mad?'

'She goes a bit crazy. It's why Grandad likes to keep an eye on her, and because of who he is.'

'Do you think he loves her?'

'Yeah.'

Britney paused, thinking, then she said, 'I think love is the one thing that matters most in life.'

'What type of love would that be?' I said.

'There is only one type of love.'

'And what's that then?' I said, taking a drink that had more vodka in it than I really wanted.

'Just love,' said Britney. 'There is no need to think about it, it just is. You know when you are in love, you just know it.'

'How do you know?'

Britney pulled herself up a little, folding her legs up against her chest.

'I suppose you don't know what love is until you have fallen in love,' she said.

It sounded like she meant I had missed out on this bit of basic, and I wasn't a follower of the 'love is everything' view of things.

'Is that you and Anthony then?'

Britney shrugged, but it didn't look to me like she was thinking about Anthony.

'Have you ever fallen in love… been in love?' she asked,

keeping her eyes on the floor.

'I don't know,' I said. 'You think you're in love and then things go wrong, and then you work out you weren't in love, it was something else.'

'Just because it goes wrong doesn't mean it wasn't love. It needs to be unconditional.'

'There's always conditions,' I said. 'There's conditions to what you want, and what they want.'

'Of course there is, silly,' she said, laughing. 'That means you're sharing. You're giving and supporting each other.'

'OK,' I said, pressing the plaster down around my nose. 'I'll make sure next time I get a fair share of that giving and sharing.'

Britney leaned towards me.

'Have you got your eye on someone then?'

'No,' I said, but she knew I wasn't being straight with her. 'Also, in my line of work, you have to be careful.'

'That's so sad,' she said, as she spread herself out on the beanbag.

Lights from outside were coming through the window. It was the only thing keeping the room lit, so I switched on the lamp next to me.

'The thing is,' I said, 'I don't want to think about how somebody else is feeling. I don't want to share my time and thoughts.'

'That sounds sad to me, like you are stuck on being on your own,' said Britney, stretching her arms and yawning.

I pushed the plaster down on my nose again.

'It would need to be the right kind of love,' I said, 'if I was to fall in love.'

'Oh!' said Britney, who swayed towards her glass and grabbed it. 'You are a softy then.'

'You sound like Greg,' I said, laughing. 'But I don't want someone just to be with someone...'

'You see!' said Britney, spilling her drink as she put it to her mouth. 'You do want to find love!'

With Britney, I didn't know what I wanted. But I didn't mind her thinking something could happen, if she hung around, which is what I needed her to do anyway.

'You know,' I said, 'I suppose I can miss things when they're staring me in the face.'

She laughed.

'Do you think we could fall in love?' she said, giving me an intense look.

'Why would we?'

'You never know, with no hang-ups, no jealousies. We could drift in and out of each other's lives without trying to control anything.'

'Do you think?'

'Yes! You can love more than one person,' said Britney, her eyes widening.

'Can you?' I said, keen to see how serious she wanted to be with me. 'It could get messy.'

'It's not just about Anthony.'

'Yeah, who else visits your planet?'

'I can't say, I don't want to say.'

'But you just have.'

'No, I haven't. We're going to forget about it.'

'Why?'

'Because I like you,' she said, finishing off her vodka.

So, there was more than one Anthony. There was another guy in her orbit, but who the fuck was it?

'Do you want to watch the film then?'

'Yeah, sure,' I said, wondering if Anthony knew his

missus had something on the side. 'But it isn't a proper film. It's something Dominique's husband did.'

'Oh, does he make films?'

'Not really, but he could prove me wrong.'

'OK, let's give it a go,' she said, as she got the DVD player out of another bag and unpacked it all.

Once we were all plugged in, she wanted to get all cuddly and settled down on the bed with me. I put my arm around her. We listened to the disc spinning before it came to life and the title of the film came up and the whole thing got going. We couldn't make much sense of it, and not just because we didn't speak French. It was all muddled up, jumping around like a jack-in-the-box. Nobody could act and we didn't know if they were meant to be acting or just being themselves. But there was a bit with Dominique in it. Britney said she was beautiful, and how she could be a real actress because she had the looks. She did, I thought to myself, but she was also sometimes psychotic and more than likely dead. And then there was a scene at the end with a load of guys piling out of a lorry and running around like crazy and pretending to be free.

'It's about immigrants,' I said, pleased with myself for getting to grips with it.

But Britney was asleep. Must be the vodka, I thought, and the useless film.

I'd learnt nothing, I decided, as I watched the word *Fini* come up. I pulled my arm from underneath her. Just as I was about to stop the thing, another scene popped up.

'Christ sake!' I said, as I looked down at the remote, checking for the pause button and pointing it at the TV.

I got my face right up close. Texas must have recorded over what was on the DVD. I played it forwards and backwards and then played it forwards again, and then paused it. Yeah, there was no doubt about it, it was Mary, smiling like the cat who'd got the cream, throwing confetti over a blushing bride and her new husband. It was a registry wedding and I was pretty sure right behind her was Dominique.

Then there was a knock on the door.

I thought about grabbing a knife but knew there was no point in being tooled-up. If it was Greg and Mickey, they would've kicked the door in.

At first, I laughed when I opened the door, because it was the cheeky kid from Tommy's den.

'Got some clothes on then,' I said.

'I saw your mate, the one you came with, the junkie guy.'

'Yeah, when was that?'

'Just now.'

'Where?'

'He was at the tube station. He was with the two guys, you know, your brother and the dumb one. He looked scared.'

'Yeah?'

Then the kid must have read my mind. 'I've got the key for the back door.'

'Stay there,' I said, keeping the door open.

I shouted at Britney to wake up.

'It's Greg and Mickey,' I said, as I pressed the eject button on the DVD player. 'The kid just told me they're on their way. Come on, we've got to get the fuck out of here.'

'Are you sure?' she said, still coming round.

'I believe the kid,' I said, as I scanned the room for my phone. 'We can sneak out the back.'

'What about Anthony?' she said, as she pushed herself up on the bed.

I found my phone on the bedside cabinet and tried to think as fast as I could.

'I need Anthony,' she said, looking as if she didn't want to go anywhere. 'He's not come back.'

'I know,' I said, hoping the kid wouldn't hear me as I said, 'he's hiding.'

She was thinking but she didn't have time to think. It was make-or-break time for her.

'You need to come with me,' I said, hoping she would get the message.

'OK, let me get my coat.'

I checked to make sure the kid was still there.

'Come on,' I said. 'We need to go.'

She was stalling.

'Come on, Britney! Trust me, if you stay here, they will do some serious damage.'

She looked shocked when I said this, then she stood next to me and looked back into the room, and then at Anthony's island painting.

'Is your girlfriend coming?' asked the kid.

'Yeah, we're coming.'

Downstairs, the kid unlocked the door to the back garden.

'Did Tommy tell you to do this?' I asked.

The kid nodded and then locked the door. I said a small prayer to the God almighty as I stuck my hand underneath the rotting table and pulled out the icebox.

'What's that?' said Britney.

'A frozen asset,' I said, making sure it felt like it had the right weight for the hand to still be in there.

'It's an icebox,' she said.

'Yeah, I know.'

'Did you put it there?'

'Yeah.'

I could tell she wanted to know more, but I wasn't about to tell her anything because we didn't have time, and I didn't want her to know.

'Follow me,' I said.

We had enough light to see shapes in front of us, but we fell over a load of rubble. I pulled Britney up and we pushed through the crap to the back gate. I yanked it open.

'Down here,' I said, looking back to make sure we were not being followed.

I could see the streetlights at the bottom of the path and had to push away a load of brambles, before we made it out onto the street.

'Are we getting the tube?' asked Britney.

'No, we can't go that way. We need to walk the other way for as long as we can. If we see a cab, we get in it.'

'Where are we going?' said Britney, as she stayed by my side.

There was only one place where I thought we could go, and where I could carry on looking for Dominique.

'Don't worry,' I said. 'It will be safe.'

'They won't find us?'

'I hope not,' I said, keeping a good pace as we walked down a street full of old town houses.

Britney was quiet after that as we kept going, looking at any car as it drove by, hoping it was a cab. Then the rain started. We were getting soaked but I wasn't about to stop. Best to keep going. Then we came across a cabbie dropping off somebody and hopped in. I told him where to go and we settled down for a journey across London. Britney laid her head in my lap. I didn't mind; it was a nice feeling. It made me think more about how much I liked her. And my fancying

Britney and not going for it, well, that was getting less, because I was thinking Anthony might not make it. Greg and Mickey must have got lucky and caught him, making his way back to the bedsit after lying low. Now that's bad luck, running into those two. But there was no way I was going to tell Britney, not just yet. And Greg and Mickey will be seriously pissed to not to find me there, and knowing them, they would take it out on Anthony. I can take a beating, but I wasn't sure Anthony was going to survive, even if they didn't want to kill him.

I messaged Grandad because I needed my little safety house ready for us when I arrived. I also told him to thank Tommy for me. Perhaps I was wrong about the little Irish pervert, who knows. But it was something I needed to think about.

I then looked down at Britney and started to stroke hair. I could feel my hands pull off some of the rain.

'That's nice,' she said. 'Has it stopped raining?'

'Yeah,' I said, as light from the street and the offices poured into the cab and lit up the side of her face.

I could feel it now: the desire, the pull of what I thought I was always going to keep to myself.

5

Texas had done his duty and let us both in. We stood in the centre of the swanky pad, thanking this strange-looking woman who was the honeypot. She was short with dyed copper hair, and all the signs her wrinkled skin was moving from middle age to old age.

'It's a lovely room,' said Britney.

'Thank you,' said Ann in a soft German accent, looking at us like we were two homeless wasters.

'Musa has told me about you, Mr Steven,' said Ann.

She could tell straight away I didn't know who she was talking about until she looked at Texas. He was like a child.

'I understand you are helping to look for Dominique?' she said. 'Have you found her then, Mr Steven?'

'No,' I said, which was about as much as I was going to say, even with an icebox in my hand.

'As you know, Musa would also like to find his wife.'

'And our friend,' chipped in Britney.

'Oh,' said Ann, who didn't know what Britney was going on about.

'It's a guy called Anthony,' I said. 'He was helping me, but he's gone missing.'

'Oh dear,' said Ann, 'so many people who go missing.'

'I like Anthony,' said Texas.

'You know him?' asked Britney.

'He paints the islands.'

I think this made Britney proud.

'We can help you,' said Ann. 'You can stay in the guest room. Musa will show you, I think.'

'Thanks,' I said, knowing Grandad would have told them they needed to help.

'While you are here, Mr Steven,' said Ann, 'we can look together.'

I was about to say no to that, when she added, 'I have arranged for you to meet a friend. Do you like art, Mr Steven?'

'Now and again,' I said.

'Good. Musa will take you tomorrow to somewhere

modern where you will meet our friend. He is a doctor, but he cannot treat your injuries, Mr Steven, but I think he will be of help to you.'

I could tell Britney was worried she'd be left on her own.

'And you, you are very pretty,' said Ann. 'I think you can go to a big shop, so you can have some dry new clothes. We all need clothes to stand in, Mr Steven.'

I was going to say no to that because I didn't want to risk Britney being out there, but she was pretty much reading my mind.

'She will be with me, Mr Steven.'

I looked at Britney, who wasn't jumping up and down about it.

'Or you can stay in the guest room. But there is no television. Will you be bored?'

'I don't know,' said Britney. 'I'm tired. I'm exhausted. I could sleep all night and day.'

'Well, go with Musa now and Mr Steven can go tomorrow.'

'Yes, yes, yes, you follow me,' said Texas, who looked keen to get us away from his client.

We went through the same painted door he had used to show me the kitchen, but at the bottom of the stairs, we ended up going through the other door, which took us into the guest room. It was like a little sea cabin room, made up of a bunk bed, painted sea-view walls and lumps of driftwood on the shelves. There was even a small round window like a porthole. It was a good hideaway, but also a trap if Greg and Mickey found us.

Texas left us sharpish, like he was under instructions not to stay, but Britney seemed a lot happier.

'Is this like your boat?' she asked, sitting on the bottom

bunk, squeezing her wet hair.

I laughed.

'If only,' I said. 'You can't swing a dead cat in my cabin.'

'I've never seen your boat,' she said.

'There's not much to see.'

'I'd like to see it.'

'Yeah?'

'How far can you go in it?'

'How far?'

'Yes, where have you gone in it?'

'Not far. Just up and down the river, along the coast a bit. But it's too dangerous to cross the channel.'

'What do you mean?'

'It's a busy place, shipping lanes…'

'What, like a zebra crossing?'

I laughed again.

'They wouldn't see you crossing,' I said.

'Oh, so it would be dangerous.'

'Yeah.'

I pulled off my shirt and trousers and climbed onto the top bunk.

'I've been thinking,' said Britney, 'about Anthony.'

'Yeah?'

'Do you think he's all right?'

I paused and then decided it was best to keep lying for a bit longer.

'Yeah, he'll be OK.'

'Are you sure? He's been gone so long. And your brother, what would he do if he found him?'

'Nothing,' I said, having thought of a good lie to keep Britney quiet. 'He hasn't done anything wrong, has he. They don't like me, that's why they had a go at me. As soon as I find Dominique, everything will sort itself out.'

'But what if you don't?'

That was a good question and I didn't have a good answer.

'Look, I think he's still laying low,' I said. 'Don't worry, we'll find him and everything will be OK.'

'Are you sure?'

'Yeah, trust me.'

'I do,' said Britney, who I could hear starting to pull off her wet clothes.

By the time she was undressed and under the bed sheets, she was asleep. It was also what I needed because there was one more thing I wanted to do.

I hadn't heard Texas or his girlfriend come downstairs, so I nipped into the kitchen to get a knife. There was no way I could carry on walking around with the bloody icebox and the only thing that was going to matter had to be the ring.

Britney was off with the fairies as I opened the icebox and looked at the hand wrapped in plastic. Even in my line of work, it was a bit gruesome having to pull the thing out and put it on the floor. The ring was frozen on, so I got the knife and put the blade as close to the ring as I could and pushed down hard. It took a few goes and the finger snapped off. It took a few wriggles to get the ring, wrap the hand and the broken finger, and put it back in the icebox.

Job done. I slid the knife under my mattress and got back on top.

So, this was what it was all about, I said to myself: a wedding ring, a gold band with an inscription inside, which made no sense to me. Just a few letters and numbers as far as I could tell. But I had what I thought Greg and Mickey wanted, as I fixed it onto my keyring. And it was going to stay there until I found Dominique, or the rest of her body.

Day 4

1

Texas seemed to think I'd never been inside an art gallery or museum as he led me into Tate Modern. Usually, the place was heaving with tourists and you couldn't get a good look at anything, but he had left me sitting on a bench with a good view of *Naked Man with Knife*, all about the struggle between Cain and Abel, good and evil. I wasn't sure on what side of the good and the evil I stood, but I liked to think of myself as being good when you added it all up. Anyway, a few minutes later, the guy I was meant to meet was sitting next to me. He wasn't as black as Texas, had a massive African nose, a bald head and a seriously expensive suit.

'Are you Mr Stevens?' he asked, in the best posh accent I'd ever heard.

'It's Steven,' I said. 'You don't have to put mister in front of it.'

He smiled as I gave him the once over. He was a big guy, nice and fat, with thick thighs and a big stomach.

'My name is Doctor Sangoma,' he said, nodding at the painting. 'What do you think?'

'It's good,' I said, wondering if I should read out the card below the painting that told you all about it.

'It is! In one word, you are right. However, people would be surprised, unless they were a student of modern art, to know such a sculptural work came from the same brush as the abstract drippings of Jackson Pollock.'

'Yeah, I like both.'

'Excellent! They all have similar meaning, origin in thought, influenced by interest in the unconscious, what lies behind our thin veneer of rational thought, our dreams and aspirations. But do you know what else I like about this painting?'

'How would I? We've just met.'

But it didn't stop him.

'I made a mistake when I viewed it for the first time. I thought it was one figure, not three. I thought, this must be a soldier, a Roman centurion.'

'Easily done.'

'Tell me, Steven,' he said, looking at the side of my face, 'is that what you are, a centurion? After all, you look as if you have been in a battle, no?'

I decided to look Sangoma in the eye, so he could see for himself the yellow bruises under the nose plaster.

'I fell down the stairs,' I said, thinking about all the times my mum used to say the same thing after she took a beating.

'Oh, a terrible accident.'

'It hurt.'

'Yes, I am sure,' he said, keeping his hands flat on his thighs. 'But time heals the flesh wounds. What about the deeper scars, Steven? Do they hurt? The less visible ones as fatigue drains us of our capability for fighting, when we can be at our most vulnerable, don't you think?'

'Not for me,' I said, thinking I was about to leave if he was going to waste my time.

'I am sorry, Steven. It is a bad habit of mine, a failing of my profession, to always want to elucidate, provide reason in the vacuous space of unreason. I know you want me to get to the point of our meeting.'

'That would help.'

'The thing is, Steven, once the thirst for knowledge has grabbed you, it is difficult to stop,' he said, which meant he was going to say what he wanted to say, the way he wanted to say it. 'But I am not an impractical man. I am aware of the world in terms of what it is, what is required to survive in it. I also suspect you have a great talent for surviving in this unreasoned world.'

'I've managed up to now.'

'I'm glad to hear it, Steven. But our poor Dominique has a greater burden than others, don't you think? And now she has disappeared.'

'It's not the first time. So, do you know where she is?'

'There is a simple answer to that: no. However, she is sorely missed by everyone.'

'Who is everyone?'

'That, I am afraid, is not a simple answer. And I know a man like you will find me annoying because I take too long to explain myself. But what we have in common here is a need to find Dominique, quickly, before it is too late.'

This got me thinking. 'Does she work for you?'

Sangoma paused and looked at the painting.

'Do you know, Steven, that in Roman times, citizenship could be obtained, even if you were a slave, even if you were a nobody, a nothing? You could eventually become a citizen of that great empire. In fact, I would even suggest to you, it was easier back then, among the barbarity and savagery, to become a citizen with rights. Take you, Steven, a centurion I think at heart, a good soldier. Had you been captured and enslaved and spent a good twenty years fighting for the empire, you could have been granted all the freedoms and privileges of a Roman citizen. There was no equivocation, no mealy-mouthed watering down of what you were entitled to. You had earned it and you deserved it!'

'You're talking about immigrants,' I said.

'They die every minute of the day, Steven. Washed down the Mediterranean drain. Thousands upon thousands: men, women, children and babies. And what is their crime? None. Just a desire, a need, a want for a better life, denied them in their own country, impoverished and raped by decades of exploitation. They are immigrants, Steven, but they are treated like slaves. The only difference is, they probably stood a better chance of citizenship two thousand years ago.'

'Is that what Dominique did for you, she helped with the immigrants?'

Sangoma just smiled. He had said it in not so many words.

'For you, Steven, I can tell you what you need to know, to help us and to help you in your search. But I must emphasise that time is against us.'

'OK,' I said, ready to see how far Sangoma wanted to go. 'Let's say for now we want the same thing, to find Dominique. But just so you know, in the past it was easy, she would just go off wandering. But this time it's different, it's turning into a spider's web and I'm thinking, are you part of that web?'

'Steven, I am not the spider.'

'You do know then,' I said, making sure he was looking at me, 'what might happen if you BS me and end up wasting my time?'

'My apologies, I have this propensity to start off superior. We all have our defences, don't you think?' he said, narrowing his eyes. 'But trust me, I would not be here if I did not think we had a mutual interest.'

'Listen, I'm not here to like you.'

'Of course not. My mistake. Our worlds collide but are forever separate.'

'Yeah, that's right, we won't be having dinner parties, me and you.'

'A shame in some ways, but you are right, that is not why we are here.'

I looked around. The floor of the gallery was filling up with a bunch of noisy school kids. The game, or whatever he was doing, had to end.

'So,' I said, 'what can you tell me?'

'Our beautiful Dominique,' he said, as he also started taking notice of who was coming and going, 'was with us two or three weeks ago. It was a wedding.'

'What sort of a wedding?'

'A wedding like any other. A man and a woman seeking to declare to the world a special type of love, giving and sharing of what they can do to help and support each other.'

'Who were they, the people getting married?'

'Ah, that, Steven, is not the point in all of this. What matters here, what is of interest, is that there were no signs of anything wrong with Dominique.'

'How do you know?'

'I know, Steven, because I am her doctor, her psychiatrist.'

That would make sense, I thought to myself.

'She was,' said Sangoma, 'if there is such a thing, normal. No signs of depression, mania, psychosis.'

'That means,' I said, making sure I understood him, 'there was no reason for her to disappear, like she has in the past.'

'It would be unusual. Dominique's pattern of behaviour always indicated she would start progressively feeling different. She had never suddenly become unwell, overnight, so to speak.'

There was good and bad in what Sangoma said because Dominique hadn't gone off on a wild one, but it also meant she was more than likely a victim.

'Was that the last time you saw her, at this wedding?'

'Yes.'

'And who else was there?'

'People who can be trusted.'

I snorted at that.

'I appreciate, Steven, that trust is a relative thing, but you do not need to know who the people are.'

'If I want to know who the people are, you will have to tell me.'

'Steven, the path you seek, the one I am about to guide you down, cannot just be strong-minded by yourself. The picture is abstract, opaque; it needs to be, I am afraid.'

I groaned.

'Nothing you've told me sounds in anyway legit,' I said. 'Which, I suppose, is why you have not contacted the police?'

Sangoma shrugged.

'But she's your patient,' I said. 'You must be on some seriously dodgy ground?'

'We are all taking a lot of risks for the greater good.

Dominique knew that.'

'So, you've got her involved in something that has put her life in danger?'

'No,' said Sangoma. 'The connections are long. These are not simple threads.'

A pack of school kids was filling up the gallery floor with a load of noise as they ran up to every painting making notes on their clipboards. It felt like we had to finish.

'The best I can offer you is this: there was a man at the wedding who nobody had seen before.'

'I thought you said these people could be trusted?'

'All those we knew,' he said. 'But this man was not part of the wedding, he was just noticed.'

'And what did he do?'

'He just watched, pretending he was not watching.'

'Was he watching Dominique? Did he follow her?'

'He left before the ceremony had finished. But we like to note these things.'

'And have you seen him since?'

'Yes,' he said. 'He has been seen one other time and now he is here, but please just continue to look at me. It is not the place to cause a fuss.'

My body tightened because I was prepared to jump up and grab the guy as soon as I knew who he was.

'Our mystery man is sitting on the bench next to the Picasso. Do you know the one I mean?'

'Yes,' I said, glancing over Sangoma's shoulder.

There was only one guy on the bench, with his back to me, wearing a black hoodie.

'I am going to leave now, Steven. I suspect he will follow me. I will lose him and you will follow him.'

'It's not that easy,' I said. 'I'm not a bloody sniffer dog.'

'No, Steven, you are a centurion, you are a soldier, and I suggest you bring the full weight of your sword down upon him, if it is required.'

'But why is the clock ticking?'

'That, Steven, is for you to ask of your master.'

And that was it. Sangoma was up and out of there like an effing ninja. And he was right, the guy in the black hoodie got up and seemed to follow him out. At last, I thought, there was something of a lead, after all the smoke and mirrors. And he would be easy to track because his hoodie had no branding.. I was on his tail, ready to grab him as soon as I got outside. However, he was a bit of a Scarlet Pimpernel because he disappeared in the crowds outside as if he'd not existed. I stood there cursing and was about to start running up to anyone wearing black when two guys walked up either side of me. It meant only one thing: coppers.

2

I was pissed they had stopped me catching up with the guy in the black hoodie, and sometimes you never really know if you've been arrested or you're just 'helping with their enquiries'. They must've picked up my scent at some point in my little journey to meet Sangoma and were keen on speaking to me about serious matters. It meant a nice little ride back to West London, settling down in a basement interview room, with the table fixed to the wall, hard plastic chairs and no air.

Now, nine times out of ten, you must keep focused on the coppers in front of you, but if you're lucky, you might get the odd carving on the table to keep you amused. However, all I had to look at, so they told me, was Detective Carter and Police Officer Hardy. It was Carter who looked corrupt; there was that look in his eyes that told me he had about the same amount of scruples as the people I meet in my regular line of business. He looked way too smug. I reckoned he was the kind of copper who thinks he lives on the edge, playing with the rules to get the job done. And I could smell him. He stank of BO, like some stagnant pond. I almost felt sorry for the little cherub, Police Officer Hardy, having to sit next to him, who had made me a cup of tea in a shiny Met Police centenary mug.

First off, Carter was all interested in why I was beaten up.

'Did your brother do this to you?' he said, as if he was on my side and was going to help bring justice and equality into my life.

'No,' I said.

'Because looking at you tells me somebody has given you a right going over.'

'It feels like it,' I said.

Then Carter paused, probably wondering why he was there, before it all came back to him.

'We know your brother has reappeared. We've had intel from our colleagues up in Manchester. So, you haven't bumped into him recently, up here or back on the estate?'

'No,' I said. 'I haven't seen him.'

Carter paused and Police Officer Hardy did his best to look interested.

'What I would like from you, Steven,' said Carter, whose cogs were back working, 'is a little bit of co-operation. It would be in your best interest.'

The easiest thing was to tell him to blow it out his arse.

However, as I wasn't too keen on being locked up for no good reason. I thought it best to let him feel I might be his friend one day.

'Well,' I said, 'to be honest with you, I haven't seen him. He doesn't even bother to see our mum any more.'

Carter didn't believe me of course, but he carried on.

'OK, so what about Mickey O'Donnell?'

'Mickey Finn!' I said, laughing. 'I thought he was still in jail? He'll have to behave himself then, Mickey, because people won't like it if he gets up to his funny stuff again.'

'What sort of funny stuff would that be, Steven?'

'You know, what he did to those young girls.'

'Is that all he does?'

'As far as I can tell,' I said.

Carter looked at his silent partner, then Police Officer Hardy said, 'Well, jail is a bit like finishing school for you lot. He's probably come out thinking he has graduated into being a proper little criminal.'

I could have given a little speech about there not being too many options available, but then it wouldn't have made much sense to either of them. But that's the thing with coppers, most of them don't seem to realise they are just like us, playing the same game, keeping everything looking normal. But deep down, they know they don't make a difference, and we don't do anything that stops most people living.

'OK, Steven,' said Carter. 'We know your brother Greg and Mickey have been seen together. Now, I find it difficult to imagine, with those two crawling out of the swamp, that no one knows what they are up to. You're a bit more intelligent than most, so you know we want information because we are hearing some rather unsavoury things.'

'Yeah, like what?'

'We were hoping you could tell us?'

'I can guess,' I said.

'Why don't you guess for us then?'

This was going to be easy.

'Well, knowing Greg,' I said, sipping my tea, 'if he's had to leave Manchester, it's because he's got right up somebody's nose. You know, it's not his territory, so he hasn't got a lot of back-up.'

'Possibly, but that's not we've heard.'

'Oh right, so what have you heard then?'

'Steven,' said Carter, smirking, 'you know that's something we are not going to discuss. You are here to help us, not us help you.'

I shrugged.

'So, there is nothing that you could add to our understanding of what Greg and his little friend are up to?'

'It's interesting,' I said, 'but we're not exactly on speaking terms.'

'We know that, Steven, which is why we think you've bumped into him, with a bang!'

'It wasn't Greg,' I said. 'It was a misunderstanding.'

'With whom?'

'Just an idiot in a pub. I deserved it, took my punishment. It's over.'

'Sounds like you were the idiot then.'

'Yeah, I don't drink much normally, so it got a bit stupid.'

'OK, we could go with that, for now, if you can help us?'

'How's that then?'

'If you see your brother, we want to know.'

'Yeah, that's fair enough,' I said.

'Here's my card,' said Carter, handing over his Met Police business card.

I took it. You never know when you might need them.

'Are you fond of art then, Steven?' asked Carter.

'Yeah, some of it.'

'Who's your favourite artist then?'

'Jackson Pollock,' I said, wondering if they had also been watching me talking to Sangoma.

'Yeah, what do you like about him?'

'I don't know, I don't think about it.'

'Well, that makes me think you don't know anything about art.'

'Yeah, and what do you know about art then?'

Carter paused, which I took to mean he didn't know anything.

'How often do you visit art galleries?' he asked.

'Not often.'

'So, that was a bit of a one off then today?'

'Yeah.'

'And you didn't meet anyone?'

'Some guy talked to me about a painting.'

'Yeah?'

'Yeah, he said he'd got it all wrong when he first saw it, but he'd read the label and so he knew he was an idiot.'

'You mean, you thought he was an idiot?'

'Yeah.'

'Because you are an expert after all.'

'No, I just read the label.'

'Clever.'

'It's not difficult.'

'I'm impressed that you can read.'

'I think it's something to do with being intelligent.'

That pissed off Carter. Then he asked me a stupid question. 'So, you didn't arrange to meet your brother Greg in the art museum?'

'If you think Greg is going to meet me in a place like that, then you really don't know anything about him.'

'We thought it unlikely, as unlikely as you knowing anything about art.'

'Are you trying to tell me that if I go to an art gallery I'll be under suspicion?'

'In your case, Steven, because you're such a dedicated criminal, I think we can safely say that everything you do should be treated with suspicion. Fortunately for you, we can accept you didn't meet your brother, and we also think that stealing a painting is it bit outside your skill set, so we are wondering why you should be there talking to strangers?'

'They talk to me.'

'Oh yes, is that because you've got such an engaging demeanour, that you don't really look like a six-foot villain who's had the shit kicked out of them?'

'Well, you know what these arty types are like, they don't discriminate.'

'Christ, Officer Hardy, I think our young Steven has been on an equality and diversity training course, and there I was thinking it was only us who had to consider every little feature of humanity before we could open our mouths.'

'He isn't going to tell us anything,' said Police Officer Hardy. 'And even if he did, he'd still be a lying git.'

'Oh, I don't know, I think our Steven is capable of telling us something, if he thought it was in our mutual interest.'

He was wrong, but there was no harm in him thinking that.

'Right, I tell you what, Steven,' said Carter. 'You want to know why we've brought you in?'

'OK,' I said.

'We think we've found a little friend of yours.'

'Yeah?'

'Yeah, he's dead.'

The point of him saying it like that was to see what kind of reaction he got, and he didn't get any.

'Well, we think you can help us, Steven. We think you might know this one we dragged out of the river in the early hours of this morning. Skinny little runt, isn't he, Officer Hardy.'

The cheeky cherub smiled.

'You see, the thing is,' said Carter, who was clearly going to enjoy the rest of this, 'we've been trying to find out who the runt is. And then, being the great detectives that we are, we did a little piece of detective work and we ended up at an address where it turns out you are in temporary residence.'

If Carter wanted me to confirm or deny, I wasn't taking the bait.

'So, what are you doing there, Steven?'

'I don't have temporary residence. I was born here.'

'He's funny, isn't he Officer Hardy.'

'Not really,' came the reply.

'But that doesn't matter, Steven, because contrary to what people like you might think, we do have a sense of humour. In fact, what's funny is I don't think you know what you've got yourself into, do you, Steven?'

'You're right,' I said. 'I do find abstract expressionism sometimes confusing.'

Carter didn't like that. His sense of humour didn't last long.

'We know what you're up to,' said Carter. 'We know you're looking for Dominique Housseyni, and so are we. The thing is, Steven, she hasn't just gone AWOL. She's disappeared, hasn't she, and no one, not even you, Steven, knows where she is, do you?'

When coppers tell you everything they know, thinking that they are cleverer than you, there's no need to say anything, so I didn't. Then they tried the silent treatment. They must have thought I was going to crack under the weight of peace and quiet, but they didn't know how much I like the quiet.

'I'll give you one more chance, Steven,' said Carter. 'Tell us anything you know about Dominique, anything you think would help us to track her down, anything in her possession, because we think she is at risk.'

I didn't and finished my tea.

'He's not saying anything,' said the super alert Police Officer Hardy.

They then looked at each other, frustrated, because I think they must have thought, before they brought me in, I was going to give in on this one. But the thing is, with coppers, you just never tell them anything, ever.

'OK, Steven,' said Carter, 'we just wanted to see if you would help. Seeing as you won't, you are free to go. You have my card. I know you never will ring me, but you never know on this one. Officer Hardy will show you the way out.'

I pushed myself up from the chair, with only one thought on my mind: who had Greg killed and thrown in the river, who was this guy in the black hoodie and why did Carter want to know what Dominique possessed?

3

The thing about coppers is they just love following you around, but I can always tell a plain-clothes copper. You see, as strange as this may sound, I always know when I'm being followed if I can get a good look at their shoes, because they always wear sensible shoes. I mean the straight type – plain, simple, sensible shoes. And the guy behind me, who I clocked as soon as I left the police station, had sensible shoes.

He kept pace with me, along the main roads, but there was no way I was going to lead him to where I was shacked up. Having visited the Tate this morning, it seemed only right that I keep up my cultural education, and the Natural History Museum was only about half a mile from the big house that Texas lived in. So, the plan was to wander around in circles in there until he gets bored, or until I give him the slip.

If it was summer, I would have been stuck outside in some boring tourist queue, but as it was the middle of winter, I just walked right in, nodding to security as they guided me through. I checked on Sensible Shoes, making sure he was keeping up, and started walking around the great big building. It didn't take me long to find they still had a load of dead birds in glass cabinets. I thought Greg and Mickey would look good in one of them, all stuffed and nicely sown up.

The thing is, it was always going to be a matter of time before the police got involved with the likes of me and Greg wandering around town. The coppers hated us, but we were their bread and butter. I mean, they don't have to be a Sherlock Holmes to work anything out. All they need do is turn us upside down, give us a good shake and something will fall out. Me and my brother, we were class A villains, and one day we will get caught and do our time. But before that happens, all I was thinking was I would like to kill Greg on the outside, before I end up on the inside, because he deserved what was coming to him.

The way I saw it, last night, he would have got back into that house just as me and Britney got out, and created all kinds of hell for anybody who was around. Greg was a great big ape with the mind of an ape, so he wouldn't have messed about. He'd be raging with me not being there, and no one would be able to give him any answers, or at least not the kind of answers he would have wanted. You know, even if Tommy's kid admitted he had helped me and Britney, he wouldn't have known where we had gone. Greg would have had the option to do one of the kids or Anthony. And the skinny runt the coppers dragged out of the river could be Anthony because Anthony is just as good a fit as any one of those kids, because he's such a wasted-looking junkie. I suppose there was even more reason for Britney to be worried about not getting a signal from Anthony's phone. That's when I had a bad image of Greg and Mickey marching Anthony back out of the house, using up a load of gear on him and washing him down the river. Christ, Mrs C would be so cut up if it turns out to be Anthony. One way or another, I needed to find out who the coppers had dragged out of the pond. I think I owed it to Britney, and I owed it to the kid.

I got to the hall where the giant bones of Dippy were supposed to hang, but there was nothing, just a closed off space. They had shipped him out and were putting something new in. With no Dippy around, I headed on through the corridors, making sure Sensible Shoes kept pace because I didn't want him to feel useless and left out. There was a load of new dinosaurs, which I followed around some dark corridors, where the boffins had put in time telling us all the things we used to know about dinosaurs weren't true any more. Which is OK, I get it, how you say one thing and later find out you're wrong, and so you have to say something else.

You know one truth and then another one comes along.

And all this looking for Dominique was full of that, like peeling an onion, layer after layer of truth and lies. But I didn't hold it against anyone for not telling me what I needed to know. There seemed to be good reasons to keep quiet about certain things, but there's only so long you can pretend before you get to the point where you need to know the truth and not lies. You know, I couldn't think of anyone who had said anything to me that didn't sound like they were hiding something from me. Nothing unusual in that, given my line of work, but there was too much hiding, too many half-truths and fake news. There were bits and pieces, and a feeling there was something back at Dominique's bedsit that I had missed. I knew Mary was part of some dodgy marriage thing. I knew Tommy was a mix of bad and good. But it was bugging me, seriously bugging me, even if I still had the best clue with me, which was the ring.

And then there was time: what Sangoma had said about how time was running out, or there was very little time left to get things sorted. Whose time, I wondered? Was it Dominique's time, the time she had left to live, if she was still alive? Had she been kidnapped by the guy in the black hoodie? Was he trying to get money off Grandad? I had no doubt he would pop up again. I know Sangoma wanted me to follow and chase like a good little doggy, but I decided, for now, he was not something I had to go chasing. I was going to keep an eye out for him and make sure the slippery bugger didn't get away from me next time.

I heard a dinosaur roar and watched the tourists laughing at this T-Rex giving it some. Yeah, that was one deadly bastard in its time, and the perfect place to give old Sensible Shoes the slip. I left him staring at the jaws of the dinosaur and hurried off to see how the mammals on the other side of the museum were getting on. I wandered around, nodding my head to my ancient relatives, and learnt how they had to adapt and survive, eat or be eaten, something which I had to do a lot of myself. There were some crazy animals back then, who worked on just the same things as me, sniffing out prey and making sure they didn't get gobbled up. At the end of the day, the clever little rodents won out. And I knew who the dinosaurs were: people like my old man and my brother, thinking being big and nasty was always going to get them what they wanted. Well, it had all fallen apart for them, and they were trying to make a bit of a comeback. But I didn't need the whole turf war thing to be breaking out again. All the loyalty BS would start up, picking sides and having to get my hands dirty, and I mean a lot dirtier than the way things are now. For me, keeping things back from Grandad to avoid the shit hitting the fan was the best way to go.

But the more I thought about it, I knew I was just part of some jigsaw puzzle, trying to make all the pieces fit together, but with Grandad holding the bigger picture. I was just pushing things along, sniffing around like a pig looking for truffles, but what was coming up to the surface wasn't some luxury food stuff. It was a whiff of lies and double dealing. However, it was not Grandad's style to tell anybody anything he did, so there was no point in asking. You had to figure it out yourself, put together the bits and pieces, and even if you came up with the right answer, you had to keep it to yourself.

I found some corner and messaged Grandad. I told him pretty much everything apart from the severed hand and the ring. As I waited to hear back, I started thinking about what Sangoma had said about me being a soldier, a centurion, how I do the bidding of my master. I'd always planned better things for myself, but there's never a right time to move on and leave all this behind. Grandad was right, when I met him at the fort: it was weird how people were desperate to come here, when most of us wanted to leave. Me, I didn't care who came over here. Perhaps Dominique had asked Grandad for help with getting immigrants their papers, just like she'd done for Texas, that is until he wanted out of the marriage. She was always wanting to help people. Grandad had the money, the contacts, the ways and means to get people across the channel if it came to it. With their little immigrant marriage scheme they had going on, with Mary providing prostitutes as brides and acting as witnesses, perhaps Sangoma, Ann and Texas wanted me to look for Dominique because she was part of it? Because there was no doubt Dominique mattered to them.

I got up and walked around for a bit, checking to see if Sensible Shoes had managed to track me down again. I couldn't see him and reckoned he had been gobbled up by the T-Rex. I was looking at a stuffed salamander when I got the message back from Grandad. It took a few minutes to scroll through it all, but he wanted me to take my foot off the pedal, even if he said time was a thing he was also worried about. He wanted me to make things look normal, hold back on looking for Dominique. He had things he needed to look into, and he also thought it was a good idea I hold off from telling Britney anything and to keep her up in London with me. But he made it clear I wasn't to follow Sangoma's wish to track down the black hoodie guy. I was working for him and I was to leave it with him. And with the police poking their noses in – one thing I was right about – Grandad said he knew all about Carter, how he was a right corrupt bastard and how the body in the river meant only one thing. He was working with Greg.

4

Britney said she had done nothing all day, just sat around waiting to hear from me.

'Texas and Ann have gone away,' she said, sitting on the bottom bunk bed and fiddling with her hair like she was a little girl.

'Did you say gone away or run away?'

'What do you mean?'

'Nothing,' I said, before I had to add, 'Let's just say if they are keen for me to find Dominique, it's odd that they have buggered off.'

'Ann said it was only for a few days and you can stay here. She didn't mind because she knows you are doing something that matters, but she also said she was doing things that are important and that matter as well.'

I sat down in what I think you would call a bath chair and puffed out my cheeks.

'And I told her,' said Britney, who was slow to finish what she was saying, 'I told her I had to go.'

'Do you?' I said, checking between Britney's legs and under the bed that the icebox was still there.

'It's my mum,' she said, as she sighed. 'She's panicking because the police have been to see her.'

'Yeah,' I said, wondering how many bent coppers there were going to be in all of this. 'Why were they talking to your mum then?'

'Because I wasn't there!' she said, getting all angry. 'They said they wanted to talk to me.'

'About what?'

'They wouldn't tell my mum, but she's freaked out.'

'Are you going to speak to them?'

'I don't know,' said Britney, who got up from the bunk bed and looked like she wanted to start pacing around the room.

'You don't have to talk to them,' I said, trying to think of a good reason to keep Britney from running off back to her mum.

'That's easy for you to say. What if they ask me about all of this?'

'All of what?'

'You know, Dominique.'

'But you don't know anything about Dominique.'

'I know she's gone missing.'

'She always goes missing.'

'She doesn't *always* go missing.'

Britney sat back down on the bunk bed, looking stressed by the whole thing.

'I can't stay here and leave my mum on her own,' she said, fidgeting with her hands. 'My dad's not around is he, and there's Anthony as well. Perhaps he's back with his mum?'

'Have you heard from him?' I asked, taking my phone out of my pocket.

'No, nothing.'

Britney then pushed her hands into her face and rubbed her eyes. That's when I noticed she had been crying. I suppose I could have said I didn't know if Anthony was dead or alive, but that would only have added to how bad she was feeling. For Britney, just at this moment, her mum came first.

'OK,' I said, 'if you have to go back because of your mum, then you'd better go back.'

Britney looked up at me with her eyes all red.

'I don't need your permission, Steven!' she said, showing me how angry she felt.

I kept quiet.

'You know,' she said, 'I've been worrying about Anthony all this time, and now there's my mum. It's not easy you know. I'm not like you, I'm not used to all of this.'

'Look,' I said, leaning forward in the chair, so I was closer to her, 'you're right, you don't need my permission to do anything, but you have to think about the risks. You have to be aware…'

'What do you mean?' she said, looking like she knew, but maybe she needed me to spell it out to her.

'There's Greg, my brother. He's dangerous and he's involved in Dominique going missing, there's no doubt about it, and…'

I paused because if I wasn't careful, I was going to end up saying something about Anthony, but Britney wasn't going to let it go.

'And what?'

'And, my brother, he's going to be looking for people involved with Dominique.'

'You mean Anthony?'

'Yeah.'

I think this made it real for Britney. I could see she was thinking, thinking about Anthony after he's been off the radar for the last few days, wondering if Greg had got hold of him and gone all nasty.

'The thing is,' I said, trying my best to think of something that could make things sound better, 'Anthony not letting you or me know where he is is a good thing…'

Britney started shaking her head, as I carried on. 'Because it could mean he's not a victim. By not telling us anything, by not letting us know anything, it means if we did get trapped by Greg, we couldn't tell him jack-shit because we just don't know anything.'

'But Greg still hurt you…'

'I know,' I said, checking on my nose plaster, as I sat back in the chair. 'But he is always going to try and do that because of other things. But for you, well, you need to be careful, because Greg is looking for something, and I think Anthony might be involved.'

'How?'

'I don't know yet, but it's what makes me think he's OK, for now.'

'Are you sure?'

I had to lie because I wanted Britney to still have faith. She didn't need to know Anthony might have been pulled out of the river, not just yet.

'Yeah, I'm pretty sure of it,' I said, doing my best to look honest.

She now knew, I hoped, if she didn't already, that she couldn't go running back to her mum's and think she just needed to answer some questions with the police. And it wasn't just the coppers she needed to be worried about because Greg would be working his way towards her if he thought Anthony hadn't given him what he wants. The only question on my mind: did Britney know anything?

'It's just Anthony,' she said. 'I do care about him.'

'I should hope so, he *is* your boyfriend.'

That's when Britney gave me this sideways look that had more meaning than just being casual.

'Let's go upstairs,' she said, taking in a deep breath. 'I hate it down here, it's like a prison. We can pretend we're rich and famous for five minutes.'

'I don't mind rich,' I said, 'but famous ain't for me.'

'You never know, Steven, you could be on one of those reality TV shows. They'd love you, all hard and masculine, with just a little soft touch to smooth off those hard edges.'

I tried to think of something snappy, but nothing came to me, and Britney was almost halfway up the stairs before I got out of my chair. However, it gave me the chance to have a quick look in the icebox. It was all there, as I had left it. So, Britney was either being a good girl and hadn't looked inside, or she didn't need to look because she knew what was there. Then, I was thinking about what Grandad had said: keep her close. But I didn't have the heart to stop her going to see her mum. I would be keeping her prisoner. Plus, it would only make operating more difficult because even if I was meant to keep my head down, I wasn't going to.

Upstairs, I found Britney with her feet up on one of the leather sofas.

'Does it still hurt?' she said, as I shut the painted door.

'What, the bruises? Not so much.'

'Let's have a look at your nose.'

'Do we have to?'

'Yes,' she said, as she stood up and pointed to the leather sofa for me to lay down on, like a proper little patient.

'Are you training to be a nurse?' I said, as I lay on the sofa.

'No, I don't want to do anything like that,' she said, as she sat on the edge next to me, her hair falling over her face.

'Yeah, what do you want then?'

'I want something like this,' she said, turning to look at

the high-end luxury we were renting for five minutes.

'There's always a price to pay for this kind of thing, if that's what you want,' I said. 'Unless you're born into it.'

'I don't mind,' she said, as she pulled back the plaster over my nose.

I made a wimpy noise, as the pain went up and along my face.

'You might have broken it,' she said.

'It wasn't me.'

'You know what I mean.'

Britney then moved over me as if she was doing a scanner, checking out all my moving parts. And then I wanted her. At that moment, all I had to do was push myself up and kiss her.

'What?' she said, as she smiled back at me.

She knew, I thought. She was waiting, waiting for me to make a move.

'Nothing,' I said.

Then she looked at me for what seemed like ages, smiling, giggling, before standing up and waving my ugly stained plaster in the air.

'You don't need this,' she said, as she moved around the room. 'The thing is, rich people don't have bins because they have people to pick things up for them.'

'Chuck it on the floor then.'

'No, that's not nice, and we – I – have some self-respect.'

Britney then folded it up and put it in her pocket.

'I'll keep it as a souvenir of our short break together.'

'Really, it means that much to you to spend time with me?'

'Yes, with you, and with Anthony, and with my mum, and with somebody else…'

So, there was someone else in Britney's life.

'Does Anthony know?' I said, trying to sound concerned for my old friend.

'About what?' said Britney, as she moved behind the piano and looked out of the windows.

'About there being someone else?'

'Anthony knows,' she said, keeping her back to me and looking out on the square below.

'And he's OK with that?'

Britney then turned to face me.

'He doesn't get to choose, Steven.'

'But you do.'

'I can, I have.'

'So, you and Anthony, you're not an item any more?'

'We're not a bloody piece of china on a shelf!' said Britney, who was staying behind the piano.

Deep down, I was well pissed. I didn't like secrets, mainly when things were so tense.

'So, who is this guy?'

'Who said it was a guy?'

'Who is this woman?'

'It's not a woman.'

'So, why is this guy a secret?'

'Because it's my life and none of your business.'

'Is he a butcher?'

'What does that mean?'

'You know, does he chop up meat, cut off hands?'

'No, he's not a butcher. Anyway, what does that mean?'

'What does what mean?'

'Why say he's a butcher and he cuts off hands?'

'Why not?'

'But you said it like it means something to me.'

'Does it?'

'No.'

I didn't believe her, and she was angry again, almost upset. I had to say something.

'Why did you tell me,' I said, 'about this other guy?'

'Don't you know?' said Britney, staring at me, her eyes demanding something from me.

'Do you want me to be jealous?' I said.

'Are you?'

'I can't get jealous about someone I don't know.'

'Can you get jealous if it's just about me?'

I eased myself up from lying down, holding my chest.

'You know, Britney,' I said, keeping my voice calm and steady, 'you're in the middle of something that is not going to end with everyone going home for tea and crumpets. You know who I work for, you know what I do, and given what I am trying to find out, secrets make me nervous, even if you think they have nothing to do with Grandad's girlfriend. Hand on heart, can you say you've had nothing to do with Dominique?'

'But you said she's just gone missing, like she always does.'

'Well, it's true to say she's gone missing, but this is not normal,' I said, getting suspicious of Britney avoiding the question. 'And your boyfriend, or your ex-boyfriend, he has also gone missing.'

'And what have you done!' said Britney, almost shouting at me. 'You don't seem to think Anthony going missing is a problem, but you're running around getting yourself beaten up for that bastard, for him, for his bloody mistress!'

Britney had told me enough.

'What do you know?' I said.

'What do you mean?'

'Britney, if you think there's something I should know, then you should tell me now. It will make things easier.'

She threw her hands up in the air and spun around on the spot.

'Come on, Steven!' she said. 'You're meant to be the clever one. You tell me what *you* know. You're the one that can make the difference, not me, not Anthony.'

I sat back on the sofa. Nothing she was saying made sense.

She was crying as she came from behind the piano and sat next to me. She took my hand.

'What if I said I want you,' she said.

'Do you?'

'Yes.'

'For how long?'

Britney burst out laughing.

'How's six months?' she said, wiping away a tear. 'Is that long enough?'

'Yeah, for me it is.'

'I'll think about it,' she said, keeping up a smile.

Britney pulled the sides of my face and kissed me on the lips.

'You still haven't answered my question,' I said.

'I know,' said Britney. 'And I will, soon, but my mum needs me.'

'Does anyone else?'

If they did, Britney wasn't saying.

5

Britney might have thought I was a gent walking her to the tube station, but I was making sure there were no predators or watchers hanging around. I got her to download the app I was using for messaging and told her I would be back on the estate in the next day or two. All I asked was she keep me updated on what the police wanted, and/or if Anthony wanders back into her life. But I told her that she should keep her head down and not go looking for Anthony round his mum's because there was a risk Greg could get hold of her. What I didn't say, but what I was thinking, was that Britney knew a lot more, which meant Greg might know by now and he'd be keen to get hold of her.

I picked up a pizza on the way back and settled down in the kitchen with a nice cup of tea. Once I'd finished munching, I had the kind of quiet I liked, which was silence. However, being the curious type, I wasn't going to let the evening go to waste. With Texas and Ann keeping out of the way, it was a bit of a gift to go and have another look around the place.

I know it sounds a bit creepy going into people's bedrooms, but that wasn't why I turned on the light to their silky red palace. One of the things that had been bugging me ever since Texas had shown me his little love nest was the connecting door to the ex-boyfriend. I had to have a look-see, and it was either going to lead me into another dimension or I would end up having to pretend I was a lost kiss-o-gram, but one way or another, I had to know what was behind that door.

I used the pencil torch on my keyring and shone it through the keyhole. From what I could tell, there was a short corridor with another door at the bottom, like an outside door, with a door number and a door knocker. I pushed down on the handle, pulled and then pushed the connecting door. It was stiff but the door opened, and the light from the bedroom lit up the rest of the tunnel. It was about ten yards long. On the left was a light switch, but I decided to just sneak down. I put my ear to the door and could hear someone moving around, coughing and singing to themselves. I was being cheeky as hell and taking a risk, but if I pissed off Ann, I didn't care, because this was going to be my last night here. I gave it a good knock and waited. There was silence and then some shuffling. That's when I noticed the spy hole in the door and so I smiled as best I could and wished I had brought with me the pizza box. I was kind of surprised, but not very, when Sangoma opened the door.

'Steven, we meet again. How nice of you to come via the tradesman's entrance.'

'Yeah, well, I ain't got any sacks of coal, if that's what you're thinking.'

'Plenty of curiosity, though.'

'All doors lead to somewhere.'

'You are right.'

I could tell he was thinking about whether to let me in or not.

'A sign of innate intelligence,' he said, 'for which the reward is to spend a little more time with me, even if I haven't asked for it.'

'I can go if you want,' I said.

'No, no,' he said, opening the door wider so I could come in. 'My flat, as you can see, is mainly for me and not visitors.'

'You mean because it's a mess?' I said, walking between piles of books and magazines stacked on the floor.

'All perfectly ordered, in my mind,' he said, almost tripping over some books that were hidden by the darkness of the place.

As far as I could tell it was just one room with a small

kitchen at the back. There was a dinginess to it, and it had anything and everything lying on the floor. But one thing that straight away caught my eye, propped up against an old wooden cabinet, was a fresh canvas of Dominique.

'Yes, Steven, your friend, my patient,' he said, as I sat down in an armchair. 'A portrait, not for me but her lover.'

'Who is her lover?' I said, hoping he would say someone else other than Grandad.

'Your master, Steven, and grand overlord of all that he surveys.'

'Yeah,' I said, not too happy if he was going to bang on again about the slave/master, soldier/sailor crap thing.

'Let me get you a drink, of whiskey perhaps?'

'No, you're all right, I'm not much of a drinker really.'

'Very wise, but I am,' he said.

This was a different Sangoma, I thought, from the one I'd met in the Tate. He was still snotty and arrogant, but I had invaded his space, which meant he couldn't pretend as much that he was somehow superior. He poured himself a drink out of a decanter (and I don't think it was his first of the night), sitting opposite me on a large two-seater. There was a wooden coffee table underneath another pile of crap, but he managed to find a few inches to put his glass.

'I know,' he said, leaning back, 'that such a portrait might have escalated in your mind that I am now elevated up the list of suspects, but I can assure you, Dominique's pictorial representation is merely for safe keeping. She wanted it done for your...'

He was going to say master again, but I gave him a face.

'For your patron, shall we say.'

'Right,' I said. 'It's very good. A good likeness and all that.'

111

'Yes, painted by someone I think we both know.'

'Oh right and who's that?'

'A young man called Anthony.'

'Anthony!' I said, sounding way too surprised. 'You know Anthony?'

'Yes, of course. Anthony was introduced to me by Dominique. A talented young artist she had said, who I understand still lives very much in your world.'

'Yeah, he lives on the estate with his mum and dad.'

'Precisely.'

He took a large gulp of whiskey before plonking it down on top of some magazines, which were piled on top of each other at odd angles. I was just waiting for it to fall on the carpet.

'But,' he said, easing back and crossing his legs, 'before I offer you my observations on your artistic friend, what can you tell me about our mystery man?'

'He remains a mystery,' I said.

'You didn't follow him after I left?'

'I tried, but the police stopped me.'

'And that stopped you from following him?'

'Yeah.'

'What did they say, the police?'

He was looking worried, so I thought it best to calm him down.

'They wanted to talk to me about other things,' I said.

'So, nothing about…'

And he paused, trying to find the right words for me.

'The things that you have probably worked out for yourself?'

This was my opportunity, I thought, to get Sangoma to say what he was up to.

'You mean the marriages?' I said.

'Yes,' he said, reaching across to get his whiskey, 'the marriages. They are necessary to help protect and secure those of us who have made it across the choppy waters.'

'Is that what you did?'

'A long time ago, yes. I was persecuted in my own country. Not for much – it doesn't take a lot to find your life and liberty in danger. For that, I am grateful to Ann.'

'She saved you?'

'Yes, she saved me.'

'And so that's what you do now, you help people like yourself get married, so they can stay here?'

'We arrange it, you could say. And for that we always need an audience, friends and family, to make things look more credible.'

'So, where do you get these people from?'

'Contacts, networks. Some paid, some giving.'

'Prostitutes?'

'Yes, Steven, even women, sometimes boys, who have to sell their bodies to survive, but can earn a little for the greater good.'

He finished off his whiskey.

'Are you sure you don't want one?' he said, as he got to his feet. 'It will be good for the injuries that have coloured your face, although, of course, that is not medically accurate, but I offer you my prescription.'

'They're just bruises.'

'Of the physical kind,' he said, pouring a load of whiskey into two glasses.

I would have preferred a cup of tea, but he'd probably lace that with alcohol.

'However, regarding my other point,' he said, as he came

back and handed me a serious amount of whiskey. 'We are all forced into an exchange of our needs and wants, Steven, be it love, marriage, freedom. We have to sell something to get a return. I sometimes wish there was purity out there, unsullied, cleansed of all the dirt that clogs up the arteries of life. But it would be naïve, utopian, to think we are better than people who must sell all or parts of themselves to survive. That is why I have pledged to myself to do the best I can, to make things better whenever I can. For instance, it would be easy to look down on a woman like Ann, to think that she is just a rich white woman who exploits young Africans for her own needs.'

I didn't say anything.

'But in an imperfect world, Ann makes a difference,' he said, sitting back down with a bump. 'She saves lives, lives that are also worth saving. Take Musa: did you know that Musa means saved from water? That is how she has helped, been there for the bodies that have floated across, smuggled through customs, treated worse than the dirty crates of goods they hide themselves in.'

'Yeah, but I'm not sure he has much of a talent for film making.'

Sangoma grinned.

'No, well, we are not perfect, and Ann deserves her little indulgences.'

I sipped the whiskey.

'So,' I said, 'you have a nice little thing going on here. You've got people on tap to come and play happy marriages, and you've got Dominique caught up in all of this through Mary?'

'Ah, Mary! Another patient of mine, I'm afraid. But you are wrong, Steven, because Dominique has been involved for many years. For instance, of her own volition, she married Musa so he could stay. Unfortunately, she was reticent to finish what she had started – she hesitated over signing the divorce papers.'

'Perhaps it was love then?'

'No, she had found happiness with your master, our puppet master, our man who holds so many lives in his hands. Hence time, Steven, time is running out.'

'Why?' I said.

'Ah, although I have the propensity to indulge you tonight, I still have things I must guard against.'

I took a sip of whiskey. That was probably as far he was going to go, so I decided to leave it. I looked at Dominique's portrait. Anthony had done a good job and caught that thing about her – the force of nature that was always present in her eyes.

'You're looking at the portrait,' he said. 'Not bad for an untrained artist, but I must say, whilst I don't approve of what you do, Steven, I like you, but with that young man, I do not approve of, or like.'

I was about to jump to his defence and let Sangoma know he might be talking ill of the dead, when he had this to say: 'You know, Steven, I think Dominique is dead.'

'How do you know?'

'I don't, I just think, instinctively, that she is no longer with us.'

When he had said that, it seemed clear. There was no point in pretending she was alive. After all, I had carried around her severed hand and to think she was still breathing was dumb.

'The question is, Steven, who did it and why?'

I was about to say I had two people at the top of my list

and then decided it was not something Sangoma needed to know.

'Well, if she's dead, I still need to find her,' I said. 'But why don't you like Anthony? They're friends.'

'Are you friends with Anthony?'

'We grew up together, went to the same school and that. The thing is, I don't think we were ever friends. I mean, it never felt like we were real friends.'

'You are perceptive, Steven. Don't you perhaps think there is something strange, odd, missing in a character at times? You must come across people who have sociopathic tendencies in abundance?'

'Who, Anthony?' I said, surprised. 'He was just a junkie who likes to paint.'

'Was?'

'Is,' I replied.

'You of all people know that you should never judge a book by the quality of its cover.'

'Well, as you say, nobody's perfect.'

'No, you are right, and I am the least perfect of them all. However, I was always worried that Dominique could not see what I could see.'

'Yeah, and what's that?'

'Duplicity, Steven. That young man is drenched in it.'

I laughed to myself because as far as I knew, he could be drenched in dirty Thames water.

'OK,' I said, thinking I'd better pin Sangoma down on this one before he wanders off on another long load of sentences. 'You just need to tell me what you know.'

'In this instance, Steven, I don't know anything. I don't have facts, just science of the mind and intuition.'

'So, you think he's a liar? Trust me, Doctor, where I come

from, everyone lies, some of the time or all of the time.'

'I don't doubt that, and there will be good social and cultural reasons for that. But in the mix, there are others who have a greater propensity to thrive in such an environment, whose frustration and anger is the fuel that feeds a distorted and dysfunctional mind.'

'You're describing my brother, not Anthony,' I said.

Sangoma paused. He certainly was keen for me to know something about Anthony.

'You remember my patronising introduction in the art gallery?' he said.

'How can I forget.'

'How art is open to interpretation, that the viewer can see one thing and the artist mean another.'

'Look,' I said, 'if you think Anthony is a liar, you just need to say, and tell me what he's lied about.'

'These are intangible threads, but they are threads, nonetheless. My only thought is that if our mysterious man does not want to be found, should you not look at and talk with all who know Dominique?'

'I usually do,' I said.

'Ah, I would take from your tone that you have yet to talk to Anthony?'

'It hasn't been easy…'

Sangoma stood up, wobbled on his feet and then stood by the painting of Dominique.

'The artist does not just draw what he or she sees. They also need to make decisions as to what they want you, the viewer, to see. I believe that young man's personality means he cannot help but reveal more in his art than he would want you to see.'

'Well, all I can see is Dominique.'

'True, I think that is a correct observation, but is that the case for all his art, for all he paints?'

The penny dropped. Sangoma was giving me the heavy hint, the bleeding obvious, that I needed to go and look at one of Anthony's island paintings again.

I let Sangoma ramble on, moaning about the failure of art to have any meaning in people's lives. Sangoma was one of those honest people, who had ideas and wanted to see things done right. It's what drove him. And he knew the rules of the game, so he wasn't stupid enough to let the rules stop him if he thought things were wrong. He had put himself at a lot of risk, but that was because he knew where he'd come from, he knew what it took to survive. People had helped him and he wasn't going to forget what people had done for him. He could pay them back by doing what he could for other people who were struggling, what Sangoma called sanctuary.

By the time he'd drunk enough whiskey to put himself to sleep, I had one thing to give him: the icebox. I trusted him because he seemed the only one who wanted answers, just as much as me. All he had to do, I said, was to not look inside and not let anyone else get hold of it, not until we had found Dominique.

6

I got a cab back to North London with a few things still rolling around in my head. Sangoma had planted the seed in my mind that I needed to get back into Dominique's bedsit, so I could see why Sangoma would call Anthony a liar. But I hadn't ever seen it in Anthony, being all bitter and twisted, because you'd have to be seriously bitter to do something to Dominique, which is also about getting back at Grandad. He was like me, just a bit trapped with things on the estate. But then there's my rule: don't trust anybody. And nobody is ever straight, and the straighter people look, the more likely they are to be hiding something.

Who knows? The more I thought about it, the more I thought I should tell the cabbie to go back, do as I was told by Grandad and put my feet up. Then I started thinking about Britney again. Riding in the cab through the night, it got me thinking about how we had run away from my brother and Mickey, and how I'd had those feelings for her, how I knew she wanted me, even if she was with Anthony or some other guy. But if there was anyone who matched the description of what Sangoma called duplicity, it was Britney. She was angry – angry about Grandad, angry about Dominique. And there I was, thinking all sorts of suspicious things about Anthony, but Britney was looking more and more like a slippery snake. The problem was, I couldn't help liking her and couldn't help thinking I wanted her to be with me. Then something else popped into my head and I wondered if she just hated me. I wondered if she hated everything I was, who I worked for, what I did. It's not like I'm the kind of person who is easy to like. I could be just as evil as my brother. Yeah, in a way she didn't need to like me, so why should she want to offer herself to me? What was in it for her and what was she trying to get out of me?

I told the cabbie to pull up a few streets away from the house, just so I could do a little recon and avoid being jumped on. Everything seemed quiet, and I had the key, so it was easy for me to get back in. There was a light on in Mary's room as I zipped up the stairs. I was going to be extra careful this time because I didn't need Greg and Mickey waiting for me. I turned the key and then kicked the door. It slammed against the wall. I left the light off and scanned the room. Everything was just the way we had left it. I saw the vodka bottle on the floor, which was half full. Perhaps it was the whiskey, or the adrenaline, but I fancied a swig. Then I lay on the bed, the wrong way up, and let the light from outside give me enough to stare at Anthony's painting.

It was just an island, a simple island like the one I dream of. There was blue sea, waves on the beach, a beach hut in the middle, a palm tree, blue sky and a sun. There was nothing special about it, no puzzle to solve. But it was bugging me, there might be something there, a hidden message. I kept looking, but I couldn't see it. Perhaps I wasn't looking, like Sangoma said? *Just don't look at the surface*, I told myself. *Look for hidden meanings*. I tried but it wasn't working. So I decided to be simple about it and put the light on. I jumped back up on the bed and got up real close. Then I noticed it, right next to the beach hut, a small wooden box, painted like a pirate's treasure chest. I laughed out loud. That was cheeky, funny. Did Anthony mean this was like *Treasure Island*, like the story? I stepped back and wondered what kind of message there was in a painting with a little treasure box by the beach hut. Well, that's what islands like this were used for, in pirate stories, hiding stolen booty. But Anthony hasn't got any money, he hasn't done any robberies, and I was pretty sure Britney or Dominique hadn't been running around holding up banks and post offices. However, before I had chance to think about it anymore, there was a very gentle tap on the door. I knew it wasn't Greg or Mickey because they would've busted it open.

'It's me...' said the voice behind the door.

It was Tommy's kid, the talkative one, the one who had given me the warning.

'Can I come in?'

There was a small chance he was with somebody, so I got ready as I opened the door. It looked like he was on his own.

'Come in then,' I said, as I took a good look down the stairs.

He stood in the room like he'd done something wrong, looking scared and frightened. I needed to know what had happened last night, so having the kid there saved me the trouble of kicking the door in to Tommy's den. However, I wasn't going to let the kid know I wanted to know, not until he'd said his piece.

'What is it?' I said.

He kept quiet, looking down on the floor.

'All right,' I said, sitting down on the bed. 'Something happened has it?'

The kid nodded.

'You need to tell me then, don't you?' I said.

He was thinking about it.

'I hoped it was you, when I heard the front door,' he said.

'Yeah, why's that?'

He shrugged.

'That's all right,' I said, thinking about offering him a vodka because he looked so scared and nervous. 'Is it all quiet downstairs then, no parties?'

He nodded.

'Where's Tommy?' I asked.

'He's in hospital,' he said, about ready to blubber.

'Yeah, what's wrong with him?'

'Your brother,' he said, almost spitting out the words. 'And they took my friend.'

I paused, watching him to make sure he was telling me the truth.

'Was there two of them – my brother and the other guy?'

'Yeah and your junkie friend was with them, but he ran away.'

That accounts for Anthony, I thought, and means he could still be alive.

'Did they beat up Tommy?'

'Yeah.'

'So, why didn't they do you?'

'I was hiding,' he said. 'In the cupboard.'

'Who let them in?'

'What?'

'Who let them into the house?'

'I don't know. They must have a key or something because Tommy wasn't going to let them back in after you had gone.'

'And they took your little buddy?'

'His name's Danny.'

'Did they say why they wanted him?'

'They wanted something, they kept going on about it. A box. And they said they were going to get it out of him because Tommy was lying.'

'Who?'

'My friend. They said he knows because Tommy didn't keep anything from…'

'From who?'

'From us…'

'Is that true?'

The kid nodded again.

'And do you know?'

'No! We don't know nothing, and Danny doesn't know

nothing, but they kept saying you had left something here and we knew where it was, but there wasn't anything so they said we must have taken it and they were going to get it out of Danny.'

'Here,' I said, picking up the vodka bottle. 'Do you want a drink?'

'Thanks,' he said.

He still stood there, still shaking.

'Sit down,' I said, pointing to the bed.

He paused.

'Don't worry,' I said, 'I won't hurt you.'

He took a big swig from the bottle and shivered as the alcohol went down.

'Is it just you then, downstairs, on your own?'

'Yeah.'

'You ever been on your own?'

He nodded.

'But you don't like it, right?'

He didn't say anything.

'Did the coppers come around this morning?' I asked.

This time he nodded.

'Did you speak to them?'

'No. The nutty woman did.'

'You mean Mary?'

'Yeah.'

'So, where were you then?'

'I was hiding. I don't like them. They'd send me back if they found me.'

'Where's that then?'

'The children's home. I hate it there, no one cares.'

I suppose I owed him, and Tommy, for letting us know about those two scumbags coming for us again the other day.

'Looks to me as if you're a bit lonely down there,' I said.

He took another swig of vodka and then put the bottle on the bedside cabinet.

'I tell you what,' I said, 'when I was beat up, I laid on that bed and looked up at that picture.'

The kid looked up.

'It's nice,' he said.

'Listen, put your feet up and lie down. They aren't going to come back for you because they've got nothing to come back for. As far as you're concerned, they don't know about you.'

'But what if Danny tells them?'

I didn't say anything. He started to whimper. I let him cry for a bit and then he did lay down on the bed. For a moment, he reminded me of myself, when I was a kid, staying around Mrs C's to escape from all the violence my old man had caused. Those were lonely times. I knew how sad and tragic life could be, and I reckoned that's how he was feeling, and not for the first time.

After about ten minutes, the kid was asleep. I got up and turned the light out. I opened the door and looked downstairs to make sure the kid hadn't been fooling me. The place was quiet. The light under Mary's door was still on. I knocked.

'It's me,' I said, 'Steven.'

I thought she'd be nervous about opening the door, so I was just about to go when I could hear her struggling with the doorknob. I waited and then she poked her head out. She didn't look too pleased to see me, perhaps because she was standing there in her nightie.

'Not out looking for angels then?' I said.

'What do you want, Steven? It looks like you've been in trouble, and I don't have any tea or milk.'

'That's all right,' I said, 'I'm just leaving.'

'Oh, are you going anywhere nice?'

'One day,' I said, 'but not tonight.'

'The police have been here,' she said, 'asking about Tommy and his boys downstairs and your friend.'

'Yeah, I know,' I said. 'But there was something else you might be able to help me with.'

'I can't help you, Steven. All these things are now in the hands of the police.'

'Not everything. There was a woman with me here the other night and all day yesterday, with red hair. She said you were the one who let her in.'

Mary didn't say anything. She just looked at me with her goofy teeth.

'Listen, it's nothing to do with the police, I just wanted to know if you'd met her, that's all.'

Again, she didn't say anything, or she didn't understand.

'OK, don't worry,' I said. 'But if you really want to help, there's a fallen angel upstairs in Dominique's room. He could do with someone who knows how to care.'

Then I left it with her, as I went back out the front door and into the night.

Day 5

1

I spent the night in a hotel, and in the morning got up nice and early. I hadn't heard from Grandad, which was good in a way because I had family business to attend to.

I messaged my old man to tell him I was on my way to see him. I knew after last night the whole Dominique thing was turning into some big battle. There was no point in trying to think it could be stopped. I now needed to hear what the old man had to say because I had no doubt he was at the heart of it all, one way or another. At least I now knew the skinny runt pulled out of the Thames was the kid's friend, and it was Greg and Mickey who must've done it, either by accident or on purpose. It meant Anthony was alive, I was sure of that, but it didn't look good for him because there was one big thing on my mind: did Anthony know about something that was probably buried? And if he did, was it on an island? And if it was on an island, was it the one we played on as kids? I even remember telling my old man about it and he was all interested, for about ten seconds, which was good going for him. Even Grandad had said something to me one day about the island out on the estuary, but that was more to do with piloting my boat.

Still, until I bump into Anthony and strangle him for being a total fucking plonker, I had to start with my old man. They'd put him in prison down South, which meant I was looking out the window on the train journey down there, thinking how going to see him was not going to be the easiest of things, but I was going to make sure I kept the visit short and sweet. When I do think about my old man, I always end up thinking about Grandad as well. That's because they are cut from the same cloth, so to speak. Grandad is only one level better than my old man, in the heaven and hell type of thing. And stand them side by side and Grandad looks straight and normal, but my old man just looks like a mean bastard, whether that's close up, far away, sideways or upside down. He has a pig's head, a nose like a long, fat snout, blond eyebrows and a massive forehead. He likes a clean shave in the morning and to look as bulked up as possible, which is good for making people scared shitless of him. If you weren't scared, he'd make sure you knew about him by giving you his dead-eyed stare, which meant he'd have you when the time was right. It was all about fear, the art of the thug and the bully, which Greg looked up to and tried his best to be like. And like Greg, it didn't take much for him to rush into a rage. He was so highly sprung he could beat a jack-in-the-box before it showed its head. *Smash, bang, wallop* pretty much said everything you needed to know about him. But he had an edge, a sharp mind, way sharper than Greg's. But my old man's problem was he thought about things a bit too late, after the event. He always knew he should have thought it through, but he would use his fist first and worry about the costs later.

What my mum saw in him, god knows, but he was the one, for better or worse, and better than Grandad so I heard, who thought he was in the reckoning before my old man said 'off limits'. That was a time when things weren't too bad between those two, their life of crime built up during the eighties, when everything was hard graft and full of opportunity. I think they loved it back then because the gloves were off. Anything goes, so they said, and nothing has changed since then. But there's a lot of rubbish talked about crime, like it's something horrible, frightening and full of menace. But a lot of it is boring, mates and family, and keeping your head above water. And at the end of the day, only a few of us take the bigger risks to make it a full-time career. But there was none of this celebrity villain stuff with either of them. I mean, they were always the run-of-the-mill, grinding it out-type villains, mixing jobs with crime, using jobs to do crime, blurring everything so there was no difference between a day's work and a day's thieving.

But that does mean you're more than likely going to end up in prison. And my old man was born for prison. It's like his home from home. It isn't a problem for him, spending ten years inside – it's all part of the game. The problem is, this time, for whatever reason, he's blamed Grandad for being there. But the old man is wrong, it was just his own stupidity. Anyway, he was never going to accept that. Also, it suited him to find a reason to blame Grandad because he was jealous of him. That's what it comes down to – deep-rooted envy.

I looked out of the window, fed up of thinking about those two. I turned my brain off and I stayed like that, from the train, from the taxi, up to the prison gates.

When I went into the visiting room, my old man had this disgusting smile on his face. I could tell he was thinking I'd come to ask for forgiveness, having seen the error of my ways. However, I was going to enjoy disappointing him, as I sat down on the plastic chair opposite. He just carried on smiling at me. I said nothing and looked as hard as I could into his eyes.

'Well, fuck me, Steven!' he said. 'I didn't think I'd see you 'ere, seeing 'ow you're all loved up with Michael now.'

By Michael, he meant Grandad.

I waited. I think then he knew why I was here and he stopped all the smiling.

'Seen yer brother?' he said, running his fingers through his greasy hair.

'Yeah, with Mickey Finn.'

'Thought so. Looks like they left their mark on you.'

'I'm a quick healer.'

'Yeah, I suppose you'd 'ave to be wouldn't you, dodging all those punches, knives and bullets.'

I leaned forward so I had my arms on the table. I didn't want to waste a load of time with him being all funny.

'What's going on?' I said.

'What's going on? You tell me, Steven. I'm locked up inside.'

'Why's Greg come back?'

'Didn't 'e tell yer?' he said, as he carried on playing innocent. 'You boys should learn to talk to each other.'

'Greg can't think for himself. He does what he's told. You must have told him to come back and do something.'

'Oh right, Steven, I forgot 'ow you think you're the only intelligent one in the family. So, knowing 'ow you're a bit of a know-it-all, shouldn't you be able to work it out for yourself?'

I leant back in the chair. I could wait, I thought. The thing about my old man is, he loves bragging. It's what got him locked up inside. It's why Grandad had to do what he did to protect himself.

'Why don't you talk properly to me, Steven?' he said. 'Instead of being all mean and nasty to your old man.'

'What do you want to know?' I said, thinking if I didn't humour him for a bit, he was going to tell me nothing.

''ow's your mum? I know we're divorced and all that, but I still think about 'er.'

'She's fine.'

'Yeah, you're keeping an eye on 'er for me then?'

'I make sure she's all right.'

'Good lad. I tell you what, Steven, for all your mistakes, you're a good lad in that way, and a lot better than your brother.'

I shook my head, thinking about all the times he had laid into her and let Greg have a go, and then pretended nothing had happened.

'Don't be like that, Steven, shaking yer 'ead at me. I loved yer mother, whatever you think went on.'

'I know what went on.'

'No, Steven, you think you do, but trust me, my son, you don't know everything.'

'I know enough.'

He shook his head.

'That's your problem, Steven. You think you know it all but there's a lot you don't know, which means it's easy to make mistakes about people.'

'Well,' I said, 'you're the one person who I know enough about.'

'Yeah? Then don't bother, Steven. Don't bother coming 'ere and thinking you going to get answers from me.'

He was making me angry and I had to be calm. The old man was always calm, even when he was beating the crap out of people.

I leant forward again, to keep things low.

'Did you have Dominique killed?'

'Who?' he said, all innocent.

'The girlfriend.'

'Oh, you mean his bit on the side? That's a terrible thing, all that infidelity. But Michael has previous on that one, something you should think about. And what must Gwen be thinking? I don't know 'ow she puts up with 'im, I really don't.'

Gwen was Grandad's wife. As for thinking about Grandad's previous, I pretty much knew what he meant, but he'd never admitted anything to me.

'Did you?' I said again.

He sighed, thinking it over for a second or two.

'I bet Michael's got you running all over town trying to track 'er down? I bet 'e's been telling you all sorts of little things, but never enough.'

'I might have found something that belongs to her.'

This pricked his interest.

''ave you now?' he said, ever so slowly. 'Well, she's a beautiful girl isn't she, so I would imagine she gets given all sorts of nice things, so it's easy to see 'ow she could lose something, 'specially if it's precious…'

'Yeah, something that most of us can't do without.'

'Is that right? Well, maybe she's a bit forgetful, being as she's a bit of a nutjob, so I 'ear.'

'She needs help sometimes.'

'Oh, I bet she does. Michael's not an easy man to get along with. I found you never know where you stand with 'im.'

'Where is she?' I said, gritting my teeth. 'Or, what's left of her?'

'Don't get angry, son. She could be anywhere, don't you think? She's French, isn't she? Perhaps she's gone back 'ome? You know, we ain't putting up with foreigners any more. Perhaps she didn't think she was welcome?'

'No.'

'Not that then? But you've gotta say though, Steven, she was one for liking all the blacks and the brownies, the Pakis and the Africans, the Asians and the Indians, then there's the Polaks and the Russkis and the Easterns. I mean, there ain't much room left for us natives.'

'Is that why you killed her,' I said, wanting to reach out and grab him by the throat, 'because she helps immigrants?'

'Nah, don't be daft. Don't get me wrong though, Steven, because if that's what she gets up to then she doesn't deserve my sympathy, but I wouldn't kill 'er because she thinks this country is for everyone.'

A few ears pricked up around us, but he didn't mind what people heard when he spoke like that. He wanted people to know.

'Anyway,' he said, giving me back a smile, 'you've found something of 'ers?'

'A ring,' I said, avoiding the detail of the hand.

'Just a ring?'

I nodded.

'And where did you find that ring?'

'In Mickey Finn's flat.'

'Yeah, that's a bit weird. Do you think she's two-timing

Michael then? Do you think that's why you found that ring of 'ers in 'is flat?'

'Mickey doesn't live there.'

'Oh, that's weird then. Sounds all Agatha Christie to me and you're 'ot on the case, like a right old detective, finding clues, putting the jigsaw puzzle together. And there I was thinking you just 'ere to see yer old man, but all you really want is just some information out of me. Tut tut, Steven.'

'Listen,' I said, getting tired of all his BS. 'I know you're behind all of this, so why don't you just tell me what's going on?'

'And why would I want to do that?'

'Because it will be in your interest. There would be consequences for you if things turn out the way they are looking.'

He started shaking his head. I knew what I said wouldn't work, but it was worth a try.

'Threats, eh, from me own son. I tell yer, things are going really out of kilter. The earth must be going all wobbly, 'specially when little urchins like you start getting above themselves.'

'OK,' I said, jumping up. 'You don't know anything. No reason why you would, would you, stuck in here, leaving everything up to Greg.'

''ang on,' he said, lifting up his arm to get me to sit back down again. 'Christ, you're nearly as bad as Greg when it comes to a bit of patience.'

I waited, wondering if he was just going to fool around with me, or if he would give me something to go on.

'Come on, son,' he said, waving his hand. 'Sit back down. You're like a turd in a blender.'

I looked around the visitors room and had one or two

looks come my way, but the POs didn't seem that bothered.

'Let me ask you,' he said, as I still stood there. 'Do you 'ave the ring?'

'No.'

I knew if I told him I had the ring, I would be met by Greg and Mickey as soon as I got back to London.

'That's a bit careless. Michael won't be 'appy about that.'

'It's just a ring,' I said.

'A ring on a finger,' he said, more to himself. 'And now that ring 'as lost its owner and gone for walkies.'

'Does that matter?'

'That depends, doesn't it, Steven, on whose side you're on?'

'Do I need to choose sides?'

'Well, we already know whose side you're on. The question for you is, can you change sides?'

'Why do I need to change sides?' I said.

'Because one way or another, you're part of me – you're a Mason. Whatever else you might think, the only people who will ever really look after you are the ones who brought you up – your family.'

'I look after myself.'

'Can you?'

'Yeah.'

'I wouldn't bet on it, son.'

'Is that a threat?'

'No, Steven, it's yer old man telling yer to stop being a fucking traitor!'

I laughed. I was ready to let rip on the whole truth, and nothing but the truth, honesty and loyalty thing. But the same rules didn't apply to him. He wouldn't understand. He just wanted it from others – loyalty from me, without ever being loyal himself.

'Enjoy the next eight years and seventy-five days,' I said, turning around to leave.

'Where do you think you're going!' he shouted. 'You've only just got 'ere.'

'Visiting time at the zoo is over,' I said.

'You cheeky…'

Then one of the POs came over as they saw him getting to his feet.

It was my turn to smile. Whether he knew it or not, I had got what I wanted. He was behind the whole Dominique thing, and I knew the severed hand was only a trophy.

2

Heading back into London on the train, I decided there wasn't much left to get out of Texas, Ann or Sangoma. Plus, Tommy was in hospital, and if Anthony had any sense, he would be getting on a plane to Spain or somewhere because his card was marked. Whatever happened next was all about Grandad's next move and I was just going to have to wait for a message from him.

As I looked out of the window at all the cold grass and trees whizzing by, I was one hundred per cent sure Dominique had become a victim, chosen because my old man was desperate to get back at Grandad. And that's the thing with a feud, it will always come to a head. Pushing it back down and hoping it will go away isn't going to happen. And killing Dominique is sure to get Grandad on the rampage. But my old man and Greg, they were also after something else, and that was the ring on her finger. But the gold ring is not worth much for all the risk. After all, what can a ring tell you: that you're married, engaged, that you're loaded, or a Freemason? I needed someone to paint a picture, a great big picture with everyone in it, with big bubbles above their heads like cartoons, telling me just what they were thinking. That's something I should have asked Anthony to do, but would he have painted me the truth?

I needed the toilet, which gave me a chance to check the carriage for any sensible shoes or anyone wearing a black hoodie. As I was rocking around and pissing into the bowl, I wondered how the guy with the black hoodie fitted into everything. He was the only one who I would call an outsider, standing around, watching and following. Perhaps that was all he was meant to do: just look and see and report back? But if that was the case, who was he reporting to? It wouldn't be Greg and Mickey because they were tools of my old man. I couldn't see Grandad hiring someone else as well as me; that wouldn't be money well spent. No, this guy was a mystery, but once I'd caught him, I reckoned it would shine a light on something I hadn't seen yet.

On my way back to my seat, I checked everyone along the carriage again for sensible shoes and a black hoodie. It looked like I wasn't being followed.. So, I took to looking out the window again and watching everything go by: the fields, the trees, the embankments, the flats, the offices and the warehouses.

When the train pulled in, I decided to walk through the city to get a train back into Essex, but as soon as I got onto London Bridge, it was like a swarm of bees or locusts coming at me, commuters all rushing on one side of the pavement to get to the train station and back home. The other side of the bridge was clear of people, so I waited for a gap in the traffic to weave my way across. That was when I caught sight of something I'd been looking for – a guy in a black hoodie with pink eyes looking straight at me. He was well over six foot, I thought, a triangle face and the whitest guy I'd ever seen, almost like an albino, but more like he'd never been under the sun. It didn't have to be him, I thought to myself, but I was dumb if I didn't think it was. And as soon as he put his head down and started walking at a good pace, going north back over the bridge, with no branding on that hoodie, I knew it had to be him.

The last thing I needed was to get myself run over trying to get across, so I decided to stick to the edge of the pavement and track him from the other side. I said to myself, *If I can keep up with you, I'm going to have you.* But then I nearly got run over, as some great big red bus came right up against the kerb. I had to throw myself back into the crowd and push my way to the edge of the bridge, so I was looking down into the river.

I looked across the road again and was losing sight of him. These commuters were moving like a load of cows, acting together, strength in numbers, pushing me against the side of the bridge. I didn't think I'd have much chance of catching up with him, pissing people off as I bumped my way along. Then there was a break in the flow, so I nipped back onto the kerb and scanned for him. Just as I thought – he'd taken advantage and disappeared. Then the traffic slowed up, which gave me a chance to get across, so I eased myself around the front and back of a few cars and a lorry.

'Bugger,' I said, as I looked both ways along the pavement. But there was just a small chance, I thought, he hadn't legged it and was still walking the way he'd been going. I picked up my pace and trotted along, checking to see if he'd crossed back over, but it was just a sea of people. He would be well out of sight by now, I reckoned, unless he had a wooden leg. But as I got over the hump of the bridge, I caught sight of him again, twenty or thirty yards ahead, walking and not running. He was either being a cocky bastard and thought he could easily get away, or he wanted me to follow. And there was only one way to find out, so I sprinted, real hard off the mark. He was no more than a few yards from me when he turned and saw me, as we came off the bridge, before I went *smack*, right into some useless tourist. That was it then. A whole load of tourists were crowding around me and helping their guy up. I said sorry, as I watched the black hoodie go down the stairs of the underground. That meant he was either going to come up on the other side of the road, or he was going to try and get a tube.

As I got to the stairs, my betting was on him coming up to surface again. I waited at the top of the underground entrance and looked across at the exits on the other side of the road. The bet with myself paid off. I wasn't going to lose him by running through the underground, so I waited for him to make his next move. He was looking for me and so I let him know I was there, waving and then pointing at him, just to make sure he knew I was coming. He kept his cool and started walking along the pavement. I followed, keeping my eyes on him, sure now he wanted me to follow because he wasn't running away from me, he was just keeping his distance. Then he gave me a quick look and he was up a side street. I was straight across, not running but keeping pace, playing his game. We went right, left and straight ahead, passing old city buildings that had been brought back from the dead, in between new massive skyscrapers poking out. I picked up the pace as we got to the iron gate entrance of Leadenhall Market. I dodged the city boys and girls drinking after a hard day of making money and was back out on the main road and the pavement.

I looked up and down, but there was no sight of him. The guy had dodged his way through the crowds better than me and I was lost for a minute or two. I couldn't lose him now, I thought, not after all this effort.

It was pot luck which way I went. I could see the dome of St Paul's in the fading light, and for whatever reason, I started heading that way. I was looking like crazy for the guy, thinking I'd messed up, when I saw him checking back as he shot down some side street again. That was it, I was off, jogging as best I could around and through people. And that's when I got there, right by the stairs of St Paul's, with tourists sitting around and the guy having disappeared. I went up the steps and was told it was closed for some service. *What a pain! Where is he? He wants me to catch him, so why disappear like that?*

I stood at the top of the stairs looking around but there was nothing. I walked back down the stairs and wandered around the side of the cathedral. That's when I saw a small sign with an arrow pointing towards an open door: The Crypt. I walked down a metal staircase into a dark and creepy place. I wasn't the only one in there as I moved around the stone graves, waiting to see if the guy would jump out and bite my neck. I did a tour of the place, and it was looking like I had lost him, when some strong light came beaming out at the back. Always curious, I made my way around the stone coffins, up to a wooden fence that went from top to bottom. I looked through into a bright lighted chapel with a hardcore altar at the back. I was going to call it a day when at the side of the chapel, a door opened and out came the guy with the black hoodie. I stared and watched him. He didn't look my way and he got down on his knees, not to pray, but to start polishing one of the candle sticks on the altar. I walked along the fancy wicker work, wondering if I should shout out before he went back into his little cubby hole, but I couldn't find a way in, so I started pushing on the woodwork, as if some secret door would open, when I heard a voice from behind me say, 'All right.'

3

The light was bad, but Anthony looked paler and pastier than usual.

'I thought you were dead,' I said, kind of happy to see him again, but also wanting to stuff him in one those coffins.

'Yeah, so did I,' he said, smiling a bit and looking behind me into the chapel.

'And now you're back from the dead,' I said, checking behind me to find our church-cleaning follower had buggered off.

'Feels like it,' he said, looking past me to make sure the guy in the black hoodie had made his exit. 'You followed him then?'

'Yeah, a friend of yours, is he?' I said, looking around the crypt to see if Anthony had been followed by anyone else.

He shrugged.

'You need to tell me what's going on,' I said, feeling like I didn't have the patience to play games with my old mate.

'Why?'

'You know why, Anthony.'

'I can't, not yet.'

This was bad – bad for him and bad for me. Now all I could think was what Sangoma had said: duplicity.

'OK,' I said, having to accept losing my rag with him wasn't going to get me anywhere, just yet. 'Why don't I ask you stuff and let's see what you can tell me.'

This made Anthony nervous and I thought for a moment he was going to run. Then he just stood there, like he knew he'd done wrong, but had good reason for everything he'd done.

'Was it you who came back and helped Britney get me into bed, after my brother and Mickey had finished with me?'

He nodded.

'So, did you come back to help me, or because you wanted to get what was in the icebox?'

'Both.'

'But why do you need a dead hand, Anthony?'

'We all need it,' he said, 'and you've still got it.'

'I haven't, I threw it away.'

'Well, it's not yours to throw away,' he said, showing he was up to having a go back.

I laughed.

'I suppose you're right, seeing how I haven't been able to ask the owner if they'd like it back. I mean, they won't be able to drink their cup of tea.'

'They didn't drink tea,' he said, quietly.

'Yeah, I'm sure Dominique liked a nice cup of tea.'

Anthony stayed quiet.

'So,' I said, wondering if Anthony had it in him to kill Dominique, 'Greg and Mickey must be pissed with you then?'

'They're not happy,' he said, looking at me as if it was my fault. 'You messed things up.'

'That was an accident.'

'Are you sure, because that's not the way they see it.'

'No, I bet they don't, but I think I got the message – on the nose, the face and in the ribs.'

'They were going to collect it, Greg and Mickey.'

'From Mickey's flat? That was you then was it? It was you who left the hand in Mickey's and put it in his freezer?'

'You got in the way. That's not my fault.'

'Yeah but it is your problem. One you have to try and make up for.'

'There was nothing I could do.'

'So, you ran away, and now one of Tommy's boys is dead.'

'Your brother did that, not me.'

My blood was beginning to boil. There was one thing he needed to tell me, which was probably going to decide if he lived.

'Did you kill her?'

Anthony shook his head a bit.

'Is that a yes or a no?' I said, ready to reach across and squeeze his neck.

I think he could tell I was going to go for him, so he stepped back a few paces.

'How's Britney?' he said, giving me a nervous twitch.

'You know how she is so don't BS me!' I said, making sure I wasn't going to let him forget this was meant to be about Dominique.

'Looks like she's taken a shine to you,' he said, which meant he knew most of what had gone on. 'She's yours, if you want her.'

I laughed again.

'Yeah, well, she's not yours to give. You've been replaced mate, and not by me. And I don't think she's the type that likes to get bought and sold.'

'I'm not offering her up for sale.'

'Then what?'

'She likes you.'

'Yeah, I don't think I'm the only one.'

'I don't know, Steven. I think she's liked you for some time. She's cared for you, tended your wounds, played with you, probably kissed and cuddled, maybe even fallen in love. Or are you going to pretend that didn't happen?'

That was when I just wanted to get hold of him, put him on the floor and beat the crap out of him.

'You know what,' I said, 'you are sick. Something's happened to you. Is it all that gear inside that's made you like this?'

Anthony snorted.

'It's not the drugs, Steven. That's my juice, my fuel. The thing is, I think I know you better than yourself. When it comes down to it, given everything you've been through, you've got a good heart.'

'Don't think a good heart makes me soft.'

'I've known you for years, Steven. I've seen you at your lowest, crying and begging on my mum's sofa because your old man is looking to beat the shit out of you. I've seen the fear in your face.'

I laughed.

'Anthony, I was a kid fighting for my life.'

'Yeah, but there aren't too many kids who would stand up to a monster like your old man. Look at your brother, he chose the other route. He wants to be like your old man. That says to me you knew right from wrong. You wanted justice. You wanted good to overcome evil.'

'Are you trying to tell me I'm a fucking Jedi? Because the thing is, Anthony, getting involved with my old man is like sucking up to Darth Vader. Do you really know what you're doing? Cutting Dominique's hand off, selling your ex to me!'

'Look!' he said, all steamed up. 'I'm not selling her to you! All I'm saying is, I won't stand in your way.'

I didn't want to hear that. I didn't want to hear that Anthony was giving up on Britney because I didn't want her to be an option in my life. But there it was, in all the mess he was involved in, he was letting me know he couldn't hold on to her, even if she had moved on.

'You know what,' I said, feeling less angry, 'what I need to know is how far in you are with all of this. How deep does this go?'

'Very,' came the reply.

I shook my head. Then it all began to make sense, all this hide and seek, and then turning up out of the blue, coming back from the dead.

He was asking for my help.

'You need me, don't you?' I said.

Anthony couldn't avoid that truth, and he nodded.

'I need to hide again,' he said. 'I know you think I'm an evil killer or something, but trust me, it's not like that.'

'Do you mean some of it is?'

'Look, I will tell you what you need to know but right now, I need your help.'

'How?'

'I need you to protect me.'

'From my brother?'

'From everybody. I need to hide… on your boat.'

'Why my boat?'

'I can't say, not yet. Then you need to come and see me and I'll tell you everything.'

I started shaking my head.

'Please!' said Anthony, who was almost begging me. 'I need you to trust me on this.'

I looked at him good and hard.

'But I don't trust you, Anthony,' I said.

'I know. I know you think I'm a liar and you want to throw me in the river, but once you've heard everything, you'll understand.'

'I want the truth now, Anthony.'

'You will, when the time is right, and then you'll understand.'

'But waiting for the truth from you, Anthony, puts me at risk, doesn't it?'

'Not for long,' he said, hoping I was about to give in. 'Let me go there tonight and then meet me there the day after.'

'And who else will be there?'

'It will be just me, waiting, I promise. As long as you're not followed.'

'But I am being followed,' I said, looking back into the chapel so he knew who I meant. 'Who is that guy in the hoodie?'

'I can't say. He doesn't want me to tell you, not yet.'

'So, he's part of it?'

Anthony just looked at me.

'All right,' I said, thinking if I give in a little it might loosen his tongue. 'I can wait, but are you working for my old man?'

'Kind of.'

'Why would you do that?' I said, wanting to add how

crazy he must be to even think it, let alone do it. 'You can't play Grandad. You know what will happen.'

'There's a lot that can happen, but no one's in control now because of what you did.'

'So it's my fault?'

'Yeah,' he said, but he didn't look too believable. 'I know you went to see your old man today. What did he tell you?'

'Not a lot,' I said, happy to keep what little I did know to myself.

Now it was Anthony's turn not to believe me.

'We can work together,' he said. 'It's not too late to sort everything out so we can all benefit.'

'How do I benefit?'

'There's a lot, for everybody. It will give us freedom.'

'I don't need freedom. I need to find Dominique, dead or alive,' I said, wondering if he was really on the same planet. 'Have you forgotten what I do and who I work for?'

'Of course not, of course I bloody know! But he's not a hero, Grandad. He just uses people.'

'We're all used, Anthony. There's always someone who is going to tell you what to do.'

'You mean there's always Grandad or your old man, telling people what to do and beating the shit out of them, but it doesn't have to be like that.'

'What are you talking about, Anthony? That's the way it is, that's the game. You find a way to live with it or else you become a victim.'

Anthony paused.

'Well, I can't live like that any more,' he said, leaning against a grave. 'You know, I learnt a lot from Dominique. She was good to me, made me think about who I was, about who I wanted to be.'

I was getting pissed with him again.

'Did she tell you then, you're just a junkie painter living with your mum and dad?'

'Is that what you think of me?' he said, his eyes bulging because I had upset him again.

'It's not what I think, Anthony, it's what you are, unless you want to tell me something different.'

I thought he was only going to get angrier, which is what I wanted, but he had worked out I was trying to provoke him into saying something.

'Dominique knew so much,' he said, pushing himself back off the gravestone he'd been leaning against. 'And she trusted me, trusted me with things. Things that I think got her into trouble with your old man.'

'Did he have her killed?'

'I thought that was your job, finding Dominique, dead or alive?'

'Well, Anthony, it looks like you've had a hand in it!'

'My god, Steven. I never thought you'd make a joke about Grandad's beloved. Then again, you have been mixing with different people. They're not like the estate, are they, Steven? They don't spend their time thinking about how they are going to shit on each other. No, they operate on a higher level, think about bigger things, spend their time on a higher plain.'

'People are all the same, and I don't think Texas and Ann are afraid to get their hands dirty.'

'Are you sure, Steven? I don't know any one off the estate who thinks about the palette to use on a bright and crispy morning.'

'No, Anthony, only you do that, but you've gone wrong in the head and got your wires crossed.'

'Don't make me out to be mad, Steven! Trust me, when I

say I have seen the light…'

'Yeah, you gone all religious then. Is that why you're hanging out in a crypt with a cleaner?'

'Oh, I think you'll find out he's a bit more than that.'

'Yeah, does he do murder as well then?'

'No, Steven, that's just you and your family.'

'So, you didn't kill her?'

'No.'

'But you know who did?'

'I know a lot of things. When the time is right, I will let you know, but you're not there yet. When you're ready, it will be time for you to know.'

'That sounds like your death sentence.'

'Maybe,' he said. 'But you know what us artists are like. Our imagination can always get the better of us, so you don't know how far I'm prepared to go.'

'Oh, I think I do, Anthony, and I think it's taken you into deep shitty water and you'll end up drowning if you're not careful.'

'I can swim all right,' he said, moving sideways, from one foot to the other, getting all jerky. 'They seek him here, they seek him there, but they ain't going to find me.'

'I found you.'

'Because I wanted you to find me.'

'Why?'

'That's it, Steven,' he said, walking backwards. 'I need to go now. You'll know a lot more in the next day or two. I'll be on the boat. Meet me there with Britney. It will change your life.'

And then he turned and walked as quickly as he could around the graves, desperate to avoid me grabbing hold of him and beating him to a pulp. The thing is, I was never going to do that – there's a time and place for that kind of thing. But knowing Anthony as well as I did, there was no need to put any more pressure on him other than my presence. He was full of it, though, trying to prove he was a big boy now, but he was still as weak as piss. Someone was controlling him, telling him what to do, he just didn't want me knowing who it was. And he wasn't asking for permission to hide on my boat. He just wanted me to be there, and the only reason he'd want me to be there was to have me pilot and sail.

I stayed down in the crypt, waiting to see if the guy in the black hoodie was going to pop his head out in the chapel again. But after a few minutes of hanging around, I was herded out with the rest of the tourists.

Back outside, there was a coffee shop opposite and so I took a good window seat looking back at the cathedral, waiting to see if the cleaning had been done and I could grab the guy and string him up by his hoodie. But I was still clueless as to how he fitted into all of this. Perhaps he was on some mission to expose sham marriages? Perhaps all he was doing for Anthony was a good Samaritan type of thing and just helping someone out? But that didn't fit because Anthony had pretty much said he had a lot more to do with it. That means, Anthony has somehow got himself involved with this guy and he was working for him, or they were working together, sharing the burden of their little plan. Well, I suppose I should count myself lucky because I now had a formal invitation to Anthony's nutjob scheme. And a day or two waiting wasn't too bad for me because I had time to try and work a few things out. The thing is, what I couldn't tell, was who was using who?

But I did know Greg and Mickey were working to my old man's instructions and they had Anthony working for them.

Which meant Anthony was in the frame, Greg and Mickey were in the frame, with my old man pulling the strings, and the weird guy in the black hoodie was somehow part of it. Perhaps they all did it. Perhaps they all kidnapped Dominique, cut off her hand and killed her? The thing is, I had to trust my instincts, trust what I knew, and everything said it was my old man getting one back on Grandad. This arty lot – Texas, Ann and Sangoma – they just wanted to help a load of immigrants. They knew Grandad through Dominique, so Grandad must be doing something else for them. But whatever Grandad put on Dominque's finger, it was more than just a ring. And that's the thing that might be cutting up Grandad bad; if it is the ring, he's like near enough signed her death sentence. And no rising from the dead type of thing for Dominique. The only question is how much of her body is left, or any of her body?

Even if Grandad wanted me to keep my head down, it was in my interest to get to the bottom of it. Either way, it was still my job to find out what had happened to Dominique, which meant finding out what Anthony had to offer. And he had hit the nail on the head: behind all the mean stuff I did, I still had a bit of a heart. He knew it, from all those days back when we were kids. I was once the frightened little boy looking for help, escaping from my old man and bastard brother. Those days were as hard as glass. But me and Anthony had taken different paths: I was Grandad's enforcer, the go-to guy to get things done, and Anthony was the sensitive artistic type. But now, it looked like Anthony was the nutjob psycho, offering up his ex-girlfriend as trade for protection. He knew Britney had got right under my skin. He knew, as soon as he said I could have her, he knew that was what I wanted. None of which makes it right. And who knows what Britney wants? But I did want to see her again, smell her again, have back those last couple of days. I should have said something to her when I had the chance, and she must have been waiting for me to say something. It was my mistake, not doing anything. She had led me to where she wanted me to be and I had bottled it. Perhaps that's why she's really gone back to her mums, because I was not giving her what she wanted.

Too late now. Plus, there was this other guy who I knew nothing about. I should have got Anthony to tell me something about who he was, not that I was going to do anything to him, but I wanted to know what the competition was going to be like. Which I suppose meant I was ready to go for it, to let Britney know I wanted her. I might be a fool to make that kind of move, when she was probably just as much a part of things as Anthony, but there must be some good somewhere in all of this, when it comes to an end. There had to be some good left over.

The full night had come on now. The lights of the city lit up bits and pieces outside the coffee shop. It was darker where I was sitting, waiting, wasting my time, waiting for the black hoodie guy to come back out again. Maybe he lived there, in the cathedral. Maybe he had lodgings. I didn't have a clue. Perhaps he was religious, all dedicated to God and that. I hope he's in there saying his prayers – for Dominique, for the kid pulled out of the river and for all the other damage that's been done. I could feel it sinking into me, a feeling that more darkness was on its way, and would more than likely keep on coming. It felt like a deep rotten hole I was falling into, with all the dirty stench of people being nasty, taking aim and trying to get one over on each other. Me, I have just put up with it and done things that keep me alive. I didn't like it, I didn't hate it, I just did it.

And then, I got a message from Grandad. I was heading back to The End of the World.

4

I had to meet Tony in the car park at The End of the World. Like the rest of us, he did what he was told by Grandad, a solid guy. His head was about two sizes too small for his body, always shaved, which made his face look like a fresh baby. Whatever the weather, rain or shine, he'd have on a sleeveless puffer. But what pissed Grandad off was his spanking bright-white trainers with the three strips (which he changed every week) because you could see him a mile off when he was meant to be all stealth like.

He was waiting in his car as I crept up behind him and he pissed himself when I knocked on his window.

'Jesus!' he said, winding down the window. 'You nearly gave me a bloody heart attack.'

'We can only hope,' I said, opening the passenger door.

'What d'yer want to see me dead for?'

'I don't,' I said, as I slid onto the cold, black leather seats in the back of the car. 'It was just a joke.'

'That ain't a joke,' said Tony, looking at me through his rear-view mirror. 'Do you know that I have to 'ave pills for me heart?'

'No, I didn't know that.'

'Yeah, I have to go for regular check-ups and everything.'

'You must be thinking about retiring then?'

'I wish,' he said, fixing the mirror so he had a full view of me. 'Who can retire now, eh? There ain't nothing left to retire on, it's all gone, like some piss-up in the brewery. Some joker's gone and pissed whatever we had down the drain and we ain't got nothing, none of us.'

'You surprise me, Tony,' I said, pulling my coat around me because it felt colder in the car than outside. 'I thought you were the sort of guy who was a dead cert for a retirement plan.'

'What are you on!' he shouted back at the windscreen. 'Retirement plan my arse! There ain't nothing like that in this business.'

I nodded, as he repeated the words 'retirement plan' to himself.

'Anyway,' he said, 'where you been hiding? I ain't seen nothing of yer for days now.'

'Up town,' I said.

'Yeah, you got some crumpet up there 'ave you?'

'No, Tony,' I said, looking out across the brightly lit car park and the entrance door to The End of the World.

'Shame because there is loads of rumours going around about you.'

'Yeah, like what?'

'Loads of stuff,' said Tony, who I could tell didn't want to say anything now that he had said it.

'Come on, Tony,' I said, 'you can tell me.'

'It's a bit close and personal,' he said, lowering his voice.

'Tony, you are not responsible for what other people say.'

'No but, you know, don't hold it against me if I tell yer.'

'I won't, I don't, and I haven't in the past have I?' I said, giving him license to repeat as much of the gossip he was desperate to get off his chest.

'Well, there's yer brother for one thing. 'E's back, isn't

'e, in and out, hanging around with that Mickey Finn. Looking at the state of you, you must 'ave run into him already.'

'Yeah.'

'Then I've heard, you know, something else is going on, with Grandad's bit of stuff, the Frenchie bird.'

'You mean Dominique?'

'Yeah, how that's not good.'

'What else?' I said, knowing full well he had more to say.

'Well, you know, I don't want you to take this the wrong way, but you and that junkie friend of yours…'

'Anthony?'

'Yeah.'

'How yous is up to something.'

That wasn't good news.

'Who's been saying that?'

'Everybody, everyone on the estate, but they've all kept their mouths shut like because, you know, no one really knows anything.'

'Have the police been about?'

'Yeah, they're looking for all sorts of people. I mean, don't go in there tonight,' he said, nodding in the direction of the pub. 'There's a load of 'em in there creeping around.'

That didn't surprise me.

'Well,' I said, 'it seems to me that nobody knows anything.'

'Well, yeah, you could say that.'

'Perfect then,' I said.

'If you're happy mate, that is all that counts.'

'Yeah, I'm happy,' I said, watching two guys come out of the pub and walk away.

'Nice one,' said Tony, as if he hadn't just said all the

things he'd said. 'So, has Grandad told you what we got to do?'

'No.'

'All right, that's OK. We just got to wait a bit, till it's not so busy and noisy.'

'What are you talking about, Tony? There's no noise, it's dead quiet, and I've only seen two people.'

'Well, you know what I mean. We don't want to be seen.'

'Yeah, not much chance of that with your trainers.'

'Ah, that's where you're wrong, Steven,' he said, lifting one leg. 'All black tonight.'

I laughed.

'Grandad must have threatened to cut your feet off then, Tony.'

'Yeah, something like that,' he said, which meant it would have been feet, legs and hands.

'So, what do we need to do?'

'There's a container,' he said, still looking out of the windscreen. 'All we have to do is find it and then drive it out of the park.'

'To where?'

'Over to the farm.'

'And what's in it?'

'Rotten vegetables. That's what Grandad said.'

'OK.'

Tony had been a crane driver before he was made redundant, so he was usually pulled in to load the lorry and drive the containers to be siphoned off. My job was to make sure nothing went wrong.

He carried on looking at the car park and waiting for the pub to empty. I sank into the leather seats and shut my eyes, but I wasn't about to start sleeping. My mind was racing, trying to work out why Grandad had only sent a simple message and nothing about Dominique, Greg or Anthony. It puzzled me because what I was doing with Tony was just normal, business as usual, rather than cracking down on the nutjobs and killers. But always with Grandad, there was a reason to everything, not that I thought there was going to be stinky vegetables in the container.

'Heh!' said Tony.

'What?'

'Keep your head down for a sec, then look.'

'What is it?' I said, remaining low in the seats.

'I think it's your brother, coming out of the pub with some geezer.'

I had to see and raised my head up to look between the passenger car seats.

'That's your brother, ain't it?'

'Yeah,' I said.

'Who's he with then?'

I didn't say anything as I watched Greg laughing with Detective Carter. I wasn't surprised. It meant keeping my mouth shut when I was interviewed had been the right thing.

'That ain't Mickey Finn,' said Tony.

'No,' I said, as I sat back again. 'Just let me know where they go.'

'They ain't going nowhere, they're just chatting. Oh, 'ang on, 'ere we go. Yeah, they're getting in their cars.'

'Are they coming this way?'

'No mate, they're still over there.'

'Keep an eye on them,' I said, 'and let me know when they've gone.'

'Heh ho, their cars are right next to each other. I tell yer, that geezer with your brother looks familiar to me.'

'Who knows,' I said, knowing that if I told Tony who it was, he'd get nervier about the job.

'I tell yer,' said Tony, 'he looks like a copper.'

'With Greg? No, I doubt it.'

'Yeah, he does.'

'You can't tell,' I said, 'unless you look at their shoes.'

'Their shoes?'

'Yeah, you can always tell by looking at their shoes.'

'I can't see his shoes,' said Tony, peering out into the dimness. 'He's got in his car.'

'There you go then, we'll never know.'

'You not bothered? That's your brother.'

'It's a free country, Tony.'

'Don't you believe it, mate. There ain't nothing free about anything 'ere.'

'No,' I said, 'you're right.'

'Heh, yeah, they're both going.'

I listened, without looking, to the two cars driving away.

'You're safe now, mate,' said Tony, 'if you were worried like, with your brother, seeing as he's a real 'ard case.'

'That's all right, Tony. It's just better they're out of the way.'

'Oh yeah, no, we don't want that, not with this little job.'

'Well, why don't we do it then?'

'Yeah, its fucking freezing in 'ere. Come on.'

As soon as he said that, he swung open the car door and jumped out. He looked down at me sitting in the back seats, as if I was now somehow holding him up.

'Let's go then,' he said, as I eased myself out of the car.

There was a track that went behind the pub and ran alongside the river. If you didn't keep your footing in the dark, it was easy to slip down and fall. The trouble was, as I kept my eye on Tony, I kept thinking about how much Carter was involved. No wonder Anthony was shitting himself and was asking for protection. If Greg and the police wanted him, he was right when he said everyone was after him. And I also had no doubt Grandad would have Anthony in his sights. But why hadn't Grandad told me to sort Anthony out, or did he think I was too close?

'Keep up,' said Tony, as we got to the wire fence around the container park.

'When's the truck coming?' I asked, standing behind him and keeping an eye out for the security car that would do its rounds.

'I'll let 'em know, ten minutes,' he said, as he started messaging.

We then slipped under the fence and stood next to the first stack of containers.

'I've got the number 'ere,' said Tony, looking at his phone. 'You go find it and I'll get the crane ready.'

'I need your phone,' I said, 'I'm not going to remember all those numbers.'

'Yeah, check the number good and proper. Grandad don't want no mistakes with this one. He said there's already been some big cock-up.'

I watched Tony walk through the container park. The thing with doing these kinds of jobs is to look casual, look as if you're meant to be there, so you don't look like a thief. Tony knew the place because he used to work here, so in a way he wasn't out of place. I threaded my way through the two stacks, using the overhead lighting to read off the numbers. There was some sort of logic to it, as I tracked it down by the time the lorry came in and Tony was driving along with the grabbers up and ready. I left it to the guys to finish and thought my job was done, until Tony said I had to follow him.

'I can't use your car,' I said.

'No, mate, in the cab with me. Grandad said you're to come with me to the farm.'

'Yeah?'

'Yeah, mate. Hop in.'

This was odd. This was what you could say went against process. It had far more meaning than just going for a ride down to the farm, but there was nothing I could do. Not that I thought I was under threat, but neither did I think things were going to be straightforward. The point was, as Tony knew, I had no choice.

I sat against the door of the cab, one of four now, all on our way to the farm. The two new guys started laughing.

'What's wrong with you?' I said.

'Christ,' said the one next to me. 'Can't you smell it?'

I sniffed the air.

'That container stinks,' he said.

'Rotten vegetables,' said Tony.

5

Grandad had bought the farm to have fresh eggs and bacon in the morning, but also to keep a lot of things a good distance away from anybody, with the woods like a barrier before you got close up to all the farm buildings. So, taking a container to the farm was nothing new.

As we pulled into the yard, there was some farm machinery, a few diggers and a tractor parked. Tony backed the lorry into a corrugated barn, so the back end of the container was out of sight. About a hundred yards away from the barn was the curtained windows of the old farmhouse, which provided dim light into the yard.

By now, the smell from the container was nasty and strong. Whatever the guys were unloading, I decided to leave it to them and leant against the front of the cab, keeping an eye on the track that led into the yard. All I was thinking about was how long it would take to get the job done, so I could get out of the cold and get back to my flat. That was until the door of the farmhouse opened and a black guy stood in the porch looking over at me. I didn't think much of it because whatever went on here had very little to do with pigs, cows and sheep. But he kept looking, steady as a rock, for a good five minutes or so, before he decided to come over. That was when I clocked it was Sangoma as he came right up close to me.

'You don't seem surprised, Steven, to see me?'

'Well, I've had a few surprises tonight,' I said. 'So, you could say I'm not surprised by who turns up.'

In truth, I was a bit surprised.

'That's a shame. I suppose I like to think I am important. However, I was hoping you would be here, with the lorry.'

'Yeah, why's that?'

'Because I wanted to share something with you.'

'Yeah?'

'Yes,' he said, looking all grave and serious.

'You have some connection with this then?' I said, nodding in the direction of the barn, which spread its light down both sides of the container.

'Yes, I do, quite a deep connection. One that cuts deep and runs all the way back to my homeland.'

I was going to say how it stinks and then checked myself. But Sangoma said, 'What do you think of the smell?'

'Nasty,' I said. 'Rotten vegetables...'

'Really, is that what you think? Is that what they told you?'

'Yeah.'

'And do you think the smell smells like rotten vegetables?'

'Probably not,' I said, wondering where this was going.

'So, are you not curious to find out what might be causing such an almighty stink?'

'It won't make a difference if I know or not. Usually best not to know.'

'I see, of course. You are a good centurion, a good soldier after all. You need only know your orders in order to act. Everything else is irrelevant.'

Having finally liked the guy, he was now pissing me off, with this effing soldier thing all over again.

'And you think that makes you better than me?' I said.

'On the contrary, Steven. I think I envy you in some way. Your clear sightedness, your arrow-like intensity, your desire to get to the truth.'

'I never get to the truth,' I said, thinking Sangoma had only shown me bits of what was true, when he knew a hell of a lot more. 'I just don't like liars.'

'Exactly! But our world is full of lying, deceits and betrayals. It makes it very difficult at times to get any sense of proportion, any sense of what matters. No moral compass, so to speak, when all around you is illusion and subterfuge.'

There was a loud clunk, which meant the guys were opening the doors of the container.

'That sounds like the rotten vegetables are ready for

disposal,' said Sangoma, who looked down into the barn.

I was going to say something about how they needed to get rid of the vegetables, when I noticed a tear running down his cheek. I thought it must be the cold because it can make you weep. But then I realised, I mean I could tell, it was a proper tear, a crying tear.

He wiped it away.

'Shall we look?' he said, walking past me.

I was going to leave it, but he wanted to show me something, however bad it was. As we slid through the small gap between the container lorry and the barn door, the smell was so strong it got right into my nostrils and filled my stomach up. I was almost ready to gag. Once Sangoma had pushed through, I slid sideways against the lorry and then into the bright light of the barn. I blinked as my eyes got used to the strip lights above my head, but in a few seconds, I could tell I was in the middle of something that came right out of a sci-fi horror. There were the three guys, covered head to foot in dark-green protective suits, with large round helmets over their heads. They were standing at the back of the container moving their arms up and down, working out who was going to do what. Sangoma ignored them and was staring at about a dozen large plastic vats that were in the corner of the barn.

I came up behind him.

'Christ!' I said. 'That's really bad, whatever's in the container.'

He ignored me, as did the guys who seemed to be settling on what they were going to do. Whatever the smell was, it must have been coming from behind the large wooden crates that were stacked up against the wide-open container doors.

'Now you will see,' said Sangoma, 'what rotten vegetables can look like in their human form.'

'You what?'

He then turned around to look at me.

'Do you remember when we first met, Steven?' he said. 'In the art gallery and I said time was important? Well, time has run its course and the mischievousness of others has brought us to this hell.'

I still hadn't quite worked it out.

'The smell you mean…'

'Yes,' said Sangoma. 'The smell of dead Africans.'

'And the vats?'

'Acid for their burial, so we leave no trace. It is better that way because we will need to continue.'

I stepped back from the container. If he wanted to show me what death looked like, I had seen it all before, but I'd never smelt it this bad. If Sangoma wanted to shock me, he had, but I wasn't going to let him think a tough soldier like me was easily shaken. But why show me and why do this to himself?

The guys had climbed into the container and were moving around at the back, then one of them came out and jumped down. I couldn't see his face through the plastic, but he looked ready to take a load. Then the first body appeared, bloated and reeking of death.

'Too many days,' said Sangoma, as he stood beside me watching, 'without food and water. We had lost them. The numbers had been switched.'

'You mean the container number?'

'Precisely.'

'So, who had the right number?'

'That we don't know, but when we find out who it is, they will go into a bath of acid, alive as you and me.'

The three guys struggled to lever the dead weight off the

container. They then placed the dead guy on a trolley and pushed it over to the vats and left it there. That's when Tony jumped down from the container and looked at me and Sangoma. He then shouted at us through his plastic visor.

'There's about a dozen bodies in there,' he said, his voice muffled, as if he was speaking into a plastic cup. 'But whoever filled them vats up was an idiot.'

'What do you mean?' I said.

'We can't put the bodies in whole,' he said. 'They'll push the acid over the lid and we'll get acid on us.'

That's when Sangoma said, 'Do you mean you need to cut them up into manageable pieces?'

I think that's when I could just about make out Tony looking a bit sheepish.

'Yeah,' he said. 'I'm gonna 'ave to get Fat Sam to come in.'

'A butcher I presume?' said Sangoma.

'Yeah, afraid so.'

'I'll ring,' I said. 'What's his number?'

'Use my phone,' said Tony. 'It's in me coat pocket back in the cab.'

Things were getting worse by the minute, with all the bodies and tubs of acid. It was like some human slaughterhouse in the barn, some bloody mini holocaust. God knows how Sangoma could stand there and watch it all, seeing as it was his people.

Then I started thinking about how bad it must have been trapped inside, not knowing anything, wondering if you were going to die, then working out you were going to die as things would have got worse and worse: no food, no water, no nothing. And all because of what, because somebody thought you were like a load of vegetables and they wanted to mess the whole thing up! It had to be the work of my old man and Greg. Only they would have known about all of this and only they would have thought it was worth doing as part of the payback for Grandad.

Once I got hold of Fat Sam, he was more than willing to come out late at night to earn a bit of extra cash. Not that I told him anything over the phone, but I reckoned he'd have seen a lot of this because of what he'd done in some of the wars he'd been in. Anyway, he'd talked a lot about all the bloody stuff and had gone straight back into butchering when he came out of the army.

I went back into the barn and told Tony to shut the container doors until Fat Sam could do his bit. I then got Sangoma to come back outside because this was only going to torture him more than it did any of us. Not that I said that to him, but I could tell he was getting upset, and the tears were in his eyes.

We stood in the middle of the yard with the lights from the farmhouse and the barn making shadows across the space.

'I can see why they do it,' I said. 'Take the risk.'

'Can you?' he said. 'Do you know what it costs to run and seek sanctuary, and I don't mean in monetary terms? No, Steven, the price is fear – fear every step of the way, fear as they balance trust with need, fear as they suffocate, fear as they realise they have been tricked into believing they had bought a better life.'

I could kind of relate, but it was not really what he wanted to hear. So I just waited as he breathed in and out, his eyes all watery from the stress of it all, and probably his own memories, until he had something else to say.

'I suspect your hunt for Dominique may be drawing to a similar conclusion?'

'I don't know,' I said.

'But if you were a betting man, it must be odds on that she is a victim in all of this?'

'Perhaps,' I said, thinking I had to ask him this question: 'Did you need to find her because she had the container number?'

Sangoma sighed.

'Yes and no,' he said. 'It was all just a vain hope, a tenuous connection. I had just been thinking about time, about the clock ticking, about what it would mean for those poor souls, and the wish that Dominique might have had some answers. Did you manage to find our mystery man and speak to him?'

'No,' I said.

'Or Anthony? For some reason I connect the two. My gut tells me they are part of this hideous conspiracy to disrupt and destroy the lives of innocent people, in some ridiculous game of revenge upon your master.'

I didn't say it, but the sight of Greg and Detective Carter coming out of The End of the World also put those two firmly in the frame.

'Don't worry,' I said. 'My master, as you like to call him, will not let something like this go.'

'No, I'm sure you are right, Steven. It is not good for business.'

I didn't say anything back. There was no need to start any moral thing when there was the stench of death waiting to be cut up and dissolved in acid.

'Well, I think I will go back in,' he said.

'Are you sure that's a good idea? You know Fat Sam is coming, and he's a butcher.'

'I must see it through, from port to port, dead or alive.

Sometimes our cargo has been lost at sea, thrown overboard by a greedy captain or a frightened crew. These people have got here and died trying, but their souls can rest in peace, in the country they hoped would give them sanctuary and a better life. We all know the risks but hope that God will see us all safely across. Alas, it is not to be this time.'

I was going to offer to go back in with him when a voice from the farmhouse called out my name.

'It seems as if you have business to attend to, Steven. I won't keep you.'

6

I sat in the kitchen of the farmhouse with Jack Henshall, who was Grandad's lawyer. He had also represented my old man at his trial because he does that for a lot of villains. Henshall was a bit of a throwback to another age, with thick ginger whiskers down both sides of his face and enough curly hair to fill a duvet. His nose was round and pockmarked, with puffed-up cheeks that I put down to all the spirits he drank. He was always in tweeds or something Scottish-looking, and loved wearing waistcoats, covering up a belly that was the size of a washing-up bowl. He used to be a big pipe smoker but had cut the tobacco out, so he just puffed on an empty pipe while talking, which meant saliva would end up dribbling down one side of his mouth.

He offered to top up my tea with a cap of brandy and we sat in silence around a large, thick wooden table. There were loads of copper pots and pans hanging down around the sides of the kitchen, which was in the front of the farmhouse. We looked through the window onto the yard, the lights from the barn making two bright columns. We didn't say much to each other for a good five or ten minutes, perhaps out of respect for the dead. But Henshall never liked to keep quiet for too long, and there would be a good reason why he was here, so I guessed he needed to talk to me about something.

'I hear you've been on a bit of mission,' he said, swilling his brandy. 'Chasing shadows, I suspect, and running into the proverbial door called Greg.'

'Yeah, you could say that.'

'Never easy,' he said, 'to find what you're looking for, with so many paths to follow and so many paths crossed.'

'Well, there's one path that's come to a dead end,' I said, as I sipped my tea, which tasted like sewage with the brandy in it. 'Do we know who did it?'

'The usual suspects I'm afraid, Steven.'

I nodded.

'How's your old man?' he asked.

That was a question I would have usually answered, but I wasn't going to let Henshall know I had been to see him, not until I knew why he was here.

'I don't know,' I said.

'But your brother's back...'

'Yeah, he was with some copper tonight at The End of the World.'

'That would be Detective Carter,' said Henshall, who knew every bent copper in London. 'It seems he has lost all sense of impartiality, especially as he was so close to tonight's scene of the crime. I wonder what has made him stray so wildly from the path?'

That sounded like a question Henshall already knew the answer to.

'It's our friend Doctor Sangoma who I feel sorry for,' said Henshall, who was now chewing his pipe. 'I can't help but admire the man's fortitude in such circumstances, with so many people gone.'

'Yeah, it's a long way to come just to be chopped up and melted down in acid.'

'Ah, but there is a bigger picture, Steven. We will not forgive or forget. Doctor Sangoma will know this.'

'Did we cock up?'

'That is rather opaque,' said Henshall, who now had saliva dripping down one side of his face. 'Are you interested in morality?'

'People have their own way of seeing things, whether it's right or wrong.'

'Correct, Steven. Morality is equivalents, usually dependent on one's material position. For instance, set adrift on a boat with only the dead carcasses of fellow passengers to feed on, our moral veil will drop in order to survive. In the comfort of our homes, eating human flesh is morally abhorrent, but a necessary expediency in a fight for survival.'

'Did they start eating each other in the container?'

'No, they could breathe, there was enough air, but they needed water. We know someone got in and poisoned them.'

'And you think that was Greg?'

Henshall didn't answer because he didn't need to.

'Do they want the business?' I asked.

'Well, it does tarnish the brand, so to speak, but there is a disturbing depth of malice to what has happened. I think they took pleasure in killing those poor souls.'

'They wanted to send a message,' I said, thinking Greg would have enjoyed fooling them into drinking poison instead of water.

'I must say,' said Henshall, who shifted his bum cheeks from one side of his chair to the other, 'that your father and brother have a rather malevolent view of the world. And they mix their criminality with an insidious political view. Had Greg inherited your own intelligence, Steven, he would probably be leading an ethnic cleansing of the estate.'

'I don't know anyone who likes immigrants,' I said. 'That's just the way it is.'

'Will they be cheering, do you think, when Fat Sam takes a chopper to their bloated bodies?'

I shrugged.

'You do know,' said Henshall, who was starting to sound like a priest, 'that this country's moral compass is spinning dangerously out of control. As the centre fails, the periphery becomes more relevant. What would have sounded intolerable becomes the norm. We are at risk of falling into the abyss!'

I laughed.

'I've always lived there,' I said. 'People think there's something nasty and different but there ain't – it's always been there. It's just people like to take notice of it now because they're afraid it might come out of the dark and bite them.'

'Old or new,' said Henshall, 'I would suggest we will all need to be vigilant.'

'I'll keep my eye out and let you know.'

Henshall bit down hard on his pipe. As much as I knew what he was talking about, I was tired and fed up, and needed my head down on a pillow and twenty-four hours' sleep.

'You have a good understanding of the wider things, Steven,' he said. 'What will be, will be, I hear you say. And perhaps you are right. Although, I still find it distressing we commodify every ounce and fibre of our being. Freedom has a price, love has a price, friendship itemised by the hour. Will there ever be a point when the bond of two people or more is not based on some form of market calculation? Like you, I think, I long for a universal truth unsullied by the distorting lens of money.'

'There's only one truth,' I said. 'It's called death.'

'Spoken like a true philosopher!' said Henshall, who seemed to be cheered up by the whole death thing. 'When the Grim Reaper is at hand, we will know all falsehoods have been jettisoned and truth has come to bury or incinerate us!'

'Yeah, I've always found liars can't stop lying, even when you give them a chance.'

'Well, they won't be able to fool their maker.'

'I doubt if they were ever bothered about God.'

'Trust me, Steven, the sinners you may be thinking of will be on a speedy transition to discuss their misdemeanours with the devil.'

'You mean Greg, my old man?'

'He is a cruel and violent man. Let us hope he stays where he is for as long as possible and does not cause any more damage.'

'But he hasn't gone away.'

'No,' said Henshall, who didn't want to commit to seeing my old man in a coffin just yet.

He then paused, and I knew I was going to find out why he had taken the risk to come to the farm and talk to me.

'You know,' he said, 'that your father and Michael grew up together, went to the same school.'

'My old man went to school?'

'They were close,' said Henshall, puffing out his red cheeks. 'As you know…'

It was the beginning of a story I had heard from people, in pubs or by the shops, people trying to tell me all about the two of them, as if I had just landed from another planet.

'So, I will not labour the point. You're right,' said Henshall, who could tell I was in no mood to hear it all over again. 'History has evolved, and we are where we are. However, as I discovered during my graduate years, history hides or it is deliberately hidden. Early on we receive the child's version, the recording of dates and events. But then, later in life, if we are lucky enough, there is a new history of discreet events, throwaway edits and cuttings from the floor. Indeed, all the best bits that had previously been left out.'

'I hope you're not saying that we've made history on the estate.'

'No. My point, Steven, is that your history, I mean your father and Michael's history, has been entwined in joint enterprise, up to the point where they separated, amicably at first, before their bitter divorce.'

'What everybody knows,' I said.

'And a child's version.'

'So, what don't I know?'

'What you don't know, Steven, is that the accumulated wealth of our erstwhile entrepreneurs needed a haven. In other words, the combined wealth of appropriation was to be collectively secured rather than divided.'

'You mean, they put all their money into one pot?'

'Exactly! A golden pot of gold coins, to be precise.'

'And where is this pot?'

'Hidden,' said Henshall.

'And you know where it is?'

'Yes, I am the only one who knows exactly where it is.'

'That's a big risk,' I said, 'for you to carry…'

'In part, but I – we – devised a suitable mitigation. Whilst I know all, your father and Michael know only half of what is needed to retrieve the gold coins. Buried treasure, evenly divided, with half a map each.'

'So, they each have a map of where you buried it?'

'A modern map,' said Henshall, who was back to enjoying munching on his pipe.

'What, Google maps?' I said, finding it hard to believe my old man coping with a smartphone.

'Close,' said Jack. 'A GPS code in fact. The letters and numbers of which are engraved on two rings.'

'And Dominique had one of those rings.'

'Precisely.'

'That is a death sentence.'

'Yes, unfortunately, that may be how things have turned out, but trust me when I say, this was not Michael's intention.'

I was struggling now to fully understand why a class A villain like Grandad would go along with such a crazy idea, and then put Dominique in the firing line.

'Yes, Steven, I can tell by your face that what I have just said might not make much sense, that it is out of character for the man you know as Grandad. But there are a few things you need to understand that will aid your comprehension. The divided kingdom, so to speak, was a necessary arbitration, facilitating relative peace between two highly motivated men. In part, it was done to prevent the violent nature of your father from becoming the dominant force, but also to diffuse a destructive turf war.'

'But it hasn't,' I said.

'No, in hindsight, it merely delayed the inevitable. We underestimated the voracious appetite of your father, which lies beneath all that has happened in the last few weeks.'

'So, my old man has the other ring?'

'We don't know who has the rings. We think your father has passed his on to Greg. Michael has a heavy burden to bear right now. He regrets the decision to give the ring to Dominique, but it was done with good intentions.'

'You mean he wanted to get rid of her?'

'No, Steven. As you know, Michael was ill and had been for some time. He's fighting his cancer, even if it is in remission, and we don't know if he'll relapse, so he wanted some insurance for Dominique. The idea behind the golden pot of coins was that when your father and Michael were ready, they would retrieve the coins for a less... how shall I say it... vigorous and demanding lifestyle. If Michael died, the intention was that Dominique would negotiate the retrieval under my authority.'

I shook my head.

'A widow's pension for his mistress? What about his wife?'

'She is catered for, but in essence, yes.'

'What did he think Dominique was going to do with the ring? As soon as my old man knew he would eat her alive. In fact, that's what he's done!'

'Possibly. We are not entirely sure who has been mischievous and who has been opportunistic.'

I was shaking my head now, as a flood of thoughts about the last five days was beginning to make my blood boil.

'I appreciate,' said Henshall, 'that you would have liked to have known all of this as soon as Michael sent you on your little mission, but we needed someone to go in blind. Sometimes you need to release the ferret to flush the vermin out of the hole.'

That was it, that was the last thing I needed to hear. I jumped out of my seat and walked fuming into the yard. As I stood there, ready to punch the first person who came near me, Fat Sam's car pulled up. He beeped his horn and I just stared. It was going to be a long walk, but I started back down the track, on my way to the estate, thinking about ferrets, soldiers and liars.

Day 6

1

When I got back to my flat, the light was just about starting to come up outside, so I grabbed the duvet and stuck it over my head. I should have gone off into some deep sleep for twenty-four hours, but my mind was full of stuff, going around and around in my head. I was sleeping but it was just a light sleep, full of dreams that were almost real. It was like my mind was going through a whole wash cycle to stop me going mad. I was in hyperdrive, dreaming about escaping from things that were holding me down and keeping me in. I needed to escape, run over fields, run up to fences, begging people I didn't know to get me out. But the dreams led me nowhere, changing scene after scene, each time starting all over again. It was a dream drug that kept everything fluid, pumping through me like a crazy trip that was never going to stop, until I woke up.

I had a load of mixed-up thoughts. I think I was raging inside my head, about Grandad, about Jack Henshall, my brother, my old man; in fact, all the people who thought they knew me better than I knew myself. I was tired of it. They always thought I'd just go along with whatever was needed because they thought I could see there was something in it for me. But not this time. Things had got twisted. I could smell it on my clothes – the smell of death. Perhaps, this time, there was just too much darkness, too much death.

I checked the time; it was around one. I threw off the duvet and stood up in the clothes I had slept in, pulled out my keys with the ring and threw them on the bed. I was surprised Henshall hadn't asked me if I had the ring, but then Henshall was all knowing, like Yoda. He would know I had the ring, even if no one had told him I had it. And he was probably the only one who knew where the gold coins were buried because anyone who had helped with the money, would have ended up finishing the job in a special resting place. He was as crooked as any villain I knew, but there was one thing he would never do: he would never cross Grandad. I suppose there must be a point of trust in our line of business, or else nothing would ever get done, and if there was one thing where trust existed, it was between those two.

Anyway, I stank after sweating away in my bed all morning, so I stripped off and chucked my clothes in the kitchen bin. I pulled out the bin liner, then went outside stark bollock naked and threw the rubbish down the chute. Then it was straight in the shower. I stayed there for a long time. I wanted to wash away everything – all the shit, all the crap, all the dirt I'd been involved in. But by the end of it, as I stood looking in the mirror, with the yellow bruising making me look like I had liver cancer, I knew there was more to come.

I checked in my wardrobe and was ready to put on another tracksuit, but then I stopped. *No more tracksuits*, I said to myself. *It is trousers and shirt*, as I picked up the keys and looked inside the ring again. At least I now knew what the engraving on the inside meant. I had thought about hiding the ring, but in the end, the simplest thing was to just hang on to it. And if I had to, I could swallow it and crap it out later. As I put my keys in my pocket, I had the security of knowing the ring gave me leverage, but it also made me a target, which meant I had to make sure I didn't end up like Dominique, because they'd probably chop off a lot more than my hand to get it.

As I did my shirt buttons up, there was a knock on the door. I could tell it was Mum. I was going to have to see her, so there was no point in pretending I wasn't in. As soon as I opened the door, she walked right walked right past me..

My mum is all chains, bangles and painted nails, about four and half feet tall, almost a midget, but a power in her that had kept her alive. She'd hung on to her looks through all those years with my old man and had the skin that made her look a good ten years younger. But it was always her eyes that told another story, of a hard life.

'Where have you been?' she said, heading straight for the sofa and giving me a look, which showed she was going to tell me off. 'You been in the wars again?'

'I've been up town,' I said, going into the kitchen to make a cup of tea.

'I suppose Michael sent you up there?'

I didn't say anything.

'I suppose you've been looking for that Frenchie woman of his?'

Again, I didn't answer. I'd made it a rule never to tell my mum what I was up to, even if she knew what I did.

'Have you found her then?' she said.

I came back out of the kitchen.

'I'll have to give you two sugars, I said. 'I haven't got any of those sweeteners.'

'I don't want tea,' she said.

'But I'm boiling the kettle.'

'Sit down, Steven.'

That was not like my mum, because she always wants a cup of tea.

'I was going to check on you today,' I said, sitting on the chair next to the sofa.

'That doesn't matter. I've come to see you.'

'What's wrong, has Greg been around?'

'No,' she said, shaking her head.

'Is it the old man?'

That's when she pulled a face.

'Has he been trying to get in touch with you?' I said.

'No,' she said, as she sighed, the way she used to after a big row with my old man. 'Did you see Jack Henshall last night?'

'Yeah.'

'Did he make any sense to you?'

'What do you mean?'

'Well, I know the man talks out of his arse. You need an effing dictionary just to understand him.'

'What's your point, Mum?'

'He probably told you something. I reckon he doesn't put himself out there unless he's got to.'

'What do you mean?'

'Don't play dumb with me, Steven. I'm your mum. You might think I don't know anything, but I know a lot more than you think.'

'Well, you know what he told me then,' I said.

'Perhaps…'

She then put her hand in her pocket looking for her fags. She kept her hand there, fiddling with the packet.

'Did he talk to you about Michael?' she said.

'No.'

'Did he say anything about me?'

'No.'

That's when she pulled out her packet of cigarettes.

'Well,' she said, 'perhaps he wasn't supposed to. It's for me to tell you then.'

She opened the packet and put it to her nose and sniffed it like some drug.

'You see, I'm being good,' she said.

'Yeah, but what do you want to tell me?'

She then looked at me.

'It's something I should have told you a long time ago. Henshall should have told you last night. Michael thought it might have been better coming from his lawyer, but it sounds like he hasn't because I was expecting you to be banging on my door.'

I waited, wondering why Henshall had failed to tell me everything, unless I hadn't given him a chance when I walked out.

'Well, there's no easy way to say it, so I'll just say it and wait and see what you think. Michael, well, he's your real old man. You know, biologically speaking…'

I didn't say anything. I kept looking in the kitchen to see if I should put the kettle on. It was a shock, a surprise. I think I always knew but still a shock because I'd never heard it said to me as being true.

My mum carried on, trying her best to give me a smile.

'He wanted me to keep it from you, for a long time, till

now really. Because of everything that's going on, he thinks you need to know now. You're going to feel angry, Steven, and you're right to feel angry. You can blame it on me if you want, for keeping it a secret.'

I didn't blame her. But I was reeling a bit, taking it all in. I was never dumb about it, but whatever I had thought in the past, I had kept it to myself. But that's how family secrets are, they just come out. *Bam!* Right between the eyes, no messing. Just one drop dead sentence that leaves you wondering how much of everything else is a lie.

'You need to say something, Steven, or else I'm going to have to have a cigarette.'

I just shook my head. I felt like a little boy again. I was meant to be a grown-up man and know everything about the world, and there was my mum telling me something she should have told me years ago.

'I can't sit here with you being all silent on me,' she said. 'It's too much.'

'Why then?' I said, doing my best to say something back. 'Why then... take so long to tell me?'

'I don't know. There never is a right time for these things.'

'Until now you mean.'

'Don't get funny with me, Steven. At least you know who your real blood is, and you should feel happy you ain't inherited anything from that evil bastard in jail.'

'But we lived with him all those years,' I said, resting my head on my hands.

'Yeah, but doesn't mean Michael could have replaced him and been a real dad. He just did what he could for us. Don't you think when I was taking a beating that all I wanted was Michael to sort it out. I wanted it more than anything, but other things had to come first.'

'And not us?'

'Michael's a good man, Steven.'

I wasn't happy. She knew I'd start thinking about all those times I was running around the estate hiding, all the times I was holed up with Mrs C, dreading who was going to knock on the door.

'You're going to need time,' she said. 'Time to think it through. But I'm glad I've done it – it's better late than never.'

'But you waited until he gave you his permission.'

'Michael's done what he could, Steven. He's looked after you as best he could. He's helped you out and given you things lots of other people wouldn't have.'

I knew that, and then I'd always pushed it to the back of mind because it didn't matter in a way, but it would have mattered when I was a kid. He could have made a difference.

'Did you ever want to tell me,' I said, 'back then, when we were trying to stay alive?'

'Sometimes, yes, I wanted you to know. When you were crying, when you were lonely and you thought nobody cared about you or loved you.'

'He could have done something,' I said, shaking my head again.

'Yes and no,' she said, sighing.

I waited. I waited for words to fill up the room. But there was just silence between us.

I got up and went over to the window, where the day was already getting dark. I watched the car lights get brighter and then dim as they went both ways down the dual carriageway. If Mum had told me this when I was younger, I thought, I would have gone straight out, crossed over the road and out onto the grasslands that ran down to the river. Perhaps I would've walked along to The End of the World and waited outside for my real dad to come out, and then he would rub my hair and make everything all right again. But that's kids' stuff, like believing in fairy godmothers and Father Christmas. I was meant to be a big man, a heart of stone, a man who could take everything on the chin, even being told your boss is your old man. I wanted to tell myself I didn't care because I was only being told what I'd already worked out for myself. But there was a load of emotion building up inside of me, getting to me, eating at me like some horrible bug. It was like a germ that had suddenly come to life and was reminding me of all the years of hell I'd had as a kid. It was the reality of how everything was a twisted mess of lies and secrets, in the past and in the present.

'Steven,' said my mum, as I kept my back to her. 'It's best it's all out there. You don't have to tell anybody anything. We can just keep it to ourselves. But you know now.'

I turned around and just looked at her. I didn't blame her for keeping it a secret. And she was right, Grandad had always done his best to look out for me, help me get by, given me things no one else would have got from him. I knew that didn't happen because he wanted to be the patron saint of abused kids. I knew I'd had privileges, but it didn't make the message any the easier to swallow.

'Who else knows?' I said.

'The only people who really know are your old man and Michael. No one else on the estate does, and even if they thought they knew, they wouldn't dare say anything. They'd only be causing trouble for themselves.'

'What about Greg?'

'No, your old man's pride would never let anyone else know. He hated you for not being his, but that didn't mean he wanted anyone else to know you wasn't.'

'So, Greg doesn't know?'

'No, he still thinks you're his little brother who should be kicked and punched whenever he feels like it.'

That was all I wanted to know.

'Listen,' I said, moving towards her. 'Thanks, but you're right, I did know, in myself. I'd be stupid if I hadn't worked it out.'

I think that made my mum feel better, in herself.

'Where're you going?' she said, as I walked towards the door.

'To sort a few things out,' I said. 'I'll catch you later.'

2

My head was a bit of mess, but there was only one person I wanted to see, and that was Britney. It took me about ten minutes to get round there and ring the doorbell.

'You can't come in,' was the first thing she said. 'My mum's here.'

'I've come to collect you,' I said, feeling the cold because I had left without my coat.

'Why, where are we going?' she said, looking like she might know, but wanted me to spell it out.

'I think you know,' I said.

She didn't like that and I thought she was going to slam the door on me. After giving me a long, hard stare, her face changed and she told me to wait.

I could hear her mum being nosey, before Britney came back and handed me a thick black trench coat.

'It used to be my dad's,' she said, as she shut the door behind her. 'He liked to wear it to funerals.'

'Nice,' I said.

'You can give it back if you want and freeze...'

'That's all right,' I said, as I slipped it over my shoulders and put my arms through the sleeves. 'It's a good fit.'

'So, where are we going?' she said.

I didn't think I had to tell her because Anthony would have told her what to do and when to do it, but I would play along.

'Why don't we sit on the swings?' I said, noticing the curtains twitching behind Britney's ground floor flat.

'That's not going very far is it!' she said. 'Are the kids there?'

'No, they only like it when its dark.'

'OK,' she said, putting her arm through mine. 'I suppose you want to talk.'

I did, I wanted to talk a lot, about all the things that had been bugging me since Britney had turned up at Dominique's bedsit. And the first thing I wanted to get straight was about her old man.

'Do you miss him?' I said, as we started walking.

'Who?'

'Your dad?'

'Yes, every day. I loved him and they took him away.'

'Who are *they*?'

'Steven, you know who *they* are! He should never have died. *They* are guilty but nothing will ever happen to them.'

'You never talked about it.'

'Not to you,' she said. 'Anyway, he lost his job and it was really hard for him. And then, when he got a job, a nothing job on the farm cleaning out muck, he fell in a pit and that killed him – toxic fumes in a pit – but they've done nothing for us, for me or my mum.'

'Why didn't you go to a lawyer?'

'We did, he was called Henshall, and then we found out he was all part of it.'

'You're still angry then?' I said, as we turned the corner to check if there was anyone messing around on the swings.

Britney stayed quiet. She didn't have to tell me any more; I could join the dots.

We both looked onto the square with the railings, surrounded by the flats on all sides. We'd be watched from the windows by the kids who did the dealing, but once it got dark, they'd want us out of there. We sat on a rotten bench, looking at the one swing that you could swing on, a play boat to sit in and a small climbing frame.

'You're not saying anything,' said Britney, who was right to wonder why I wasn't speaking.

I was thinking, or trying to think, but I was also suffering, from the aftershock, from the big news from my mum. The reality was sinking in – the truth and lies and the world of secrets. I thought I'd had it all sussed when I left the flat, but now my head was filling up with rubbish, angry rubbish, like the anger that Britney still hung on to because of what had happened to her dad.

'You know I saw Anthony yesterday?' I said, as the traffic along the dual carriageway was humming in the background.

'Yes, he told me,' she said, looking down on the gravel, which she started to push with her feet. 'He said he was hiding from your brother. He said you were helping him.'

'Have you told anyone else that?'

'No.'

'Is the other guy you're involved with part of all of this?'

'What guy?'

'The other guy you're with. The one who's replaced Anthony.'

'It isn't like that, he hasn't replaced him. He's different.'

'Does he wear a black hoodie?'

'Why do you ask?'

'Because there is a guy who has been following me who wears a black hoodie and he led me to Anthony.'

'Oh…'

'Is that a yes?'

'I don't know.'

'But you do know…'

'In a way, but I will tell you when the time is right.'

'That's what Anthony said.'

'Sorry.'

'I need to know,' I said. 'It's truth time now. No more BS.'

'I know, and you will know, I promise. I just can't say anything yet, but I want you to believe and I want you to help us.'

'Why should I do that?'

'Because I think you want to.'

'To do your dirty work?'

'No. I need you…'

I wanted to believe her. I wanted to believe she wanted me, that there was something true and not false. It was why I had run down to see to her, to find out if there was any truth left.

'The thing is,' she said, putting her fingers together and moving them around in a knot, 'I trusted somebody and now I don't know if I can trust them, because I'm afraid…'

'Afraid of what?'

'Afraid of everybody, afraid of everything, of what might happen to me.'

'Why, what do you think is going to happen to you?'

'I don't know,' she said, untying her hands. 'Don't you ever feel afraid of things?'

'Sometimes, but you learn to control it, fear.'

'You're lucky,' she said, going back to twisting her hands together. 'You must be used to it. But me and Anthony, this is all new, all different.'

'So, you've done this together?'

'We've tried to do something and it's all gone wrong,' she said, giving me a shifty glance.

'What's gone wrong?'

'You kind of know,' she said, looking at me. 'But it can go right again.'

'What does that mean?'

Britney stared at the empty swing seats.

'Look at this place,' she said. 'It's horrible. I can't live like this, with nothing. I want something better, better than this.'

'Is that what you and Anthony have been up to? Trying to get a way out of this place?'

'Aren't you?' she said, looking at me as if I should own up to it.

I didn't answer, because anyone with half a brain cell would want to leave the estate behind. I know I did. I just hadn't forced myself to do anything about it.

'You know,' she said, as she carried on staring at the empty swings, 'even if you think you can't trust me, or Anthony, he is your friend. He told me how his parents looked after you, how they would hide you from your dad.'

She was right, Anthony was my friend, and because of

that I'd already given him a free pass. But if it had been anyone else, I would have dragged them back to Grandad and he would never have been seen again. Then I wondered if she knew Anthony had tried to offer her to me, in exchange for safety and protection. But that was no good. She wasn't going to listen to me making Anthony look like a liar and a cheat. Something had to come from me now – how I felt, what I wanted.

'OK,' I said. 'Do you want to know the truth?'

'What do you mean?'

'I mean, do you want me to be honest with you?'

'Of course,' she said, looking at me.

'So, do you want to hear how I feel about you?'

She hesitated. I could see it in her face, weighing up the pros and cons of what I might say. And then she looked away, down at her boots.

'Or is that too much for you?' I said.

'No…' she said, crunching the gravel with her heels. 'I just didn't think…'

'Think what?'

'I just didn't think you would say anything.'

'Well, I am now.'

'Go on then. How do you feel?'

'About you?'

'Yes.'

'I have feelings…' I said, 'for you.'

'Oh…'

'Yeah… I can't stop thinking about you. You keep coming back into my mind, whatever crazy stuff is going on. You're always there, and I end up thinking about you.'

I hadn't said as much as I wanted. I hadn't used the words I had used in my head when walking back from the farm to the estate, but I was getting there.

'But am I part of those crazy things?' she said.

'I think you are,' I said. 'So, I can't promise anything, except me, here, with you now, and needing to be with you.'

'Oh,' she said again, carrying on grinding the gravel. 'Why do you like me then?'

'I don't know. Do I need a reason?'

'No…'

We were both silent for a bit. It's not easy to tell someone how you feel about them, but I think we were both on the same level and words weren't going to make a lot of difference.

'Can we go somewhere else?' she said. 'I really don't like it here.'

'Where do you want to go?'

'I don't know, let's just go, in my car…'

And then she jumped up from the bench, taking charge.

'Do you trust me?' she said.

I laughed.

'As long as we're not going to see Anthony,' I said.

'No, not yet.'

That was good enough for me, for now.

I stood up and Britney moved towards me and put her arm through mine. We looked at all the windows of the flats around us and we both hated them. They were just like ugly faces, full of hate, full of anger, full of sadness and no hope.

'Let's just go,' she said.

We walked back around the corner and got into her little run-around. The light had almost gone now, as she turned the engine on, fiddled with the heating and reversed out of the parking space. I didn't want to say anything. I just wanted to look outside the window as we drove out of the estate.

We were soon on the country roads that are a;; over Essex. It doesn't take too long to get away from all the dull and boring housing estates, which spread out along the river or sits in pockets of messed-up new towns. I bet Britney had done this loads of times, just getting in her car and driving, coming up to a junction and on instinct, turning left or right.

For the rest of the car journey, for a good hour, we drove along lanes with hedges, with ploughed up fields either side of them, through villages with cottages either side of the road, or over the odd train crossing. I watched the telephone lines go up and down from one pole to another, and the sun fall and the moon shine in the clouds.

I didn't think about Britney all that time. I thought about my mum. Why had she put up with it for so long, all the violence, all the terror? For what? For a few moments when we were like a proper family. Why did she put up with it when she had a way out? I couldn't figure it out. There was Grandad, my real old man, just keeping quiet, pretending nothing ever happened. But why couldn't he tell me to my face?

I had always thought I was in control. I had always thought I knew what was going on, why people did certain things, what made them do what they did. Now, I wasn't sure of anything. All I had been was a good centurion, as Sangoma had said, taking orders and doing what a good soldier was meant to do – obey and don't think.

Well, I was not going to put up with it. It was time things changed.

Day 7

1

Britney had paid for the room last night, which was in an old country house, with red carpets everywhere and creaky floorboards. I was lying in bed, looking at the sunlight coming through the gap between the thick curtains that covered the high window. I thought Britney was sound asleep, with her back to me and her head on the pillow, until she asked if I'd had any dreams.

'I don't know, I can't remember,' I said, rubbing her back with my hand.

'Don't you have dreams?' she said, into the pillow.

'Yeah, I have dreams.'

'What sort of dreams?'

There was only one dream I ever had. A real dream in real life, about a desert island, getting away from everything and being free and feeling safe.

'I don't remember,' I said, rolling onto my back. 'None of it ever makes sense anyway. We just dream to work things out.'

'Did you dream about me?'

I wanted to tell Britney she was in my dreams, but it had been one long, deep sleep.

'Probably,' was the best I could say.

'I had a dream about Anthony,' she said, sounding like she was confessing.

'Yeah?' I said, trying to make out I didn't care.

'You were in it as well.'

'So, no room for the other guy in your life?'

'No.'

'Is he not your boyfriend now then?'

'He is,' she said, sighing.

'OK, just checking.'

'We were all on a boat,' she said, keen to get back to her dream.

'What sort of boat?'

'It was dirty and small.'

'Sounds like my boat.'

Britney then turned over so she was looking at me, holding the sheet to cover her body.

'You were sailing the boat,' she said, 'and then you said there was a storm coming and we had to do all these things, but we didn't know what to do, so you got angry with us.'

'And then what happened?'

'I think the storm came, and me and Anthony got thrown into the sea, but you were trying to save us, but each time you threw a rope into the water we couldn't hold on, our hands kept slipping.'

'Did you drown?'

'It felt like drowning. I was going down and down and I didn't think I was going to wake up.'

'Sounds like a nightmare.'

Britney didn't say anything, as she looked up at the ceiling.

'As long as you wake up, you'll live,' I said, resting my head in my hand.

'You mean, if you don't wake up you die?'

'Perhaps, but nobody knows, do they?'

'You mean, nobody has come back to say they dreamt their own death and survived?'

'Yeah. We always wake up and work out what's real.'

'Do we?'

'I like to think so. You'd have a problem if you didn't know what a dream was and what wasn't.'

'I'm not sure I can,' said Britney, who was still staring at the ceiling.

'This is real,' I said. 'Me and you, here, in this bed.'

'I know,' she said, pulling the sheet up to her chin.

'Or is this a nightmare for you?'

'It could be.'

'Didn't you want this to happen?'

'I don't know…'

'But it has…'

Britney then looked at me as if all she wanted to do was turn the clock back, and rewrite the bit at the end so we just said goodbye. I'd go to my flat and Britney would go back to her mum and watch TV for the rest of the evening.

'You know,' I said, 'you shouldn't feel guilty about this.'

'I don't. It's not guilt…'

'What is it then?'

'I don't want to say… You'll hate me.'

'I won't hate you,' I said. And just to make sure she knew how I wanted things to be between us, I said, 'Whatever it is,

I won't hate you.'

'Will you promise you won't hate me?' she said, keeping her eyes still firmly fixed on the ceiling.

'Britney,' I said, laughing. 'Even if I had a good reason to hate you, I don't think I could.'

That seemed to put her at ease.

'I know what Anthony said to you,' she said, 'in the church, when you met.'

'He told you?'

'Yes.'

'Did he tell you to sleep with me?'

'No.'

'Did you want to sleep with me?'

'Yes.'

'That's all that matters then. What you think and feel, you did it because you wanted to.'

'I think so,' she said. 'But I don't want you to do things for Anthony, just because I slept with you.'

'I don't see it like that, plus I owe his family, his mum.'

'Anthony said they were staying in their caravan out of the way of things.'

'It's as good a place as any.'

'Like your boat?'

'Yeah, people know about it, but it doesn't mean they'd go there straight off.'

'What about me?' she said. 'What if I asked if you could help me?'

'Why, what kind of help do you need?'

Then she looked up at me.

'I need you to help me and Anthony.'

I didn't say anything. I just looked at her.

'Please, Steven, I really need you to help.'

'I am. Anthony wanted me to collect you and I have, and we'll go and see him today.'

'But are you really going to help or are you just doing this for him?'

'You mean Grandad?'

'Yes.'

'I work for Grandad,' I said. 'What you are asking me to do is a bit of freelance, and that carries a big risk for me because of what I think you did.'

'That doesn't answer my question.'

'That's because I don't have an answer, but once you tell me the truth, then I can make a decision.'

Britney paused and rolled over, so her body was free of the bed sheet.

'I think you know my secret,' she said, as she put a hand on my chest.

'Maybe,' I said, as I kissed her.

Then she pushed my body back a little.

'I know you can't promise things,' she said, 'but promise me you'll remember this, whatever happens.'

I looked at her, her eyes glowing. I knew I would remember everything about her, whatever happened.

2

Britney told me she had agreed to meet Anthony before twelve, and so we were back in her car, driving out to the estuary where my boat was moored. It meant I looked out of the car window at the same flat earth I had looked at last night, only this time it was covered in a thick white frost. We were also back to being silent. Ever since we had gone down for breakfast, she'd hardly said a word. I reckoned she was keeping quiet in case she said anything that might change my mind. I was going to see it through as far as I could, until I knew what I needed. But I still didn't know how far I was going to go to help either Britney or Anthony. I just wanted to get on my boat and get them both starting to talk, because the last thing I needed was Anthony being tracked down before I had got to him. And knowing Anthony, he would say anything to save his own skin.

As we got closer to my boat, Britney pulled up at a supermarket so she could get some food for Anthony – he'd told her he was starving. She came out with two bulging bags and threw them in the back of the boot.

'There's only a couple of gas rings on the boat,' I said, 'and a few plates.'

'That's all right,' said Britney, who was focused on her little mission. 'It's only soup.'

'That's a lot a soup for three.'

'You never know,' she said, as she got ready to set off.

I didn't say anything. Whatever Britney and Anthony's plans, it looked like spending days eating soup.

We carried on until I had to start directing her for the last few miles. As we got closer, we turned off the road, and Britney's little run-around bumped over mud and gravel, and then down a narrow concrete track, which passed a small store used by the locals and boaters. It was also the last place where you could get a phone signal. Out in front of us was a wide spread of grasses and marsh, which stretched to the estuary. As we jumped up and down the concrete track, we could see there was no more than a dozen boats and dinghies moored in the inlet. Most of the boats were like mine – for sailing up and down the estuary or along the coastline and back again. It's what I did now and then, to make it look like I was a proper little sailor, but the boat was owned by Grandad and had a different purpose, which we called 'our fishing trips'.

I told Britney to carry on down to the end of track and park up next to a square, white mooring office with a clanking flagpole, which in the summer had Captain Birdseye keeping a lookout. Britney spotted Anthony, sitting on the bank with his back to us, looking out across the estuary, which was wide and marshy on both sides.

'Why is he not on the boat?' said Britney, as she pulled up on the gravel car park.

'He would've brought the dinghy back, so we can row over to the boat,' I said. 'Plus, he'll be cold being out on the water.'

'You mean, it's warmer to sit there?'

I shrugged.

'Which boat is yours then?' said Britney.

'My boat's there,' I said, pointing. '*Haven.*'

'Oh, did you name it?'

'No, that's just the name.'

For whatever reason, Britney wasn't jumping out of the car yet and Antony hadn't turned around to greet us.

'Do you think he'll be angry?' she asked.

'Who, Anthony, about last night? Have you told him?'

'No, but he'll guess.'

'Britney, he's not your boyfriend. You've finished with him.'

She sighed as she opened the car door and went around to open the boot to get the shopping.

I could tell last night was eating into Britney as I watched her walk over to Anthony. She stood beside him, talking, holding the shopping bags, and then looked over at me in the car. After a few minutes, she mouthed for me to come over.

'Bit chilly,' I said, as Anthony turned around to face me.

'I'll row,' said Anthony, all aggressive.

The cheeky bugger, I said to myself. He didn't seem too appreciative I'd let him hide away down here.

'Be my guest,' I said.

We all sat in the dinghy and Anthony pushed off. With the oars in the water, he then gave me and Britney a cold, dark stare. I wasn't going to say anything about sleeping with Britney unless he wanted me to, but I was sure Britney would have told him while I was waiting in the car. As he rowed, Britney clapped him for a skill she didn't think he had, but it didn't crack his stiff face. He carried on rowing in silence. Britney dipped her hand in the water and said the bleeding obvious: it was cold. After twenty strokes, the front end of the dinghy bumped into the side of my boat, and I pulled us back down the stern and hauled myself in. I tied the dinghy and then hauled Britney, Anthony and the shopping up.

'Let's have a cup of tea,' I said, as I dived down into the cabin.

There wasn't a great deal of space, just a bunk on one side, which Anthony had been freezing in, some shelving, cupboards and the gas rings on the other side. Anthony and Britney sat down on the bunk, like two naughty kids, while I got out a pan and some bottled water for the brew.

'Here,' said Britney, as she pulled out some vodka from the shopping bags. 'It will warm us up.'

'I'll need that,' said Anthony, who was shaking from the intense cold he had put up with.

I just grinned.

I moved up to the narrow port end and stood with my head bent down because of the low decking. There was nothing for me to say. It all had to come from them.

They looked at each other, then looked over at me.

'What do you want to know?' said Anthony.

'Why don't you start at the beginning?' I said. 'Most stories start at the beginning, and after you've finished lying, you can then tell me the truth, you know, the whole truth and nothing but...'

'You can't judge us,' said Anthony, who was trying to prove he could stand up for himself. 'If we've done wrong, so have you – all the time..'

'Listen,' I said, feeling my patience hit close to zero, 'I can put you both over the side and leave you to look after yourselves.'

'We know,' said Britney, who stood and picked up a couple of mugs on the side to see if they were clean.

'Well, if you want my help,' I said, 'I need to know what you've been up to, what you want me to do and why you want me to do it.'

'It's an offer,' said Anthony, who picked up the vodka bottle lying on the bed next to him and unscrewed the top. 'It's an offer to join us, for a better life.'

'Yeah, and what makes you think I need a better life?'

'We all do, Steven,' said Britney, as she pulled a face when she looked inside the mugs.

'At any price?' I said.

'Sometimes,' said Anthony, as he took a serious swig and felt the vodka slip down his body, 'you know, opportunities come along that can be hard to refuse.'

'And you've got an offer I can't refuse?'

Britney wiped her hands around the inside of the mugs

and kept quiet, but I wondered for how long, seeing as I knew Anthony couldn't negotiate his way out of his front door most of the time.

'How much do you know?' he said.

'I thought it was you who was meant to be telling the story.'

'We know you know a lot more, Steven,' said Britney, who looked as if she was ready to help with the tea making.

'Then you know how much I know,' I said, taking a step forward to see if the water had started to boil in the pan.

'Do you know about the gold rings?' said Anthony.

'Yeah.'

'And you have one?' he said, taking another swig.

I kept a blank face. I wasn't going to say yes to that, just in case they both lunged at me with some hidden meat cleaver.

'It doesn't matter,' said Anthony, who was being warmed and made lucid by the rush of alcohol into his empty stomach. 'We know you have it.'

I looked at Britney, who was also keeping her eyes on the pan of water. She didn't want to look at me. I knew now she must have checked in the icebox after I had taken the ring. Once she knew I had it, there would've been no point in hanging around with me. She could head back home. And there I was thinking I was keeping an eye on Britney up in London, when she probably had a closer eye on me.

'The thing is,' I said, leaning back, 'you don't know if I have the ring. You think you know, but you can't be sure. And, at the end of the day, my job is not to find the ring, but to find Dominique. So, what I need to know is, who killed her, or did you do it together?'

'We haven't killed anyone!' said Anthony, who seemed

to think I had offended him.

'Anthony, it was you who dropped off Dominique's hand in Mickey Finn's old fridge. Was it that you just happened to come across it and thought, I'll seal it in a plastic bag, post it in a fridge and hope I get an annual subscription for *Junkie Unlimited*? I mean, I ain't no Sherlock Holmes, but I would think you are a prime suspect for her disappearance and murder.'

'We didn't kill her,' said Anthony, this time looking at Britney.

'OK,' I said, reading between the lines. 'Based on what you're *not* saying, you got her off the radar so someone else could do it. And it wasn't Greg because he was waiting for a hand with a fat gold ring still attached to the finger. What I can't figure out is, why give up the ring and let Greg walk away with all the money?'

Anthony wanted help from Britney, but she was pretending making tea was a lot more interesting.

'I wasn't leaving it for him,' said Anthony, who was coming over all guilty. 'I was meant to be meeting Greg and Mickey there. I just thought…'

That was when Britney dropped a teaspoon in a mug, which sounded angry and pissed.

'…that it wouldn't hurt, five minutes, instead of waiting, to just to get a quick fix…'

'From the grocers?' I added.

'Yeah.'

'And so you thought the hand would be all right in the freezer until you got back, and then you and my brother could ride off into the distance, hugging each other as you go, waiting for Google maps to update, all the way to the buried treasure like a couple of useless fucking pirates!'

After I said that, the silence from both seemed painful.

'OK, so why didn't you take the ring off Dominique's finger and write the GPS code down on a piece of paper?'

'We tried,' said Anthony, 'but we couldn't get the ring off because her fingers were swollen. Also, we had to give Greg the hand because he thought it was the only way of making sure we hadn't taken the ring off her finger to get the code.'

'That's Greg, the criminal mastermind,' I said laughing. 'But I can't believe you guys thought you could get away with it. I mean, you're getting into bed with the devil, a nasty evil bastard! My brother is not someone who would ever keep his word. Even if you had got as far as finding something, he would stab you in the head, chop you up into little pieces and feed you to his dogs.'

'He gave up his dogs,' said Anthony.

'That's not funny,' I said.

'When he moved to Manchester.'

'I know,' I said, struggling to understand how these two could be so effing dumb. 'Well, for whatever reason, you were stupid enough to lose the ring of plenty, which we know had been given to Dominique, who we all know is dead, along with one of Tommy's kids and a load of immigrants fermenting in tubs of acid.'

'We didn't know anything about the immigrants,' said Britney, chipping in.

'That's your old man's thing,' said Anthony. 'He wants to do as much damage as he can. He wants to destroy everything Grandad has. It's just that Dominique was...'

'Was what?'

'An accident.'

'You mean, you didn't mean to kill her, but you just couldn't help it?'

'It got out of hand…'

'Is that a joke?'

'No, just the truth.'

'But you got in the way,' said Britney, who bit down on her lip.

'And you lied to me twenty-four seven,' I said, keeping my eye fixed firmly on Britney. 'I bet you had the key to Dominique's bedsit all that time. I bet you let Greg have the key, so he could beat the crap out of me, and you let Greg snatch the kid and throw him in the river because he couldn't or wouldn't talk, and you let Greg put Tommy in hospital.'

Britney couldn't or didn't want to look at me.

'We had to think,' said Anthony, 'what was in our best interest. You messed up our plans…'

'But there's an opportunity,' said Britney. 'We have the other ring.'

'You stole it from Greg?'

'That's why I had to run,' said Anthony. 'I got the ring off him when they were threatening me. I knew he was never going to share anything. It was easy – I just put my hand in his pocket. It was a gift!'

I had to laugh again.

'Please don't tell me you only worked that one out a few days ago?'

'There was a plan,' said Anthony, who wanted to prove he was not as stupid as I made it all sound. 'There was a plan A and now there is a plan B.'

'You mean, rip off Greg and do it for yourselves?'

'Yes and no…'

'It's fluid,' said Britney.

'A rivers flows,' I said, 'but it always leads to the sea. Where do you think this is leading?'

'To a better life,' said Britney.

'If you live,' I said. 'You've got two violent gangs after you. How do you think you are going to survive?'

'They've got to find us first,' said Britney.

'That won't be difficult,' I said. 'This boat is not a hiding place.'

'We know,' said Anthony. 'We don't need the boat to hide. We need it to go somewhere, with you, because you can sail and because you have the other ring.'

'Well,' I said, 'offer me a good price and the boat is yours.'

'We don't want to buy it. We want you to sail it.'

'Yeah, and what makes you think I would do anything for you when the price is a cruel and unpleasant end?'

'Because we think you want what we want,' said Anthony.

'No,' I said, 'I really don't want to die.'

'Money,' said Anthony.

'I get by,' I said.

'More money than you'd ever have working for Grandad.'

'But it's his money and it's my old man's money,' I said.

'And your old man, he must owe you a thousand times for what he did to you, but he'll never give you anything.'

'The thing is, Anthony, because of what he did, I would never take anything he offered. The only thing he owes me is staying out of my life.'

'But you must want to change things?' said Britney. 'We have a chance to change everything for ourselves and to take it from people who don't care about anybody except themselves.'

The saucepan on the gas ring vibrated and we all looked.

'Don't bother,' I said. 'It takes ten years to boil.'

That seemed to be a good excuse for Anthony to down some more vodka.

'What's the plan then?' I said, sounding like I might think about their death wish.

This seemed to change their mood straight away. They had everything riding on me going along with it, whatever it was they had come up with.

'You know the rings have a GPS code?' said Anthony.

'No shit Sherlock!'

'Well, I always knew where the coins were basically hidden,' said Anthony. 'Dominique told me.'

'Her fatal mistake,' I added.

'It wasn't personal,' said Anthony.

'But it is now,' I said.

'The point,' said Anthony, who wanted to move on from the depths of his betrayal, 'was not where the coins are buried, but *exactly* where they are buried.'

'Which needs GPS,' said Britney.

'Which is why,' I added, 'she must have thought she could tell you without any risk of you looking for the money, unless of course you chopped her hand off.'

'Look,' said Anthony, 'I liked her. That's what I mean, it wasn't personal.'

'But she helped you, Anthony,' I said, having trouble getting to grips with what was driving him. 'Dominique and Grandad, they turned you into an artist.'

'Is that what you think!' said Anthony, giving me back that cold, hard stare. 'What's wrong with you, Steven? Do you really think Grandad has any interest in art, in me?'

'No,' I said. 'That's up to you, isn't it. But he didn't turn you into a junkie or make you live at home with your mum and dad.'

'He exploits me,' said Anthony. 'He uses my art sales to launder his drug money. Do you know how much I get for a painting? Five per cent!'

'And all the gear you need,' I offered.

'Which keeps Anthony in his place,' said Britney. 'Anthony will never be anything stuck on the estate with Grandad ruling over him.'

I paused. It just didn't add up, but then I had to go with it, just to find out what they wanted from me.

'OK,' I said, 'you have a plan that means you kill a few people, then rob some of the biggest villains in Essex, so you can live in luxury. Oh, and Anthony is free to become a famous artist.'

'Don't laugh at us, Steven,' said Anthony. 'We can't go back now. We can only go forward.'

'Well, it's true you can't go back,' I said, sneering.

'And what makes you think you're not a target?' said Anthony. 'Greg will come for you, just as much as he will come for us. He'll think you're part of it now, whatever you say.'

'But that's between me and him, something that was always going to happen. Your problem is, I'm not going to get in his way when he catches up with you.'

'Please, you need to help us,' said Britney, who was almost begging. 'This is our one chance and we've got to take it. All you have to do is sail the boat to the island and share the ring with us.'

'Oh right, you mean as in *Treasure Island*?'

'It's not made-up,' said Anthony. 'It's the one out in the estuary.'

That's when the penny dropped. Everything, or quite a few things, fell into place.

3

By the time they had told me all about plan B, I had to get out of the tiny cabin and stand by the wheel to get some air, to think it through. They wanted three things from me: sail to the island, which they could do anyway by themselves in a dinghy, give them the other half of the GPS code and then sail them across the channel, which is where my boat really comes in. For those three things, I could take equal shares in the money, split evenly they said. It didn't seem to cross their minds that I could have mugged them there and then and taken the other ring and sorted it out for myself. I said the whole thing was crazy, but they were stuck because there was no way they could unwind what they had done. And they can't turn around and say to Grandad: we killed your girlfriend and we're sorry, because our eyes were bigger than our stomachs. Which is why they have no choice. They must go with it, try and recruit me, even if it means I could turn against them at any minute.

Getting to the island was no problem because me and Anthony used to do it as kids. And there was not much there, just some old war defences and a shack, which some nutjob had built because he thought he could live there on his own with the birds for company. The last I had heard it had some wildlife protection, but for those of us who had boats, it was a lump of land to navigate around before heading out to sea. Anthony must have known it was where the gold coins were hidden because he'd painted that little treasure chest in Dominique's island above her bed. And he must've gained her trust for her to tell him the pension pot had been buried on the island. God knows why she did it. Perhaps she told him because she wanted him to know that one day, she'd have the money to help him with his painting. Dominique was like that – always giving, helping other people. If only she had known what a traitor Anthony would turn out to be. But that's the thing, the thing you learn: no one thanks you once you've helped them. It's like they hate you for it because you knew them when they were weak. And that's the one thing they can't stand, knowing that you knew them when they were helpless.

Anyway, I needed to decide things for myself. I was on nobody's side just yet. I reckoned the only reason Grandad fessed up about claiming me as his was because he knew I would find out what was going on and he would know I'd be pissed about being used like some effing sniffer dog. He'd be worried about how I might react, in case I decided to take advantage of the opportunity that had presented itself. Well, he always wants loyalty, and he wants me to know where the real family ties lay. But the thing is, I was only on his side of the turf if I thought he was going to win, not because I needed to be loyal. And with the way things were with Anthony and Britney, I had another side I could be on, which gave me another option, something in the middle – not with Grandad and not against Grandad. And as for my old man and Greg, well, I was always against them.

I had also worked out most of what had gone on. But there were still a few bits missing, which was stopping me from joining one side or the other. The problem was, Anthony and Britney had told me nothing about how Dominique had died. I could kind of believe it wasn't them; they were crazy, but not that crazy. Killing someone isn't easy. It's messy, complicated, it leaves a sick feeling in your stomach, if you're normal. And they didn't have those eyes, which could tell me if they had done that kind of thing. But I needed to know, for my own interests, who it was who had killed Dominique. And the only person left in the snake pit, who I couldn't swear by, was the guy in the black hoodie skulking around in the shadows – he had to be Britney's new boyfriend. And seeing how Britney hadn't said anything about this boyfriend before, maybe he was part of it from the beginning? Maybe he was the one who had messed up when they were dealing with Dominique? Yeah, I was keen on knowing more about him, when Britney poked her head up from the cabin.

'I've made you tea,' she said, pushing the cabin door shut. 'Anthony's doing something.'

I nodded.

'Not the best thing to be doing right now, is it?' I said, taking the tea.

'Not for me or you to say, but it's what makes him tick.'

She was probably right. I was always amazed how junkies could do a lot more stoned than when they were straight.

Britney sat down on the bench, which ran around the inside of the tiny deck.

'Are you disappointed in me?' she asked.

'About what?'

'About everything.'

'Yes,' I said. 'I am disappointed about everything.'

'I thought you were,' she said. 'But you shouldn't judge us. I know from Anthony that you've done all sorts of things.'

'I'm not judging you,' I said, which was a half-truth. 'But whatever I have done, I've always made sure I get out of it in one piece. You guys have thrown yourselves in at the deep end, and you could both get killed.'

'Is it you then, who's going to kill us?'

'I don't know,' I said, honestly.

'You can choose, you know. You don't have to do Grandad's dirty work for him. You don't have to feed off the crumbs Grandad gives you. There's a great big piece cake for all of us.'

'What makes you think I only feed off the crumbs?'

'Come on!' said Britney, who pushed her hands out in frustration. 'You live in a shitty flat two floors down from your mum.'

'It's got a good view of the dual carriageway,' I said, smiling.

'Is that what you really want, to live the rest of your life in a shithole? I don't believe you, Steven. I know you have dreams, just like me and Anthony. You wouldn't do the things you do if you didn't want something better.'

'I do what I'm good at.'

'Well, if you come with us, you wouldn't have to do all that horrible stuff.'

'No, Britney, you're wrong. That's all I would have left because they would come after us.'

'We can hide. We'd have enough money to pay for anything.'

'It wouldn't be like that,' I said, sipping the tea, which was another poor cuppa. 'Where do you think we could hide so no one could find us?'

Britney stared.

'You're wrong,' she said, perhaps more to herself than me. 'You can stay if you want, but you know there's nothing here for people like us. You need to be rich in this world because there's no more in between. And I don't want to end up like my dad, with nothing but a day of hell to get through.'

'Swapping one hell for another doesn't sound like much of an offer to me.'

'It won't be like that, I promise.'

'Yeah? The thing is, Britney, I can't help thinking that we were together last night, so what happens to things like that?'

'That's different,' she said, looking pissed because I had brought it up. 'That's something that just happens. I don't know if it will happen again. Is that what you want? Do you just want me?'

'Like you said, maybe...'

I could have said yes, if she had said something different, but that was not where Britney's head was at right now. All she wanted was for me to pull up the rope, sail out to the island, get hold of the gold coins and somehow get across the channel.

Then she looked down at the floor, the same way she had looked down when we were sitting on the bench on the estate.

'You know the guy you followed to meet Anthony in the church?' she said.

'Not really, he likes to run away.'

'Well,' she said, lifting her head up, 'he's not Anthony's friend...'

'But he helped him?'

'Yes, he did it for me.'

'Yeah?'

'He's my guardian angel. He saved me... He saved me from killing myself...'

Some truth, at last. And I straight away started thinking that could've been at a time when all sorts of crazy ideas had got into her brain.

'He found me,' she said, turning her head to look back at

the embankment. 'He found me in London, on the river. I was going to do it and he stopped me...'

'When was that?'

'After my dad died. Everything was dark. I couldn't see a way out. All I thought about was trying to stop the pain, feeling awful and sad all the time. Every minute, every second of the day.'

'And how much does he want?' I said.

'What do you mean?'

'His cut, your boyfriend?'

'How do you know he's my boyfriend?'

'I think you've just told me.'

'It's not like that.'

'So, he doesn't want a bag of gold and you believe him?'

'It's three ways,' she said.

'The split?'

'Yes. You get one third, the rest is for us.'

'Who's us?'

'Me and Anthony.'

'And the boyfriend?'

'He doesn't want anything. I mean, I am going to share it with him. It's now a third for you, a third for Anthony and a third for us.'

So the guy in the black hoodie was Britney's boyfriend. I didn't like the sound of that, not because I was unhappy about splits or any other fantasy that came into her head. It was the boyfriend, the one who must have been watching everything right from the start, who had been at the weddings, watching Dominique. It was like finding that missing jigsaw piece for the picture to be complete. Every time I looked, I hadn't seen it, but it had been there all along, the one piece I needed to make sense of all the craziness.

'So, where is he? What's his name?'

'He's coming,' she said.

'And you trust him?'

'What does that mean?'

'Well, it's just that I remember, before you went back to your mum's, you had said you had lost trust in someone. There really is only one person that could be.'

'He just wants to help.'

'Yeah? Does that include killing and chopping off hands?'

'What do you mean?'

'You heard the question, Britney. Was it your boyfriend who killed Dominique?'

She started shaking her head, and then she started crying.

'It just went wrong,' she said, as the tears ran down her cheeks.

'How wrong?'

'Very wrong, and then it's too late, for me and for Anthony…'

'So, he wasn't just helping?'

Britney was now in floods of tears. It was getting to her – all the seriousness, all the mistakes, all the damage, but with no way out, no way of turning back the tide.

'We haven't got much time,' she said, wiping the tears across her face.

'We've got time,' I said, sipping the horrible tea again. 'I need to know…'

'Not now,' she said. 'There's only one way out now. So, will help us or will you stop us?'

'I'm not here to stop you. I'm only here to find what's left of Dominique. But I just don't believe it will work out for you. I think all three of you will end up dead, as dead as

Dominique.'

'It could work if you helped us,' she said, back to a little bit of begging. 'I know we could do it.'

'You mean with my boat so you can get across the channel?'

'No, it's more than that,' she said. 'I mean, I want you to be part of everything. Last night did mean something to me. I always wanted it to happen.'

'And you're not just saying that?'

'No, I'm not just saying that.'

'So, your offer has changed then, it's me and you taking all the money?'

Britney shrugged. She was slippery and desperate, desperate to offer anything because she knew her life was on the line, even if she had tried to end it in the past.

'But who means more to you, me or the boyfriend?'

'You can't do things like that. You can't add it all up, or weigh it, and say something is sixty/forty.'

'But if you did,' I said, 'would I be sixty or forty?'

Britney shook her head. All she had to do was commit. Like her, I had been waiting for last night to happen.

'OK,' I said

'OK, what?'

And just as I was about to say what I wanted, we both looked up because we could hear the engine of a car and the front of it come into sight along the track.

Britney's eyes widened.

'Don't worry,' I said, watching as the car pulled up next to Britney's. 'Just stay where you are and don't turn around. I can watch who it is from here.'

'Who?' she said, squeezing out the word.

I didn't say anything because I knew whose car it was.

Then, all at the same time, the driver's door and both passenger doors flew open.

'Is it Greg?'

I shook my head.

The three guys strode over to the bank. Tony cupped his hands and shouted at us: 'So, who ordered a taxi then?'

4

We were lined up and tied up, our arms behind our backs, standing in the farmhouse kitchen with Greg and Mickey at one end, me in the middle, and Anthony and Britney on the other. The large kitchen table had gone and we were squeezed in tight. Fat Sam was right behind us, breathing down our necks, with Tony standing in the kitchen doorway and the two guys from the other night hovering around outside. Grandad was still in his anorak sitting in a chair, looking at us all, his keen and mean eyes ready to make some judgements. It was reckoning time – no more BS. He had brought us all in and we were going to have to answer for what we did or didn't know, and for what we did or didn't do.

'Well, well, Mickey,' said Grandad, leaning back on his chair, 'I 'ad 'eard you were out and about cosying up to our friend Gregory, getting up to no good like.'

'Fuck off!' said Mickey.

''eh!' shouted Grandad. 'Less of the mouth. I ain't said nothing yet and yous already being rude.'

Then it was my brother's turn to add to the mix.

'How about you go fuck yourself,' he said, 'and let us go

before this gets seriously out of hand.'

'Out of 'and, yous say,' said Grandad. 'Now that's funny coming from yous, seeing as I think we're all positively aware of what an 'and can do.'

I looked along the line. Greg and Mickey were fuming and ready to make a fight of it, Anthony was bricking it, but Britney looked like she was keeping it together.

'Tony,' said Grandad, ''ow about yous go and get my new friend Alan, seeing as we're all 'ere for a bit of a truth party.'

Grandad loved to play games with people once he knew what he wanted from them. And having Fat Sam behind us kept us wondering what was next. I had no idea how I would come out at the end of all this, but I was banking on my biological link to save me from the worst. Ten years in Siberia would be a result.

Tony came back in, holding what looked like a large bell covered in a green blanket.

'Yeah, well done, Tony, thanks,' said Grandad. 'Yeah, just put 'im up there.'

Tony placed what I thought might be a birdcage on the kitchen bench.

'As yous all know,' said Grandad, 'I ain't been too well lately, but I've 'ad good news, which means I could be around for a lot longer than I'd ever thought possible. I tell yous what, the country may be a shithole most of the time, but yous can't fault the NHS. So, first off, I thought that would cheers all of yous up, knowing that I was going to live a lot longer. Yeah, nasty thing that cancer. Affects yous all mentally like, makes yous do stupid things, looking back. Still, fit as fiddle now, so they say, the doctors.'

I could hear Greg swear to himself.

'No need for that,' said Grandad, who leant forward in his

217

chair. 'It's been difficult times for me and loved ones 'aving to carry the burden. Of course, yous lot 'aven't been too caring now, 'ave you?'

It looked like I was going to remain on the naughty step, even if he had tried to reach out to me.

'Which brings us to the point of all of this,' said Grandad, who started to raise his voice. 'Because one or more of yous 'orrible people has done something terrible to me.'

He then turned and looked hard at Britney.

'Do you know what that is, pretty lady?'

Britney showed no fear, but I didn't think she was going to speak because it wouldn't be in her interest.

'Terrible, terrible thing to do, to take from me my beautiful Dominique. And for what, eh? To get back at me because of your daddy. I tell yous what, pretty little girl, your daddy's accident on this farm wasn't my fault. Trouble was, 'e was snooping around, wasn't 'e, Tony? Spying for the other side.'

Grandad looked back along the line to Greg.

'Now, in my book of good and bad, that means 'e doesn't deserve nothing back for being a traitor, not 'im or 'is family.'

The penny dropped. Britney's motive, her anger towards Grandad, it all came down to that day her dad had died. She wanted payback, and that came through Anthony, who must have told her about Grandad's ring on Dominique's finger.

'So, do yous all think yous can make yourselves rich?' said Grandad, acting as headteacher. 'Well, let me tell yous, not of one of yous is going to get rich, not on the back of my 'ard work and not on the back of killing the one thing I loved!'

'That ain't your money,' said Greg.

'Oh, ain't it? Is that right, Gregory? I suppose yous going to tell me 'ows your old man deserves it all 'cause I 'elped put 'im in jail? Well, let me tell yer, son, your old man is in that place because 'e put 'imself there and nobody else. And I'll tell yous another thing. If something 'ad 'appened to me, Jack 'enshall would 'ave sorted it all out for your old man once 'e was out. But somebody 'ere, perhaps all of yous shites, 'ad other ideas, didn't yous!'

Grandad looked back across the line again to make sure we all knew we could pay a heavy price.

'So, there is two things on my mind. What is it people say, Tony?'

'The elephant…'

'Yeah, the great big fat elephant in the room, because no one is going anywhere any time soon until I 'ave got to the bottom of it. In fact, I reckon not all of yous know everything, so we could all benefit from this open and transparent session. A bit of team building, eh?'

Greg snorted.

'Don't yous want to be in my team, Gregory? Yous must 'ave been feeling all lost and lonely living up in them northern parts. Why else would yous come down from Manchester if yous didn't want to join the best team in Essex? 'owever, it only took yous five minutes and you're beating up again on your little brother. What's 'e ever done to yous?'

'He's a traitor.'

'Oh, another traitor. Strong words, Gregory. Getting all a bit Shakespeare on us, isn't it? But I think our Steven 'ere 'as only been trying to do 'is best. After all, 'e might be the only 'onest one among yous. But it's 'ard to tell, isn't it. It's like fishing in the muddy river. Yous look and look, but yous can't see any of them little fishes below the surface. What yous need is a stick of dynamite, and yous throw it in and *bang! Boom!* There's all them dead fish that yous knew was there all along come floating to the top.'

The 'bang' and the 'boom' had made Anthony jump, which caught Grandad's attention.

'I mean,' said Grandad, 'we've 'eard, Anthony, that yous been swimming around in the river, and 'ad to be so cruel as to get some poor nipper drowned…'

I could see Anthony look down the line towards Greg.

'Oh, I see, that was your stroke of genius was it, Gregory?' said Grandad, as he looked back at Tony. 'That's a shame because my good friend Tommy – yous know Irish Tommy, don't you, Tony?'

'Yeah.'

'Poor old Irish Tommy, well, 'e 'as a liking for the young boys, but e's not all bad is Tommy, better e's doing something for them than them useless social services? Now, look what's 'appened to 'im, all busted up and broken, and now the rest of them boys, theys just fresh prey with no one around to look after them.'

Grandad was shaking his head like a concerned vicar for his wayward flock.

'So, my lovely people, everything's so murky, 'ard to see what's truth and lies 'ere! Which got me thinking about my friend Alan. Whats we need, I thought to myself, was a neutral judge, someone who's going to sort the fact from the fiction…'

'So, where is he then?' said Greg.

'Oh, Gregory, so good of yous to ask, but 'e is right 'ere,' said Grandad, as he nodded at Tony.

Tony then lifted the green blanket off the bell. It was a birdcage with a rainbow-coloured parrot inside it, which flapped and blinked in the light. No one said anything at first, but I could see Tony grinning all over his face. And then I remembered, at the old fort, the guy with the caged parrot on his back. He must have been delivering it for Grandad.

'All right, Alan,' said Grandad, who was now smiling away at his new friend.

'You're fucking nuts,' offered Greg.

'Well, you could say that, Gregory, my boy, but there ain't no risk of Alan 'ere killing my girlfriend and stealing all me money.'

'That's because it's a fucking parrot,' said Greg.

'And ain't that a sad state of affairs when the only person yous can trust is a parrot?' said Grandad, who pulled out of his anorak pocket some bird feed.

'Yous see,' he said, as he went up to the cage and got the parrot to peck through the bars, 'yous lot is probably too young to remember, but I loved that sketch about the dead parrot, 'eh, Tony?'

'Yeah.'

'That was so funny, weren't it?' said Grandad, who then repeated some of the lines. 'This parrot is dead, oh no it isn't, it's a Norwegian Blue, but it's dead, 'eh, Tony? Cracks me up every time.'

'Yeah.'

'So, you've dragged me here,' said Greg, who was seething, 'just so you can tell us your only friend is a fucking parrot?'

'If only, Gregory,' said Grandad, who poured the bird feed into the feeding tray, 'that was all we was 'ere to discuss. But there is some shameless, despicable behaviour, where I think my good friend Alan can 'elp out.'

Greg then spat on the floor. Grandad's face changed, from

the jokey menace to the rage that was inside him. He walked up to Greg and slapped him hard across the face. Mickey tried to head-butt Grandad because he was close, but Fat Sam grabbed him with a headlock. Mickey wriggled and fought, so Fat Sam put him on his knees.

'That's the sort of manners, Gregory, that really won't do,' said Grandad, as he calmed himself down.

I looked at Anthony and Britney and they had their heads bowed. They were probably hoping the more Greg and Mickey made a fuss, the less chance Grandad would have to focus on them. However, I knew that wasn't going to happen.

'Stand 'im up,' said Grandad to Fat Sam.

Grandad was now up close and personal, and walked along the line, looking into our eyes to work out the level of guilt. He just grinned at me, but his look told me nothing about what he thought I deserved for hiding Anthony. He then got hold of Anthony's face and pulled it up. There was no pity from Grandad, just a burning rage. Britney did the right thing and had pulled her head up, ready to face whatever was coming her way.

'Right,' said Grandad, who was now staring into the face of Britney. 'Because yous 'erberts are a bunch of lying, twisted, no-good fuck-ups, there's only one thing to do when it comes to getting at the truth. Let the parrot speak, that's what I say, ain't that right, Tony?'

Tony nodded.

'Because as yous say, Gregory,' said Grandad, still looking into the face of Britney, 'with only Alan as my real friend, who can I rely on to tell me the truth? It 'as to be the parrot, don't yous think?'

'You're nuts,' said Greg, 'like your nutjob girlfriend.'

'The thing is, Gregory,' said Grandad, moving back down

the line to look into the eyes of Greg, 'whatever a person is, if yous love them, yous take them as they are, good and bad.'

'Yeah,' replied Greg. 'Is that what you tell your wife then?'

That was another big mistake by Greg, as Grandad threw a punch into his stomach. Fat Sam then used his other hand to hold both Greg upright and keep Mickey held by the back of his neck.

''eh, Alan,' said Grandad, who turned to look at the parrot, 'what are these 'orrible little urchins like, eh?'

Alan the parrot flapped its wings.

'Shall we play our game, Alan?'

Grandad then stood in front of Mickey.

''as Mickey Finn 'ere got the rings, Alan? What do yous think? True or false?'

'False!' squawked the parrot.

'You're fucking joking me…' said Greg.

Then Grandad looked at Greg.

'Well,' said Grandad, 'if Mickey ain't got the rings, that means yous ain't got them either. Oh dear, Gregory, seems like yous ain't the criminal genius that yous like to think you are.'

Then I thought it would be my turn to get the parrot treatment, but Grandad just walked past me and focused on Anthony. I wanted to tell him to keep his head up, but it was no good, he just kept his head down, expecting the worst.

'And Anthony 'ere, the next Picasso, I don't think. The boy who I 'elped, the boy who Dominique 'elped, and then decided that wasn't enough for 'im. So ungrateful ain't yous, Anthony. What must your parents think? Yous 'ad a future there, Anthony, but yous just gone and given yourself a bit of a death sentence. What do yous think, Alan? Does Anthony 'ave the rings, true or false?'

'True!' squawked the parrot.

'Stop it!' screamed Britney, either to protect herself or Anthony.

But Grandad wasn't going to stop.

'And as for yous, little lady,' said Grandad, who now had the boiling rage full in his face. 'We know all about yous. We don't even 'ave to ask our friend Alan 'ere.'

I looked at Britney and saw that she had a strength I had never thought possible, given the mess we were in. But then that was it, Grandad suddenly switched focus and just said one word: 'Sam…'

The sound of the compressed air going off and the steel bolt going into the back of Mickey's head stunned everyone into silence. I suppose you could say it was painless and simple, just like it was for the animals on the farm. I think the few seconds that followed, before all hell broke loose, lasted a lot longer than it really did. It was a strange silence, the sort of quiet that most people get when they've been in an accident. We spent those seconds staring at Mickey's body, which was lying flat out and turned over on one side, his dead face looking right back up at all of us. But what got me was, he couldn't have landed a better way, dead Mickey giving us his final words: you better tell Grandad what he wants to know, or else you're all going to die.

It was Greg who tried to react first, but Fat Sam was quick to get him under control and pushed him in the back of his legs. Greg was down on his knees, then gave it a mouthful. Britney stayed cool, but Anthony was blabbering away, swearing he had never done anything wrong.

'Pipe down!' shouted Grandad, who was standing over Mickey, making sure he was dead.

Greg was still giving it some, as best he could, so Fat Sam whacked him across the back of his head with the stun gun.

'Listen, Gregory,' said Grandad, as he moved up close to Greg, who started to heave, 'don't yous start making out yous give a diddly squat about your play pal 'ere. This piece of shite 'ad it coming to 'im ever since 'Er Majesty let the scumbag back on the streets.'

I looked over at Tony, who was still blocking the door. There was no way any of us could make a run for it.

'So, where was we, Alan?' said Grandad, as he stepped back from the puking Greg. 'Oh yeah, Anthony, yous was saying 'ows yous all innocent. Now, I think it's time, Picasso, yous 'anded them rings over, unless yous want to go and 'ave a chat with Mickey 'ere up in 'eaven, or probs down in 'ell.'

The parrot flapped its wings with a bit more energy than before, almost pleased with itself. However, the problem for Anthony was the fear had got to him and he wasn't saying anything, like a rabbit in headlights.

'Sam...' said Grandad again.

'No!' shouted Britney.

But she didn't have to worry just yet because I knew Fat Sam would have to load the stun gun again with a bolt. Anyway, he held Anthony up and gave him a quick rub down and went through his pockets. Fat Sam shook his head.

'OK, Anthony,' said Grandad, 'seeing as yous said yous 'aven't done anything wrong – oh, apart from killing my beautiful Dominique and trying to run off with all my money – 'ows about yous be a good 'onest boy and tell us what's been going on?'

Anthony's body was shaking, and his head was shaking so much I thought it might drop off. But this was my problem now. Anthony knew I had one of the rings and he was supposed to have the other one. It wouldn't take too long for Anthony to put me in the shit.

'Not saying much are yous, Picasso?' said Grandad. 'But I appreciate what just 'appened may be a bit of a shock to yous. So, just to make sure I'm asking the right person 'ere, let's go back to our friend Alan and see what 'e 'as to say, eh?'

Alan the parrot flapped its wings at the sound of his name.

'Alan,' said Grandad, as he pulled out more bird seed, 'did Anthony 'ere plan all of this with his girlfriend and conspire with my worst enemy to steal me beloved's ring? True or false?'

'True!' squawked Alan, who went on to squawk again. 'True!'

''eh, yous can't argue with that, can yous, Picasso?'

Anthony just shook.

'So, I reckon yous could tell me who 'as those rings?'

'He hasn't got them,' said Britney.

'Oh,' said Grandad, 'that's a shame, because if there was one thing 'e could do to keep 'imself alive for a few more seconds, it was to tell us where them rings is.'

'You can't kill us all,' said Britney, 'not if you want the rings back.'

Britney was right. They could kill Mickey because he had nothing to offer or bargain with, but Grandad wanted the rings back before the rest of us were killed.

''ave a look,' said Grandad to Fat Sam.

As Fat Sam checked on Anthony and Britney, Grandad sat back down in his chair.

'Nothing,' said Fat Sam.

Grandad scratched his chin, which meant he was having a think. It also gave me time to think as well, how I was going to come out in of all of this. I didn't think I had massively betrayed Grandad yet, and the other thing I had going for me, I hoped, was I also happened to be his one and only son.

'Tony,' said Grandad, 'I don't suppose yous got any laxatives on yous?'

Tony shook his head. They would be for Anthony and Britney to see if they had swallowed the rings.

Then Greg seemed to come around a bit.

'If you want me to take a shit,' he said, 'I can do it on your head.'

'No, Gregory, the laxatives are not for yous, my son, although the offer is awfully kind. But the thing is, yous is as stupid as your old man, ain't yer. Yous let these two little buggers over 'ere shaft yous good and proper.'

For once, Greg kept quiet.

'That's the thing, Gregory,' said Grandad, 'with this little conspiracy. It 'as so many permutations yous just don't know who the 'ell is telling the truth, which is why yous need a parrot!'

Greg spat a load of gunk on the floor.

It was then that we all heard a noise, like a rumble or a small earthquake. I thought it was coming from outside and turned to look out the kitchen window. The two guys were just standing there smoking. But the noise was still there and it was getting louder, and it was coming from inside the farmhouse. We all heard it, and the weird thing was, it sounded like a bunch of animals coming right towards us. I could see Grandad give Tony a strange look, who then turned his head to look back into the farmhouse and said about two words: 'What the…'

That's when the rumble became something that made sense. I could see a cow, and then another cow, and even more behind those two, all wandering through from the living room. Tony started shouting at the first one, with its big face and wide eyes looking scared and confused, but it wasn't going anywhere other than forwards. Tony turned back to look at Grandad, who realised the kitchen was about to be invaded.

'Tony!' shouted Grandad. 'Someone's pushing them through. Get the lads in 'ere!'

But it was too late, a bit like a wave of water that you know is coming and there is nothing you can do except get ready for the flood to swallow you. As the first and second cow came through, we all stepped back against the kitchen window. That's when Greg seized the opportunity. He was still on the floor and started crawling through the cows' legs. And that was our chance to escape. I didn't think there were any other weapons that could be used, unless Tony or Fat Sam got up close, so I looked at Anthony and Britney and nodded. Fat Sam was the biggest threat and I turned and gave him the hardest head-butt I could manage. It knocked him straight down onto the floor.

Britney bolted and pushed her way through with Anthony right behind her. Tony was trying to shove the cows back and Grandad was shouting at him to get hold of Greg, who was somewhere on the floor. And that's when I looked straight into Grandad's eyes. It was only for a second, but as always with Grandad, he just stared straight back and gave nothing away. Well, that was enough for me and I was off. I could hear Grandad banging on the kitchen window to get the two guys in, as I started pushing through the cows who had filled up the kitchen.

'Don't go down!' I shouted to Anthony and Britney, as I pushed up against the stinking beasts.

With our hands tied behind our backs, squeezing between the cows also helped keep our balance. Tony was on the floor trying to find Greg, who as far as I knew, could have been kicked in the head and out cold. It just made sense to keep going the way the cows were coming, which meant pushing on into the living room. As I looked behind me, the two guys had opened the front door, which meant the cows had somewhere to aim for. They were pushed back outside, as there were more cows coming through and the animals had an exit to aim for.

'Keep going,' I said, as Anthony and Britney looked back at me.

Britney was on a mission as she made it through the door at the back of the living room. I got up to Anthony and pushed him.

'Come on,' I said, 'they don't bite!'

'Are they going to shoot us?'

'What are you talking about! Let's get the fuck out of here!'

We both slid past two more cows and into a corridor and found Britney next to an outside door letting in the daylight. Then a face appeared. It was the guy with the black hoodie, with those pink-looking eyes staring straight back at me.

'This way!' he shouted. 'Push through them! Come on! Let's go!'

I had no idea where Greg and Tony were, but all I cared about was getting out. Pink Eyes was yelping and clapping as we pushed through and out into the backyard, which looked onto the woods. There was a sea of cows in front of us, swarming all around and seriously out of control.

'This way,' he said, pushing through the cows again, as we all followed him towards the woods at the back of the farm.

That's when I noticed he had a cattle prod, which he was using on them to part the waves. I was laughing as we moved easily through.

'What's so funny?' said Anthony.

'Well, he's just like Moses,' I said.

Anthony pulled a face. I reckoned he was glad to be out, but not as happy as he should have been.

'What's wrong?' I said.

But before he had chance to say anything, we were up against the wire fence.

'Quick, quick, quick!' said Pink Eyes, as he pulled up the top of the barbed wire and we went under.

Being in the woods changed everything. The noise of the cows had gone and there was a quiet peace.

'No time, follow me,' said Pink Eyes, who shot off through the woods.

We did our best to keep our balance but with our hands still tied behind our backs, we were wobbling all over the place, and then Anthony fell over.

'I hope he knows where he's going,' I said to Anthony, as I tried to help him get to his feet. 'What's his name?'

'Jan Nowak, he's Polish, and we don't have a choice,' said Anthony.

I shrugged.

Jan Nowak shouted back for us to hurry up, with Britney standing by his side. Anthony rolled over a few more times, covering himself in mud.

'He needs help!' I shouted.

The two of them stood there for a few seconds, and too long for my liking, before they came back. They must have twigged: they couldn't run without us because I still had the other ring.

'Come on,' said Jan Nowak. 'I've got a car.'

'Yeah,' I said, 'and where are we going?'

'To the island!'

5

Jan Nowak, who had a load of tools in the boot, cut our plastic ties and had us all in the car in five minutes. Britney took the passenger seat, and I was up close and personal with Anthony in the back.

'You guys are so lucky,' he said, as he pulled the car out of the woods and got us on the road. 'Now, you all lie down.'

We did as he said and ducked down on the floor of the car.

'I grew up on a farm,' said Jan, as we rocked around and gained speed. 'For me it's easy to move the cows.'

I looked up at the driver's seat.

'Slow down,' I said. 'You need to drive normal.'

'No,' he said, looking back down at me. 'When you run, you run, and when you hide, you hide. We are running.'

'Slow the fuck down!' I said, ready to sit up and put my hand on the wheel and my foot on the brake.

He was a stubborn bugger because he started gaining speed.

'Jan!' said Britney, which meant listen to what I had just said.

He kept his speed going for a few seconds and then started to ease off.

'They know where to go,' said Anthony.

'Anthony is right,' said Jan. 'We have to run to beat them.'

'Look,' I said. 'We get there by not being spotted, that's how we beat them.'

I waited to hear if anyone had a better idea. Jan drove on in silence.

'Does he know where he's going?' I said to Anthony.

He nodded, which told me all I wanted to know. If Jan Nowak knew where it was, then he's been in on it right from the beginning. In fact, he sounded like the captain of their little ship.

'You do not have to like me, Steven,' he said, as if he had been reading my mind, 'for us to work together.'

'That's OK then, I won't.'

This brought a chuckle out of our 'guardian angel'.

'Has God not given you all another chance?' he said.

'You saved our lives, Jan,' I said, wondering if that was something he would remind me of later. 'But the only place I think your God will want to see us is in a room called hell.'

'We have chosen the path that suits us on this earth,' he said. 'We wait for the judgement, when it is time to meet our maker.'

'Is that God according to Jan or one you found in a children's book?'

'He saved our lives!' snapped Britney.

'Praise the Lord,' whispered Anthony.

'We don't need an argument about religion,' she said. 'Jan is part of this.'

'Since when?' I asked.

'From the beginning,' said Britney.

'So,' I said to Jan, 'was it you and God who planned it all?'

'No, he didn't,' said Britney. 'The person who started all of this is the one trying to kill us.'

'You could hardly blame him,' I said.

'It is what is in our heart,' said Jan, 'that determines the quantity of our guilt.'

'Sounds like there's plenty of space for a lot for sin then?'

'It can add up,' he said.

'Good job we're not counting.'

'Hopefully, we will all have something to count,' said Britney. 'We just need to get there.'

'Then take a right,' I said, as I looked up at a road sign, because I wanted to take a zig-zag route.

I could see Jan look down at Britney and get the nod from her to follow my directions.

'I will drive like an old English gentleman,' he said.

'As long as that means steady as she goes.'

Jan let out a great big laugh.

'I like you, Steven,' he said. 'Even if you don't like me. Where I am from, people would like you.'

'And where are you from, Jan?'

'Poland,' he said. 'And other places.'

'So, why did you come here?'

He laughed again.

'To drive a bus...'

'Steven!' said Britney. 'Let Jan drive.'

'He's a bus driver,' I said. 'Just like driving a taxi, he knows how to talk and drive, don't you, Jan?'

'Today, Steven,' he said, 'I am a taxi, yes, and tomorrow we can buy lots of taxis!'

'If any of us see tomorrow.'

'If you can see today,' he said, 'there is always a chance you will see tomorrow.'

I looked again at Anthony.

'Cheery bugger, isn't he?'

'You could say that,' he said.

'The thing is, Jan,' I said, 'I am not sure why I should trust a guy who watches weddings, cleans churches and earns a living as a bus driver. Why don't you want any of the money?'

'That is a good question, Steven,' he said, as we lurched over to one side, which meant Anthony was pushing his face into mine. 'Perhaps there are things with no reason.'

'Not in this world,' I said.

'He's doing it for me,' said Britney. 'I told you.'

'That's a lot to put on the line, Jan,' I said.

'Maybe,' he said, finding another corner, as we all leaned over.

'Well, you've proved one thing, Jan.'

'Yes, Steven?'

'You drive like a bloody bus driver.'

That eased the tension for everyone. For the next half-hour, we kept below the seating and Jan put on the radio. With the music on, we all had time to think, work out how we thought things were going to go – if we were going to get rich or end up like Mickey Finn with a bolt in the back of our heads.

I watched the clouds in the sky, the phone poles and the phone lines go by, the same things I had watched in the morning when Britney had driven us down to the boat. Then it started raining and I watched the water on the car window make channels down to the rubber, and then leak inside. Perhaps Jan was right: somehow, somewhere, the gods were smiling on us and letting us live a little bit longer. The only question in my mind was for how long, and would they let any of us off for good behaviour? I didn't think Anthony, Britney or Jan Nowak had much of a chance of getting out of this alive. And my lifeline was beginning to look like it had been stretched to breaking point. I had to do something, I decided, if I wanted to give myself half a chance of breathing tomorrow.

As we got closer to my boat, I eased myself up onto the car seat and leaned in.

'We're going to need a few things,' I said.

'We have everything,' said Jan.

'No, you don't,' I said. 'You're not getting on my boat without more supplies and torches.'

Jan looked down at Britney, who had also pushed herself up onto the car seat.

'Do we have torches?' she asked.

Jan shook his head.

'So, you need to listen to me,' I said. 'First things first, you let me get what we need for this little boat trip, park the car behind the store and then we walk down to my boat. That's the best way to see if they are waiting for us.'

'And what if they are there?' asked Britney.

'Then there's not much we can do,' I said.

'We've got a head start,' said Anthony, as he also raised himself up from the floor.

'It's not a head start we need,' I said, 'but a shed load of luck.'

'We will have the luck!' said Jan, who I was beginning to think really did believe he had God on his side.

'Let's hope so,' I said, as Jan started bumping the car over the ridges of the concrete track.

'Should we keep our heads down?' asked Anthony.

'No,' I said, 'just keep looking around for anyone. And

Jan, if we see somebody, put your foot down. We need to run, not fight, if we want to live a bit longer.'

'But we need to get to the island,' he said.

'I know,' I said. 'We can think about that after, but we have what they want – the rings – don't we, so we've always got something to trade.'

It was question for all of them, but no one said anything.

'I need to know,' I said.

Jan did that thing again, where he looked at Britney.

'Yes, Steven,' he said. 'I have the ring.'

I grinned.

'Good job you came to our rescue then,' I said, 'because we could have all died for nothing.'

'My question for you, Steven: do you have the other one?'

I nodded. They looked relieved.

'Remember, Steven,' said Jan, smiling, 'only the bad people are dead. The good people have lived.'

I was about to say there was nothing bad about Dominique, immigrants or Tommy's boy, when Anthony shouted, 'Who's that!'

We all looked at a guy ahead of us in long green waders.

'He's all right,' I said. 'Just keep driving.'

'Are you sure he's all right?' asked Britney.

'Yeah, he's a local.'

They were on edge as I told Jan to pull up behind the store.

'I'll come with you,' said Britney.

'No,' I said, as I was opening the car door. 'Just wait.'

She didn't like that.

'Look,' I said, 'none of this is going to work if you don't do what I say. If you don't trust me…'

'We will wait, Steven,' said Jan. 'We trust you.'

I slammed the car door as the rain went straight into my

eyes. I walked around to the front of the store and the guy in the green waders strolled past. He saluted as I went inside and did what I needed. Ten minutes later I was banging on the car window. Anthony opened it.

'I've changed my mind,' I said. 'We can't carry all the stuff down like this. Plus, I've had a quick look and I can't see anyone hanging around by the boat.'

'So, I will drive down,' said Jan. 'We can run away faster in a car than on our legs.'

I ignored him and threw the carrier bags into the boot, which was full of gardening tools, a pickaxe and a few spades.

'Are you sure there's no one there?' asked Britney, as I got back into the car.

'No,' I said, 'I'm not sure, but we can risk it.'

'I think we've got here first,' said Anthony.

'You don't know that,' said Britney.

'I did not see anything on the road that looked like them,' said Jan.

'I want to go,' said Anthony. 'I don't want to wait.'

'We're not waiting,' said Britney. 'But I don't want to drive into a trap.'

'Why is it a trap?' said Anthony.

'Because she doesn't trust me,' I said.

'But you're on our side now,' he said.

'We have no choice,' said Jan. 'We cannot wait, we can only trust. We must do it now.'

'Come on!' said Anthony.

'Go and look for yourself,' I said to Britney.

Then she looked at me. She wanted to know if I was on her side, if she could believe in me.

'OK,' she said. 'We all know it is a fair split. Me and Jan, the same for you, Anthony, and the same for you, Steven.'

'Sounds fair,' said Anthony.

'It is fair!' said Jan, who was getting all excited and turned the engine on.

Then Britney gave me one last look, in the hope she might still be able to read my mind.

6

I had been doing a fair bit of sailing at night to do pick-ups for Grandad out in the channel. I would usually only go a few miles out, using the small motor to navigate my way along the estuary and out to sea, but this time, though, I wasn't going too far to get to the island, even if they wanted me to get across the channel should we find the money.

Once we were all on the boat, I needed headspace, so made out to all three of them they had to keep out of my way until we had got to the little island. With the rain coming down in buckets, I hoped that would keep them in the cabin, but it didn't take long before Jan was poking his head up. I kept my eye on the banks in the darkness, checking the line I took, hoping he would think I couldn't talk.

'What will you do with your money?' he said, blinking in the rain washing over his face.

'I won't do anything,' I said, looking ahead of me.

'You mean, you will put it in the ground again?'

'Why not? It's my old man's pension, so I might as well keep it as a pension.'

Jan shook his head.

'I don't believe you, Steven.'

'You don't have to believe me,' I said, spinning the wheel hard. 'What will you and Britney do with it?'

'Not me,' he said, holding his hands up like I had pointed a gun at him. 'She will have the money.'

'So, you're not going to build a church then?'

That made Jan chuckle.

'No, no, no churches. I only clean them for extra money. Chapels can get very dusty you know.'

'Is that because people don't use them anymore?'

That made Jan burst out laughing.

'Many were built on greed,' he said, 'but they all point to God.'

He then steadied himself, as we felt a wave, which meant we were heading into the wider bit of the estuary.

'You are a strange contradiction, Steven.'

'Yeah, why's that?'

'For a man, so Britney tells me, who is capable of anything, you like to think you know right from wrong. I think you have a moral core in your backbone, which keeps you separate from others.'

'Yeah,' I said, licking the rain from my lips. 'If you mean I don't like liars and cheats, I won't argue with you.'

'So, there is never any doubt, there is never any grey, it is always black and white for you?'

'To get things done,' I said.

'And after?'

'There is no after.'

'But how can you be sure?'

'Sure of what?'

'That this person or people deserve what they get?'

'That's simple,' I said. 'It's not my job.'

'Never?'

I knew what he meant, I knew what he was getting at, because they would all be worried if I was still working for Grandad.

'Listen, Jan,' I said, now moving up and down as we chugged over a few small waves. 'I am not taking orders from anyone, so you don't need to worry.'

'I am not worried, Steven. I trust you. You are with us now, I know.'

That seemed to keep him happy, and he was ready to head back down into the cabin when I decided it was my time to find out a few things.

'Tell me,' I said, 'how come you showed your face at the last minute?'

It was Jan's turn to wonder what the question meant.

'I see with big eyes,' he said. 'I watch. When it is time, I come and join.'

'So, you have been watching everything for a long time, and you do all this out of your love for Britney?'

'Yes,' he said smiling. 'Are you jealous?'

I pulled a face.

'Maybe,' I said.

'But all is fair in love and war, no?'

'What counts in your favour,' I said, pulling on the wheel, 'is you saved her life.'

'OK, so we are even? You will think twice before you try to kill me?'

I nodded.

He gave me one more look, as I kept my eyes on what was in front of me.

'Tell them five minutes,' I said. 'And bring the torches.'

Apart from the rain, it had been an easy trip out of the inlet, into the estuary and then as close as I could get the boat to the island. While I put the anchor down, I didn't want too much light going on, so I told Jan to keep just one torch shining where we needed to land. We then dragged the dinghy alongside and agreed that Anthony ferry us off the boat.

We were all cold and wet by the time we stood there on the shingle, with a couple of spades, a pickaxe and a rucksack. Jan started shining the torch across the small island and we all told him to turn the light out, just like in some old war movie. Anthony said he would take the lead and we followed in single-line, trudging through the tall grasses and stumbling over the mud. About two hundred yards in, we came across the old war defences – a concrete bunker that had sunk into the ground by about forty-five degrees. I don't know what it is about these things that makes people jump up on them, but Jan did it, so he said, to look around. There was no need because we all knew where we were going and left him to catch up with us as we headed for the shelter of the abandoned shack.

About five hundred yards in we got there, checked as best as we could in the dark and the rain for any surprises, before we pulled open the plywood door. We waited for a few seconds just in case someone or something jumped out, but all was good as we switched on the torches, desperate for some shelter. The place stank of rotting wood and petrol, with a load of gear stacked in piles on the chipboard floor. You could tell where the leaks were because the rain dripped down in puddles all around us. For whatever reason, the guy who had built it hadn't bothered with a window. Still, it wasn't too hard to look out through the slats of the wooden plank walls to see if we had company.

'We're the only ones here,' said Anthony.

'You see, Steven,' said Jan, holding the pickaxe in both hands and pretending to dig, 'we have beaten them to it!'

'For now,' I said, taking off the heavy overcoat, which was like a tonne weight with the all the rain it had soaked in.

'We will all dig,' said Jan.

'Why?' asked Britney.

'Because we need a big hole,' said Anthony, pulling out of the rucksack a GPS locator. 'This is military grade, accurate to two or three metres.'

'So, we need a hole that is this wide,' said Jan, who spread his arms.

'That could take some time,' I said.

'We don't have a choice,' said Anthony, who looked at me because he needed what was engraved on Grandad's ring.

'Steven,' said Britney, 'do you have it?'

I could have played with them, made them worry again, but time was also something that mattered to me. I pulled out my key ring and the gold band sparkled in the torch light. I wasn't about to hand it over, and so I read the coordinates out to Anthony.

'Come on,' said Jan. 'Let's do it.'

'Wait,' I said, as I used my torch to poke around the shack and find what I was looking for.

'What is it?' asked Britney.

'Some waterproofs,' I said, pulling out a load of plastic sheeting. 'If we're going back out there.'

'Good idea,' said Jan.

'Is there a knife in that rucksack?'

Anthony stuck his hand in and pulled out a nice chunky Swiss blade. I cut four equal strips and left them to shape their own holes for their arms.

'No more pneumonia,' said Jan, smiling.

'Even less,' said Anthony, as he stood there with the locator, like he had just found water in the desert. 'It's here!'

'The gold?' said Jan.

'Right beneath our feet,' said Anthony, as he stepped back to make the area wider.

I looked at all their faces, their eyes getting bigger, as they must have all thought the risk had now been worth it.

'Clever,' said Jan. 'Now we know who built the shack.'

'They must have paid that guy to come and live on the island and build this useless thing,' said Anthony, who was checking he was right about the location.

'It's not useless,' said Jan. 'It will keep us dry while we work.'

Jan then moved into the centre and jumped up and down on the floorboards.

'We can lift them up,' he said, 'and then dig underneath.'

He picked up a rusty iron stake and wedged it into the join between the chipboards, and with a few pulls, had levered up one side. Jan was on a mission, so we all stood back and waited for him to finish pulling up the flooring. The space he created took up almost the whole of the front end of the shack, about three metres long and filled with hardcore and mud.

'Perhaps they have buried someone,' said Jan, laughing.

It was a joke that we all thought could be true.

'I will loosen the soil,' said Jan, 'then we all dig.'

'Let's take it in turns,' I said. 'Two in, two out – space to work and time to rest.'

'You are our foreman, no?' said Jan, who had the bit between his teeth.

'Let's just get it done,' I said.

Jan swung the pickaxe with a serious amount of muscle. I

243

jumped in and told him to stop because all we needed to do was to start picking up the lumps of hardcore.

'How long will it take?' asked Britney.

'A few hours maybe,' said Jan, who stepped out of the mud. 'In Poland, I used to dig holes.'

It wasn't long before we realised we had nothing to keep up our energy apart from adrenaline. Anthony went back to the boat to get water and anything we could eat. It was now me and Britney or Jan pulling up hardcore and digging up earth. And the deeper we got, so the thought started to creep in: what if we didn't find anything? As we all took a breather, munching on some nut bars and sharing a large bottle of water, Anthony turned on the locator.

'I was just checking,' he said.

'Don't worry,' said Jan, again full of belief. 'I know it is here.'

'How long have we been digging?' asked Britney.

'I don't think that matters,' said Anthony.

'We dig until we reach Australia!' said Jan, who jumped back into the hole and swung the pickaxe.

As the hole got deeper and wider, the hardcore gave way to damp waterlogged earth, which meant we had to loosen, shovel and dig. The amount of effort kept our minds off thinking too much. Even Anthony joined in with the manual labour, before he said that we'd been at it for well over two hours, which meant it was time for another break. But this time, as we all gulped down a load of water, we didn't say anything, because we were all thinking the same thing: nobody wanted a plan C.

Then Jan suddenly threw his bottle down, picked up one of the torches and jumped into the hole. He was up to his waist as he shone the torch around, using his foot to scrape away at the bottom. He then looked for a shovel, put the torch so it was shining down into the hole and hit the earth hard. It made a sound that had us all looking at each other. It sounded like metal.

We stood staring into the hole, watching Jan dig around, until most of a green lid was showing. If we were lucky, if we all kept believing, because we had all said our prayers before we went to bed at night, we might just find the pot of gold at the end of the rainbow.

There was a padlock, which Jan ripped off with the pole.

'Are you ready?' he said.

'Yes…' said Britney, as she breathed out.

'OK,' said Jan, who was enjoying the moment. 'Do you want to be rich?'

'Let's hope it's bloody worth it,' said Anthony.

'Of course, you will see,' said Jan.

He got down on his knees and tried to use his fingers to open up the metal lid. It wasn't moving.

'Do you have the knife, Steven?'

I gave him the blade to side it around the inside of the lid.

'Use the pickaxe as a lever,' I said.

Jan then got the end of the pickaxe, squeezed the axe under the lid and lent on the handle. He was using so much force, he fell against the side of the hole as the lid flew open and came crashing back down.

'Well done!' said Britney.

Jan was now caked in mud, as he bent down to ease open the lid.

We all looked down at a pile of cloth bags. Jan grabbed one by its neck and used all his strength to lift it up, as we heard a tell-tale noise which sounded just like coins.

'It's heavy,' he said, as he plonked it down in front of

Britney.

'That's a good sign,' she said, kneeling by what we all hoped was the first bag of gold.

'Put your hand in,' said Jan.

This was it, the moment of truth. We just needed Britney to pull one out.

Then she did, all bright and shiny.

'Oh my god!' said Anthony.

Britney was shaking her head, maybe because she couldn't believe it was true, that whatever they had done to get to this point, it was now, for sure, reality. She handed the coin to Jan, who started to inspect it.

'No need to bite it,' said Anthony, 'that looks real to me.'

'How much is in there?' asked Britney, as she looked back down at the metal chest.

'How much is a lot?' said Anthony.

'There must be enough,' said Britney, 'for all of us.'

I jumped down into the hole and pulled up another bag.

'Come on,' I said, 'we need to think how we're going to get this all back on the boat.'

'What's the rush?' said Anthony, who must have been thinking he could now pay his way out of anything.

Britney picked up the first bag.

'You know,' she said, 'I never thought about how heavy it was going to be.'

'It won't sink the boat, will it?' said Anthony.

'No,' I said, putting the bag down next to the first.

'Should we count it?' asked Anthony.

'You are joking!' I said. 'It's gold, not pennies, and we need to get out of here!'

'Steven's right,' said Britney. 'They're bound to be here soon.'

That seemed to focus everybody's mind and put to a stop the moment of glory. We had hit the jackpot, but none of us thought it was over. It was like having a winning lottery ticket but not wanting to celebrate until the you had the numbers checked.

The only way to get the gold coins back to the boat was to do it in relays. We agreed that two stay while two transport. We emptied out Anthony's rucksack and came up with the plan of two bags in the rucksack and another bag carried in the arms. But the one thing I wasn't going to have was Britney and Jan pairing up. It meant Britney and Anthony went first.

We watched them from the shack, struggling through the rain, falling over the ruts in the dark.

'That's not good,' said Jan. 'It will be morning before we finish.'

'We'll go next,' I said, walking back into the shack and needing to sit down.

Jan stood by the door for a bit longer then came inside and sat with his legs in the hole.

'I think your friends will be coming,' he said.

'Perhaps,' I said, still looking for something that I could use to sit on.

'And what will you do?' he said, picking off some of the mud that was caked over his bare chest.

'Well,' I said, finding a short wooden stool, 'that's a question we all need to ask ourselves, if it happens.'

'I trust you, Steven,' he said, slapping his hand down on the canvas bags of gold. 'But if they come, should we not think of a negotiating position?'

I laughed, as I plonked the stool down by the open door, so I could keep an eye on what was outside.

'If it's Grandad's crew or Greg, and whoever else gets here, none of them will be negotiating anything.'

'But you and me,' he said, 'we are strong. Britney and Anthony, they are weak.'

'Does that matter?' I said.

'It could,' he said, picking up his jumper and squeezing all the water out of it into the hole. 'After all, I think your grandad knows everything. You were part of his crew. He may still like you. But he will not like the people who killed his girlfriend.'

'So, it wasn't you then?'

He shrugged.

'You cannot help amateurs who think they know better than you,' he said, spreading out his jumper on the floor. 'They were silly.'

'How's that then?'

'This little island,' he said, spreading out his arms, 'holds more than one secret.'

'Yeah?'

'Believe me, Steven, I was not here before. And perhaps we are only here to find this secret,' he said, again patting the bags of gold coins. 'We are two strong men. We can fight. We can share.'

'I think you mean sharing but not caring.'

That got Jan laughing.

'OK,' he said, changing his tone so he was all serious. 'If we get the gold on your boat, we do not need Anthony, we do not need Britney. There will be less weight on the boat and we can give them the two bodies. Then, they will not want so much to look for us.'

'Jan, you carry on like this and I might begin to lose faith.'

'But you know, I think, Steven, God moves in mysterious

ways…'

'Your God does.'

'Can we agree?'

'To what?' I said, carrying on looking into the rain and the night.

'That I am right.'

I looked back at him. I didn't know if he was just trying to make the best out of a bad situation or he had planned this all along.

'There's no one here yet,' I said.

'We don't have to wait.'

'We can wait,' I said, as I stood up in case the faithless boyfriend got physical. 'But you would sell out Britney for the right price?'

'Like you,' he said, 'I wait to see.'

'And you let Britney think she was the only one that mattered?'

'I saved her,' he said. 'She has had more time to live than she wanted.'

'Well, I'm sure she would like to live little bit longer now.'

'We can let them live; we can help them die.'

I said nothing after that. It was best not to let him know which way I would go. He made me a final offer, thinking that was going to somehow clinch my loyalty. Of course, all he really wanted was to make sure I wasn't a threat. But now I knew I could trust him about as far as I could throw him, and his love of God and Britney was a bit on the temporary side. He was also keen on me thinking he had nothing to do with killing Dominique, which I found hard to believe. If Britney and Anthony had messed up when they took Dominique off the streets, I couldn't see why Jan would have nothing to do with it. Everything he did since the farmhouse told me he was the kind of guy who would follow through with something without blinking, which meant he was the one who more than likely had a lot to do with the accident that killed Dominique, not that I thought it ever was an accident. As far as I was concerned, it was clear to me Jan was pulling all the strings. And when we were trudging across the island in the dark, he didn't look to me as if he didn't know where he was going. It all meant there was more to navigate than just the channel across the sea.

7

The rain had eased off as we all had a go at stumbling in the dark, getting in the dinghy and stashing the gold bags. We had one more trip to go when it ended up with just me and Britney in the cabin.

'Do you have anything dry?' asked Britney, pulling off her plastic cover. 'It would be just our luck to get pneumonia as soon as we get rich.'

'There's not much,' I said, bending down to pull out a greasy hooded top from a cupboard.

'I don't care,' she said, putting it against her body. 'What about you?'

'I'm OK,' I said. 'Anyway, I think you should stay here.'

'But we haven't finished.'

'Near enough,' I said. 'We need someone on the boat, to keep an eye on things.'

'You trust me then?' she said, pulling the top over her head.

'It's not about trust, is it?' I said. 'More the case that you can't go anywhere unless you think you know how to sail a boat across the channel.'

Britney threw herself down on the bed and laughed.

'You never know, Steven,' she said. 'I think I could do anything!'

'Yeah, well, it's one thing to think it and another to pull it off.'

'But we've done this!' she said, showing for the first time her relief and excitement.

'Britney,' I said, 'you've had the luck of the gods, or God, on your side.'

'It's more than luck,' she said, pissed that I was not giving her the credit she thought she deserved. 'And it's not just me, there's Anthony, Jan and you.'

'Yeah, well, the only thing I know about luck is it runs out, just like what goes up must come down.'

'I'm not coming down,' she said, like she was on some serious high. 'I know now, if you don't take risks, you don't get anything in life.'

'I would work on that risk thing,' I said, using a towel to dry my hair, 'before you go jumping in.'

'I did,' she said, cocksure.

'Is that right?'

'Yes.'

'Let's hope so,' I said, getting ready to leave.

Britney bit her lip, as she started to think about what I'd just said.

'I always believed in you,' she said. 'I knew you would come through.'

This made me stop and turn back to look at her.

'And what do you think now?' I said.

'You've kept your promise.'

'I didn't promise anything, Britney.'

'Not in words...'

I smiled.

'Rule of thumb,' I said, with half a foot on the step to get back outside, 'never take your eye off anybody.'

'I trust Anthony,' she said, sitting back up.

'Then you've got everything, haven't you?' I said. 'Love, money and a friend.'

'And what are you?'

I paused.

'I don't know yet,' I said, pushing up onto the deck and then poking my head back down. 'Just stay out of sight.'

And with that, I shut the cabin door.

I pulled the dinghy back alongside and was about to climb down when I heard Britney's voice again.

'Steven...'

'Yeah?'

She kept herself just inside the cabin and then watched as I got ready to go back onto the island for the last time.

'Do you think we will make it?'

'What do you mean?'

'Across the channel?'

'Maybe, maybe not. There's a load of weight, which isn't going to make things easy.'

'You mean we might sink?'

'You can get big waves out there,' I said. 'But it's the big ships we need to watch out for, and they don't see you.'

I started to lift myself down.

'I'll look out for you,' she said, as she stepped onto the decking.

I balanced myself on the dinghy and undid it from the

boat.

'It won't be long,' I said.

'But what if someone else comes?'

'Then it's all over,' I said, as I sat down and pushed out.

I started to row, looking back at her. I could have said something about Jan and his little plan, but there was no need to because I didn't know what I was going to face when I got back to the shack. The rain had stopped and a bit of moonlight had come down through the clouds. Britney kept looking at me as I rowed, and for the first time, without the torches, I could see her face. I kept looking at her for the next five minutes, wondering where her heart was, her loyalty to herself and to others, before I pulled up onto the shore. Once my feet were on the shingle and I'd dragged the dinghy out of the water, Britney was gone.

I had already decided there was no way I was heading straight back along the path we had all been on. So, I walked along the shingle for a bit, a good two or three hundred yards, then made my way back into the island. I looked for the old war defences as a bit of a marker, and was going to carry on right up to the shack when my gut told me to just turn around and look back at the boat. Sure enough, there was someone there, a bright torch out in front of them and getting closer to the water. I crouched down and headed in a straight line towards them, running like a crazed monkey, falling over once or twice, spitting grass and mud out of my mouth. By the time I got close enough, I could tell it wasn't Anthony or Jan. But whoever it was, they were shining the light towards the boat. I only had a few seconds before they got into the dinghy and started rowing. I didn't have a choice. I pulled out the torch and ran at them. I was only a few yards away when they must have heard me coming and turned.

Carter's face was all shock and awe as I swung the torch and whacked him as hard as I could across the forehead. He didn't go down at first and stood there all dazed. Somehow, the torch was still in one piece, so I spun him around and hit him as hard as could on the back of his head. It was risky because I didn't want to kill him, but I wanted him out cold. The stubborn bastard fell to the floor, on his knees, spluttering away. I looked around for something else I could use to hit him with. A few yards away was a large bit of driftwood, about the length of a railway sleeper. I picked it up and went straight up to him. He had his head down, mumbling.

'Here, Carter!' I said, swinging the great big lump of wood. 'It's the end of the world for you, mate!'

This time the blow across his head knocked him over. He was either dead or out cold, face down in the shingle. I rolled him over. There was blood coming from his forehead. I bent down to see if he was breathing and there seemed to be something going on. I looked back at the boat and could make out Britney still in the cabin. She was none the wiser as I pulled Carter up the shingle and into the grassland. I took one last look at him and thought that was going to be it, he was going to live or die there, when something else caught my eye. It looked like a finger, but not Carter's because it was sticking out from just underneath his chest. I rolled him again, a good two or three feet, and bent down with my torch. No doubt about it, but it was a fleshy, bony finger, sticking out of the turf. Like I was some sort of fossil hunter, I started scraping away until I could see there was a hand. It was a slim hand, a woman's hand, which some rodents and birds had probably had a good go at. The way it was sticking out meant she was buried a good few feet down.

It had to be the dead hand of Dominique.

There was no time to dig anything up and make certain. I just needed to mark the spot as best I could. The wood I'd used on Carter would do, and I pushed it down as best I could into the soaking wet ground. There it stood, a piece of driftwood, a kind of gravestone for Dominique's last resting place.

In a way, she had sown the seeds of her own destruction. The undercurrents beneath the surface had dragged her down. Perhaps she was always too innocent, not wary enough about the kind of waters she was swimming in. Everyone off the estate operated on another level. It was always instinct, survival, to get what you needed out of people before they got what they wanted out of you. If you were born on the estate, you knew from day one you were different. You were cut off from what was normal and you had to live by another code. But Dominique had made the mistake of thinking we were normal, if we were treated like human beings, but we weren't really. We were wild animals who would never be tamed and would bite that hand that feeds us if there was ever a chance to eat more.

Still, it was a stroke of luck coming across Carter when I did and finding Dominique's muddy grave. I now knew what I needed to know. But time was running out to get everything done because coming across Carter meant only one thing: Greg was on the island.

8

I was banking on Greg only having Carter to help him out,

and with Carter out of action, I would have a good chance of dealing with whatever was left. I headed back towards the shack using the light of the moon to track my way through the grasses. From about fifty yards out, I did a quick circle to check if there was anyone hanging around. I got down low and crept up to the side of the wooden slats of the shack. I had no idea where Anthony was, but it was no surprise to see Greg standing over Jan, who was lying on the floor and looking scared shitless. I moved a few feet along to a nice little hole, so I could get a better look in. Greg had a knife, which he had by his side and looked ready to use. I really needed to hear what they were saying, but the wind had got up and it was making listening hard. I pushed my ear against the hole and covered my other ear to try and keep the noise of the wind down. And the first thing I heard, told me all I needed to know.

'You traitorous fucking bastard!' screamed Greg.

'No, Greg,' I heard Jan begging. 'I have done it all. You can thank me later, but we have it all.'

'What's this? That's nothing. That's nowhere near what's meant to be here.'

'I told you, I told you, I had to move it onto the boat, but we have your brother now, he is on our side, but he is dangerous.'

'You don't say, you stupid fucking twat head! He's not having anything. That's the rule, dumb fuck!'

'Well, we can kill him.'

'You want me to kill my own brother?'

'You hate him, you told me you hate him.'

'Shut up! I need to think…'

That was never one of Greg's strong points, as I took my ear away and looked through the hole into the shack. Jan was trying to ease himself back so he was ready to deal with Greg stabbing him, but Greg was having none of it, as he trod on Jan's leg. The bus-driving church cleaner screamed out in pain as his leg looked close to breaking.

'I'm not the enemy, Greg!' he shouted. 'I saved you, in the farmhouse. You are here now because of me...'

'Fuck you!' shouted Greg.

He then bent down close to Jan's face and I could only make out a few words: 'stupid girlfriend' and 'not for me'.

I pushed my ear again close to the hole.

'I will do it,' I heard Jan say.

'Where is he?'

'He is with Britney. They took some bags back onto the boat.'

'How long ago was that?'

'It depends. The bags are heavy.'

'How long?'

'They should be back.'

I could hear more movement and so took a quick look through the hole. Then I saw Greg say something else and heard Carter's name. I had to listen.

'How did you get here?' asked Jan.

'Trust me, you Polack fuck-up, we didn't swim. We saw my brother's boat and came around from the other side.'

'And where is your friend, Carter?'

'That's a good question. Hopefully, he's drowned your girlfriend and has got my little bro handcuffed.'

'I don't think we should wait.'

'Shut up! It's not for you to say.'

'But we should go and help. They are two, even if one is Britney.'

I knew Greg needed to think again and so used my eye. I

could tell Greg felt trapped. If he made a move outside, he wasn't sure what he was going to get, but if he stayed put, he could manage the situation for a bit longer. If I was stupid enough to walk in, he'd be able to fight back, and killing me was not going to be problem, whatever he said to Jan. And the only weapon I had was the torch. I might be able to surprise Greg, but Jan was another thing. I decided the best thing to do was just wait and let Greg make his move. If Britney stayed on the boat and Carter stayed unconscious, I was in the better position.

I started to shuffle around the shack, hoping to get more of a view and a better opening to hear what Greg was up to. But the wind was also making things difficult, not just with listening, but the cold biting into my body. One way or another, I could do with getting into the shack. I was at the back of it now and could hear things moving about, which maybe meant Jan had a few more minutes to live. I made my way around the rest of the shack and skipped past the door, which was closed. I was back at the hole in the wooden slats. It was going to be my best view of what was going on inside.

I looked in and Greg was down on the floor taking a few gold coins out of a bag, with his knife pointing at Jan. He started to say something again.

'Daft bastards. What's wrong with taking out a proper pension?'

'I think gold is safe, no?'

'Yeah, until somebody finds it. Still, me old man will be well chuffed.'

'But we share?'

'Who said anything about sharing.'

I then heard Jan laughing.

'Greg, you joke with me, but you are not like your brother.

I like his jokes but you, you will not make me laugh much more.'

This was getting interesting, I thought, as I took another quick look.

Jan had changed from looking like a frightened rabbit to someone who might be a lot meaner. He was trying to get up, but Greg was having none of it. He quickly moved to stand over him again with his knife pointing downwards.

'This is not fair,' said Jan.

'Yeah, well, you'd know all about that wouldn't you.'

'I gave her to you. I gave you Britney, I make it all happen for you, I put all the story together for your old man so he can get back what he wants, but we share, we said we share...'

'You did, mate, but not me.'

'This is a mistake, Greg. For you, for me...'

'It ain't no mistake, Polack,' said Greg, as he moved in for the kill.

But it was a blade from Jan, the one I had given him, that came out of nowhere and went straight into Greg's leg. Greg's head went up in the air as he screamed out in pain. Jan looked shocked by what he'd done, but Greg was a hard bastard, who used all his rage as he fell on Jan, with the blade going right into his chest. Greg carried on using all his body weight, pressing down and keeping the knife in. Jan was struggling, trying to push up, but it looked all over for him, with the blood pumping out of his heart and pouring onto the chipboard. I looked at his face,, and knew it was all coming to end for him.

A few minutes went by as Greg just kept everything as it was, looking into the dying eyes of the man who had given my old man and Greg what they wanted: a gift to get back at Grandad. I knew now, for sure, Jan must have heard the story from Britney about the rings and then put the whole package together. He'd been trying to make out to me he was an innocent passenger in all of this, but it looked like the scheming bastard had seriously miscalculated.

And a good time, I decided, to make my entrance.

I think Greg must have thought I was Carter as I pushed the door open because he didn't move from lying on Jan.

'Don't get up,' I said, ready to whack him on the head with the torch.

Greg didn't move and just smiled.

As I walked around the large hole, there was Anthony's body lying at the bottom of it, like a thin reminder of what he once was, his face looking up, his hope for a better future now dead.

I had to keep my focus.

'Just a thought,' I said to Greg, 'but I suppose you can't move that much with a dodgy leg.'

I could see the knife sticking out of his right thigh and touching the floor. That was going to hurt. And I now had Greg just as I wanted him. He couldn't move and he couldn't fight back.

I bent down to take a closer look at Jan. There was no life left in him.

'He deserved it...' said Greg, squeezing out the words, struggling to speak because of the pain.

'And I suppose you're going to tell me Anthony did?'

'That wasn't me...'

'Well, you would say that, wouldn't you.'

'Trust me, little bro, I don't need to lie to you about who I killed.'

It probably was Jan, I decided.

'This is going to hurt,' I said, as I rolled Greg over onto

his back.

He screamed out in pain. He was like some helpless insect lying on its back. I stood a few yards away, just in case he had some energy to have a go at me.

'Doesn't look good,' I said.

'Nah... just a flesh wound...'

'Shame,' I said, 'but I don't have any plasters on me.'

'Do you think that will fix it?'

'Not really. Looks like you're going to bleed out... Best keep the knife in.'

Greg then looked over at Jan.

'It's all his fault,' he said.

'Yeah, why's that?'

'Don't you know?' he said, pushing himself up on his hands, trying to find somewhere to lean.

'I'm all ears,' I said, as I watched a spurt of blood from his knife wound, which had Greg creasing up for a bit.

'Stupid bastard,' he said. 'Went to see the old man and told 'im all about that bitch.'

'You mean Britney?'

'Yeah, crazy cow, was fuming about her dad.'

'Who's dead...'

'That's the point, little bro, useless git fell into some septic tank on Grandad's farm. Anyway, she was mad as hell, couldn't get over it, you know, was going to kill herself...'

'But she didn't...'

'No,' said Greg, who looked down at his wound. 'The mad Polack saved her.'

'And planted the seed?'

'Yeah, little bro. His mind must have been going like a thousand miles an hour, like he's found the pot of gold at the end of the rainbow and all that...'

'You mean, once he knew about the ring Dominique had?'

Greg shrugged.

'So, Anthony had told Britney, and Britney had told Jan, and Jan told our old man?'

'Something like that.'

'Why the hand?' I said, waving my torch in front of him.

'Nothing to do with me. These guys you're mixed up with, let me tell yer, little bro, they're crazy. For me, just get me the ring.'

I didn't believe him.

'And the money,' I said, 'how were you going to share it?'

'Funny you should say that, little bro, but we were all going to meet here,' he said, looking down again at the knife sticking out of his leg. 'Yeah, take the money and stab all three of them. After all, there was only Carter to pay off and he'd be at a discount…'

'Then there's only Britney left to get rid of now,' I said. 'Things have still gone the way you would have wanted it to go.'

'Trust me, little bro, it was that Polack who did all the thinking. You know me, I don't need to do any of that, just tell me what needs doing and I do it.'

'So, what did need doing?'

'Not a lot, little bro, until you turned up. We were five minutes away from popping into Mickey's old flat.'

'And what would you have done if you'd found me there?'

Greg laughed.

'The same as we did when we did get to you.'

'You mean in Dominique's place?'

'Yeah, you know how it is, just like the old days. Don't

tell me I hurt yer feelings…'

'Just my face,' I said, as I quickly looked behind me at Anthony lying in the hole.

'So, I suppose Anthony told you I still had the hand with the ring on it?'

'Yeah, the cheeky bastard, him and that crazy bitch, they've been playing you, you know that, little bro? They tricked me too when that fucking junkie nicked the old man's ring. Then they got paranoid about Grandad and me and what we would all do to them once we caught them. They needed you. They thought you could protect them, being as you've been on both sides of the fence like.'

'Yeah, well, I haven't done a very good job of that,' I said.

Then I wondered if he was playing me, by giving me his version and hoping Carter would turn up. I looked back at the door and then gave him the bad news.

'I came across Carter by the way,' I said.

'Yeah?'

'Afraid so…'

'Well, he was always a useless bastard. Listen, little bro, not a good idea to go killing coppers.'

'Who knows, maybe he'll live. Not that he deserves it.'

'Yeah, he told me you had a chat, said he didn't like you much.'

'You know how it is, Greg. Never talk to coppers.'

He cringed, probably because of the pain in his leg.

'Well,' he said, 'it's just me and you, little bro. Not a bad ending, eh?'

'There's Britney,' I said.

He started to cough and I waited for him to sort himself out.

'You can't trust her,' he said, spitting out snot and blood.

'Where is she, on that boat of yours?'

'Yeah.'

'I'll tell yer, I bet she's halfway across the channel. We're wasting time sitting around here.'

'We've got time.'

'You might, little bro. I haven't. We need to sort things out, me and you, see what's in our best interests…'

'Yeah, do you have a plan?'

'Like I said, that's not me strong point, but let's face it, things ain't too good for me here, but that don't mean we can't sort things out together. After all, little bro, blood's thicker than water…'

I looked around him. There was a lot of blood on the chipboard, most of it from Jan, but there was plenty now coming out of Greg's leg.

However, he seemed to have a plan for me.

'It's a shame about the people, you know, dying and all of that,' he said. 'But you know, if they want to swim with the big boys, there's going to be things that they ain't going to win at…'

He paused, fighting off the effects of his blood loss.

'So,' he said, 'this is the way I see it. With the gold dug up, there's no need to put it back. It's ours now, just you and me. It's like what parents do these days, you know, they help the kids out, give 'em a bit of money to get them started.'

'Oh, I see,' I said. 'We buy a mansion together?'

'Why not, little bro!' he said, trying to breathe. 'Let's face it, we've both had it tough. We've had to fight for everything. This is like winning the lottery. You don't go giving it away to charity.'

'And what about Britney?'

'Me? I'll be honest, little bro, I would kill her. I mean, you can't trust her. She'll be saying this and saying that and before you know it, you'd be doing all this shit all over again.'

'You might be right.'

'That's it, Steven! You see, we're brothers, me and you. All that other stuff, you know, with the old man, that's just about getting by. But we're older now, you and me, and together we'd be a force, you know. The force is strong…'

'I don't know,' I said. 'With all this money, there's no need to live the way we do. I was thinking of a nice quiet life, on an island, with the sea and the sun.'

'Go on holiday, little bro! Have a thousand holidays, but this never stops,' he said, looking over at Jan. 'All this stuff just keeps on coming. Once you're in, there's no getting out.'

'I suppose there's Grandad,' I said. 'He'd want this money back.'

'That's it, little bro, of course he would, but we'd sort it, me and you. We'd be like Batman and Robin, Gotham City and all that. We'd take over. He's half dead anyway. You never get rid of that cancer thing, it always comes back…'

It was my turn to pause.

Then I bent down.

'Let me give you a hand,' I said.

'That's it, Steven…'

'Use your good leg,' I said, 'and push up.'

He tried, but he was totally stuffed.

I got behind him and put my arms through his back. I then said, on the count. The effort had Greg screaming out in pain, but I managed to keep him standing.

'Fuck me, little bro! That's not good…'

'You'll be all right,' I said. 'Now try and walk.'

'Let me breathe… I'm gonna need yer to hold me.'

'OK, but you need to try and walk.'

I was still behind him, with my face by the side of his. We were close now, with all the rain and the mud, the blood and the sweat shared between our faces.

'Come on, push…' I said.

I held him and got him a couple of yards forward so we were right on the edge of the hole. I let him get his breath back, as we both looked down at Anthony.

'Did Jan kill him?' I said.

'I tell you what, little bro, seeing as we're now brothers again, it was me…'

'Yeah, well, the thing is, Greg,' I said, talking quietly into his ear. 'I'm not your brother…'

Then I pushed him and he fell into the hole face down.

The knife jammed into his leg and he let out a load of pain. I didn't wait for him to try anything and turned to grab Jan's body. I dragged it to the hole and rolled it on top of Greg and Anthony. Then I started throwing the hardcore down with Greg screaming and swearing and doing his best to stay alive. I grabbed the spade and started piling the mud on top of everything. There wasn't much room with the three bodies, but I was packing it down real tight, working like crazy, trying to get as much on top of him to stop him escaping and to shut him up. But I did want him to hear one more thing, before I finished.

'Greg, you ain't just going to die, you're going to know what it's like to drown in your own vomit, in the dark, alone with dead bodies, you piece of shit!'

Jan's body started to bob up and down, so I got back to piling the mud on. After a few minutes, it went quiet. I got hold of the chipboards and put them back over the hole and then got as much weight as I could from around the shack to put over it. I couldn't be sure he was dead, but even if he had any time left down there, it was going to be the worst way to go.

9

It was still dark as I sat near the stern and watched the lights of a ship passing through the shipping lanes. The sea was calm but the boat was heavy, and it dipped down low enough so I could run my hand through the cold water. I splashed some on my face to keep awake and spat out the salt, but I didn't think I would have too long to wait for the pick-up. Plus, Tony and his guys would be on the island by now, cleaning up after me, and I was heading off to keep out of the way for a few years. That was the deal with Grandad, over the phone in the store, and the best deal I could have struck. I was just lucky that most of the killing was done by everyone else, although Greg had done most of that. At least between me and Jan we had managed to kill Greg.

That was the one death I had no issue with, my half-brother. It was payback, not just for what he had done to the immigrants in the container, but for all the times he'd had a go at Mum, or joined in when there was violence, or tortured me. Greg had always loved the anger. He thought that was what made him a hard man. But when I'd pushed him into the hole, all the fear he had created in others came flooding back onto him. Covered with mud, burying him alive, was everything he deserved. Of course, my old man will be seriously cut up about it. He will have to live with losing his proper son, and when he finds out I had done it, he will badly want to see me dead. What I didn't know was how Mum was going to take it. She didn't hate Greg, she just didn't like him, but Greg was still hers. It meant she would have to think if she would still want to have anything to do with me.

So it made sense, for a whole load of reasons, to be well away from things for a good long time, keeping away from the police and keeping well away from the estate. I mean, it wouldn't have been easy to look people like Mrs C in the eye, because she'd think I'd betrayed her because Anthony was dead. I thought I'd done my best, considering what he'd been up to, but I knew she wouldn't see it like that. She'd think I was the one person who could've saved him, whatever he had done. But that was never going to happen. Once Dominique had told Anthony about the ring, and he had told Britney, he had sown the seeds of his own downfall. And it only took Jan Nowak – mystery man, bus driver and church cleaner – to seriously mess things up. He was the one with the balls, the big idea, or the stupidity, to set the whole thing off. But his plan was always fluid, with way too many things that could go wrong. He had to be always trying to work out how long he could spin a story, how long he could get someone to trust him, before it was the right time to stab them in the back, or right between the eyes. His biggest problem had been getting involved with my old man and Greg, but then that was the only way he was ever going to get hold of the other ring. For my old man, it must have been too good an opportunity to turn down – the chance to get back at Grandad and destroy as much as he could.

But the one thing that hurts Grandad the most was losing Dominique. I still didn't know who had killed her, but Jan Nowak was top of my list, and that's the way Grandad sees it. Even if Dominique had previous with wandering off, I think he always knew something had gone badly wrong. He would've known there were no signs of there being anything wrong with her because Sangoma would have told him as much. And I was the ferret, the means to start flushing everything out, just like Jack Henshall had said. I think Grandad knew most of what was going on, who was behind it. There was just the unknown factor, the trigger, the mystery man that needed bringing to the surface.

However, I still felt there was another side to all of this because none of it needed to have happened. Grandad could've got Henshall to agree something with my old man, to step in and get the coins back. But I think Grandad needed to know how strong the stench of lies was, who was involved and who was guilty. And that was my job. It meant Grandad now had enough on my old man to hold a million grudges against him, and there would be plenty of people lining up to offer their services at the right price.

As I said, right at the beginning, everyone has a price. We all like to think that there are some things that don't cost money, like love or friendship, loyalty or a better life. But that's not the way it is. Everything has a price on it, even if we can't see it. We pay in all sorts of ways, with whatever we have got, even with our own lives if we must, because dreams make us do crazy things, desperate stuff. We cash in our bodies, our love, our needs so we can get the things we want, looking for a fair deal on the market. I'm not saying it's right, and maybe it's wrong, but that's just the way I see it, and I haven't seen anything yet to tell me different.

I started laughing to myself as I got to thinking back to Tommy's den, the two kids, crazy Mary. I'd even pretty much forgotten about Dominique's husband. I wondered if Texas was trapped in the marriage now, with Dominique listed as missing, unless Jack Henshall was doing something for them on the quiet. Still, Texas had enough going for him. Ann would sort him out. But there was one thing that kept bugging me: how he just had this belief in himself as a filmmaker, when he had as much talent as a two-year-old with a camcorder. At least Anthony had talent as an artist, even if he had a poor judgement on everything else. But it seemed like nothing would stop Texas from making his 'filums', however bad they were, however useless the whole set up was. I kind of admired him for that – his belief, his faith. Even if it was a million miles away from reality, he just kept going.

It made me think about myself, about who I was, about what I should be doing. Should I be like this for the rest of my life, or should I try and get out of all the dirt and muck? I was leaving the estate, so perhaps I should also make sure I didn't bring too much of it with me.

I dipped my hand in the sea, watching it move through the thin, cold water. I moved my hand backwards and forwards, fed up of thinking about the past, ready to move on. Then the signal started, the light from the pick-up, beaming into the boat and forcing me to shade my eyes. I pulled the torch out of my pocket and sent back a signal. That was it, the big boat was coming in, usually for the drug imports, but this time to pick up.

Once they were alongside, it wasn't long before we were lifting the bags with the gold coins onto their deck. I couldn't wait now to get it all over and done with. It had been a long night, from the hole underneath the shack, filled with three dead bodies, to the boat that would take me safely across the shipping lanes, maybe around the coast and down into some sunshine. And these were guys I could trust, guys who I had built up a nice trading relationship with, because I was banking on that, when they asked if that was everything.

Seven days and six months later

Seven days and six months later and I am living on an island. I've been on the beach but there's not much of a beach, and there are no palm trees or a mountain with fresh water running down to the sea. The thing is, where I'm staying, I can't hear the sea. And the insects in the trees are always making a racket. But I can shut my eyes and dream, in the afternoon, when the sun is hot.

So, all I do is breathe.

And then my phone rings.

'Yeah?'

'Is that you?'

'Yeah.'

'It's Grandad.'

'OK.'

''ow's business?'

'Going well…'

'Good investments then?'

'Yeah, a few more things, then it should all be done.'

'Good lad. Must be nice out there, lots of sun?'

'Yeah.'

'And they like the Brits out there, for what we done for them in the war.'

'I think so.'

'OK, well, let's see 'ow much needs managing. No point coming back if things ain't right for yous 'ere. Anyways, I tell yous what, get yer self a nice new phone, nothing too fancy though.'

'OK.'

'Good boy...'

There was a pause before Grandad had one more thing he wanted to say.

'Just remember...'

'Yeah?'

'No man's an island, is 'e, son?'

'I'm not trying to be.'

'Of course, yous not. It's family that counts, eh? OK, son, speak later.'

And that was the end of it, making sure all the money was back in the system, building up the business here and looking for other opportunities.

Over the last six months I hadn't asked Grandad too much about what was going on back home. As far as I could tell, there was no arrest warrants out for me, and the bodies had been disposed of. The only thing Grandad had said about anyone was my mum, and how she wanted me to look after myself because she didn't want to lose another son. I know, it's funny how things turn out. I've also taken to writing things down, which is how you've got to read this story. It's because I've had time on my hands, living in one of the villas I had bought, kind of in the middle of nowhere, and keeping a low profile.

Anyway, with Grandad having disturbed me, I checked the time because I needed to head off into town. I decided to walk instead of getting a taxi and felt the heat of the sun as soon as I was outside. I had a tourist-type summer hat on, shorts and a t-shirt, and a pair of sandals that I'd had since the first day I'd arrived. As I walked along the narrow tarmac road, I looked across the burnt grass and all the way up to the edge of the blue of sea. It wasn't the type of island I'd dreamt about back on the estate, but it was close enough for now. I had probably got something like my dream, even if it wasn't perfect.

Once I had got into town, I had to walk through all the modern bits of the island, full holiday hotels and car fumes, across the inlet and through the old city. I think it had taken me a good two hours or so and hoped I wasn't too late. But Britney was there, waiting by a boat for me so she could say goodbye.

'I didn't think you were coming,' she said, her face glowing and sad at the same time.

'It's a long walk from the villa.'

'You could have got a taxi.'

'I know, but I like to walk. I like the freedom.'

'I know what you mean,' she said. 'I can't believe it really.'

'What, that you made it out alive?'

'No, that we've had these six months together, just like you said when we were in London.'

'Well, it wasn't planned.'

'Are you sure?'

'Yeah, we've had as long as we can together before anyone found out. And now you can be free to be who you want to be.'

'You mean my new passport?'

'Yeah.'

'And thanks for the money.'

'It's just a little bit to get you going. Just remember, there's no going back.'

'I know. It's just my mum. She thinks I'm dead.'

'It's best for her and for you. That way you both get to live.'

'I'm going to miss you,' she said, as she hugged me.

'Is that the truth?'

'Yes,' she said, stepping back and looking behind her at the boat she was leaving on.

'I was just wondering,' she said, giving me a bit of a cheeky smile. 'Have you given it all back to him?'

'What, the money? No, it's all invested, and the investments are locked away in my name.'

'If it's locked away, that means you have a key. Have you brought me a ring?'

'No, I'd be stupid to do that, wouldn't I? Decided to go a bit modern and come up with a password.'

'And only you know that?'

'Of course!' I said laughing. 'That's what will keep me alive. Grandad won't like anything I've done, even if I am his own blood. Villains like that never forget or forgive.'

'But he's your real dad.'

'Trust me, blood is not thicker than water. Anyway, no need to go over all that again.'

Britney looked at me, smiling all over her face.

'So, what's the password then?'

I thought for a second.

'I could give you a clue…' I said.

'Go on then…'

But I realised, a second later, I was just trying to be too clever, and that's not good for a centurion.

'Hmmm, well, maybe not.'

'Cheeky,' she said, as she moved forward and kissed me on the lips. 'Just remember, don't write it down or put it in a book.'

'Nah, I wouldn't do that,' I said, tapping my head.

'I'll miss you…'

'Yeah, me too.'

'So, it's goodbye then…'

'I think so…'

Britney sighed and stepped back from me.

'You'd better go then, or else you might just stay here,' I said, putting my hands in my pockets.

Britney laughed.

'We both know that can't happen,' she said. 'And we know who won't let that happen.'

'Well, six months isn't bad. I think that's a record for me.'

'Good. Promise to keep it that way?'

'I don't think I need to promise.'

I looked at her one last time. I had avoided saying to her how much I loved her for six months. I wanted to say it now, but to do so would be a death sentence. She looked at me again and I was happy to keep looking for as long as we could.

'I think I better go now,' she said, bowing her head to hide her tears.

'Yeah…'

'I know we can't say it,' she said. 'But I do agree with

you.'

And then she turned and hopped up the gangway. I waited, but she disappeared inside the boat.

That was it, the end so to speak. I walked back along the harbour, sad but also happy Britney had got something out of it. And if I was honest with myself, I didn't feel I had really paid for her love for the last six months. So, perhaps I was wrong to think that everybody was the same, but only time will tell on that one.

Printed in Great Britain
by Amazon

41189264R00162